Joy Comes in the Morning

Joy Comes in the Morning

Ashea S. Goldson

www.urbanchristianonline.net

Urban Books, LLC
78 East Industry Court
Deer Park, NY 11729

ISBN 13: 978-1-60162-860-2
ISBN 10: 1-60162-860-9

First Printing July 2010
Printed in the United States of America

10 9 8 7 6 5 4 3 2 1

Distributed by Kensington Corp.
Submit Wholesale Orders to:
Kensington Publishing Corp.
C/O Penguin Group (USA) Inc.
Attention: Order Processing
405 Murray Hill Parkway
East Rutherford, NJ 07073-2316
Phone: 1-800-526-0275
Fax: 1-800-227-9604

Joy Comes in the Morning

By Ashea S. Goldson

Dedication page

This book is dedicated to Mommy, whose youth and marital status neither afforded you luxury, nor prestige, yet you persevered with motherhood. Thank you, Mommy, for life and love.

Acknowledgments

To my Heavenly Father, who has made this kingdom writing possible, I give all honor and glory.

To my husband, Donovan, thank you for twenty-three years of growing with you, and learning what real love is. The best is yet to come.

To my children, Anais, Safiya, Jamal (my son-in-law), and Syriah (my granddaughter), I love you all with an endless love. Keep on making me proud.

To Mommy (Evangelist Janet Sloan); what can I say? A mother's love is special. Where would I be without it? Thank you for being in my corner when it seemed like no one else was, and thank you for allowing me to be me.

To Grandma Ruthell, thanks for always believing in me, and for reading my books, even when it seemed like your strength would not allow you to.

To my business partner and friend, Tamicka Mccloud and your family, Darryl, Lashydra Cameron, and my godchildren, Emmanuel, Hannah, and Faith—you are forever members of my family. Thank you for the daily laughter you all bring into my life.

Acknowledgments

To my editor, Joylynn Jossel, you have been a Godsend in every sense of the word. Thank you for helping me in my publication journey.

To my Urban Christian family, thank you for allowing my words to be heard, and for being supportive of those words.

To my literary agent, Sha Shana Crichton of Crichton and Associates, thanks for doing what you do; keeping my literary business in order.

To the Faith Based Fiction Writers Group, thanks for helping me by critiquing, uplifting, teaching, promoting, informing, and praying. What a literary sisterhood-truly a force to be reckoned with.

To my World Changers Church family, and for Pastor Creflo and Taffi Dollar, for continuing to teach the Word of God with simplicity and understanding. To the WCCI marriage maintenance ministry for accepting us in with open arms, and allowing us the opportunity to serve.

To The Anointed Minds students, who light up each day with smiles. And to one of my very special students, Michael Brown, whose potential is clearly recognizable and whose destiny is just beginning. I expect great things.

To all the Christian fiction authors who have stayed true to the genre; bloggers, book clubs, social media organizers, and radio hosts who have either paved the way for me or promoted me, thank you for being examples of literary and professional excellence to which I can aspire.

To all family, friends, or writer-sisters who have not yet been

Acknowledgments

mentioned, whether you be from World Changers Church, from Brooklyn Technical High School, from Fordham University, from the family in North Carolina, from New York; whether our paths have crossed in Atlanta, whether you be blood relatives, relatives by law, or whether you're a fellow author, I love and appreciate you all.

To my readers and fans, thank you for supporting me in this kingdom writing venture. What a journey it has been so far.

Prologue

(Ten years ago)

I arrived at the clinic a shivering mess. I never imagined I'd feel so alone. Ahmad was supposed to meet me there at ten o'clock, to hold my hand, even though he had never held my hands before, to talk me out of it. Ahmad was supposed to marry me and make this thing right, make this problem disappear. In my mind there was never anything fancy, just us and a judge, covering this mistake with eternal vows. It had already been at least three months, and he hadn't even asked.

The sky bulged with dark, angry looking clouds, clouds that threatened to explode in magnificent fury. I imagined that it was God's way of expressing His disapproval. As if disapproval was a strong enough word for what God must've been feeling toward me. It had rained all morning as if the heavens had opened up and my clothes were soaked, but not because I didn't have an umbrella. Oh, I had an umbrella tucked away neatly in my little canvas backpack. Believe it or not I wanted to walk in the rain and be cleansed. I wanted to feel the drops, one by one, piercing my skin, chastising me. To me the rain was a kind of baptism, a cleansing for the sin I knew I was about to commit. I waited an hour before I snuck inside the building, trying to reason away what was already dying inside of me. A solitary tear fell from my eye, and it meant nothing because nothing was all there was left. I glanced down at the watch on my wrist, knowing that he had missed his deadline. It was finally clear that Ahmad wasn't coming; that he had made his choice. Unfortunately, here beneath the open sky and the eyes of God, I had to make mine.

Chapter One

It was barely past eight o'clock, and already I felt like I had taken a trip to the pit of hell. It should have been the happiest day of my life, but the flip flopping in my stomach, when Joshua popped that huge rock out of that Tiffany's box, told me that it wasn't. I couldn't stop feeling that there was no coming back from this. Here I was sitting in one of the finest restaurants in New York City being proposed to by a very eligible bachelor, yet I couldn't even look into the eyes of the one I claimed to love. Guilt, torment, and confusion all wrapped themselves around my heart, paralyzing me. Why did the words I had waited thirty long years to hear turn my stomach inside out? Not that I didn't love Joshua, because everything that was woman about me screamed out his name in my dreams. Yes, I loved him, but I wasn't sure he'd still love me if he knew the truth.

He looked into my big, dark eyes with his chestnut brown ones and grinned, revealing two deep dimples. "Alex, will you be my wife?" Joshua kneeled down next to the table. The white linen tablecloth draped itself over his well toned legs. Two waiters, dressed in black and white, stopped and stared as an attractive hostess passed by.

I was speechless. Instead of the joyous leap into his arms that I had always imagined, terror consumed me. Perspiration began to trickle down my eyebrows. He seemed to be waiting for an answer. "Alex, are you okay?"

All I could do was sit still and wonder if I could do it.

Could I marry this wonderful, sanctified man and bury the past once and for all? "I . . . I don't know what to say."

Joshua chuckled. "I hope you'll say yes."

"Yes, I . . . I . . ." I fumbled with my fork.

"Well?" Joshua's eyes sparkled under the light of the crystal chandelier.

"Of course I'll marry you." I gave in. Afterall, how could I turn away the only man that was peanut butter to my jelly?

"Wow, you had me afraid for a moment there." Joshua loosened his tie and collar.

"I'm sorry . . . it's just that I'm so happy and so surprised." I forced my lips into a smile.

"You had to see this coming. We're together all the time. I love you." Joshua took my hand in his. "You're one of the few people I can trust."

His confidence in me made me cringe. "I love you too."

"You've made me a happy man." Joshua kissed my lips softly. "I'm going to take care of you."

For a moment I felt sorry for him because I knew he'd try to take care of me, but there was that pain in me he wouldn't know how to take care of; that pain he knew nothing about. Only God could settle that. Nevertheless, Joshua was a special sort of man, a thirty-five-year-old widower, a distinguished deacon, a son of a bishop, and a ministerial student himself. He was on the fast track into ministry, the future heir to one of the biggest churches in New York City. By day he was the brilliant bank manager for one of the largest banks on the East side and an MBA graduate of MIT. His most important job, however, and the one which impressed me the most, was being a father to his three-year-old daughter, Lilah, although she seemed a bit spoiled for my taste. Fortunately, none of these things were the reasons why I loved him. I loved him for his dedication to the things of God, for how he made me a better person, and for how his sweet smile could bring tears to my eyes.

Joshua and I continued to dine that evening, and I was careful not to let him see worry in my face. I only wanted to enjoy the moment, to be swept away in the romance of my engagement, to envision my wedding day and all the happiness we would share. He grasped my hand. "I'll be right back."

Then he excused himself to the restroom, and I whispered a prayer. "Lord, please help me to focus on the present." A shallow calmness fell over me for the remainder of the evening as we ate, laughed, and talked. Still there was uncertainty hidden behind my smile.

The magical night continued with Joshua and me riding in his Chevy Tahoe over the majestic Brooklyn Bridge, with its Gothic Piers lit up in all their urban splendor. I looked out at The Empire State Building, Lady Liberty holding her torch, and numerous other skyscrapers towering over the flowing waters. For a moment I thought of September eleventh as I pictured The World Trade Center, once a dominant force in my world, now just an eerie remembrance lurking behind the clouds. The water glistened under a sky streaked with lights, and I felt God's presence. When we finally arrived at my apartment building, Joshua jumped out and ran over to my side to open the car door as he always did, then we walked up the front steps holding hands. There in front of the metal door to the lobby, he held me in his arms, tucked my hair behind my ears, and planted a goodnight kiss on my lips. It was a gentle kiss, one that reminded me of all the reasons I loved him, and I was shaken by its affect on me. "Tomorrow we'll discuss the wedding plans," Joshua said. I smiled at the mention of our wedding. "I can't wait."

"Goodnight." Joshua started walking back to his car which was double parked.

"Goodnight." I watched him walk away and admired his gallant stride. The form of his slightly bow shaped legs could be seen through his tailored suit, and I had to fan myself to stay in the Spirit and not fulfill the lust of the flesh.

So I walked into the building, quietly up the flights of stairs leading to the small, two bedroom apartment I shared with my twin sister. Before I could turn the key in the lock, Taylor swung the door open.

"You're back already?" Taylor confronted me, as she often did, with one hand on her hip.

"I should be saying the same thing about you." I was surprised she wasn't out with one of her many scandalous suitors.

"I was a little tired tonight so I cancelled." Taylor sat down on the velour couch. "But what's up with that smile on your face, girl?"

I showed her the diamond on my ring finger. "Joshua purposed tonight."

"Nice bling," Taylor said, grabbing my hand. "I guess Deacon has got some sweet taste, huh?"

"Oh, yes." I looked down at it, still admiring the ring. "I said . . . yes."

"That ain't no surprise, but why do you sound so funny about it?"

"What do you mean?"

"I mean this is Deacon Joshua Bennings we're talking about here. You been all up on him for months now. He's so this and he's so that."

"I have not." I put my hands on my cheeks to hide my embarrassment.

"Seems like you would be jumping up and down with joy. And all I get is a ring in my face and a fake smile." Taylor smirked. "Uh-uh. Something is up."

"Oh, it's nothing. I'm just happy, that's all." It wasn't easy trying to fool my sister. After thirty years of living together, in addition to the nine months we shared in the womb, she knew me all too well.

"Good, 'cause I'm all for couples getting their groove on, especially my almost identical twin." Taylor hugged me tightly, and then let me go. She was a jazzier, more muscular, weave wearing, tough mouthed version of me; a diva from the beginning to the end. "Hey, better you than me. I ain't tryin' to let nobody lock me down."

"Well, the way you run, there is little chance anyone would be able to catch up to you in the first place." I laughed heartily.

"Yeah, girl, but I've got to hand it to you; you work fast." Taylor smacked her gum like gum was going out of style.

"What do you mean?"

"You've only been dating homeboy for three months."

"Oh, come on, we've known each other for much longer than that." Now I was on the defensive.

"Yeah, I know he has been around for a while, but every female in the church had their eyes on him too." Taylor snapped her fingers. "You really worked it, girl."

"He worked it; God, I mean."

"Whatever." Taylor rolled her eyes. "Yeah, yeah, I know you and Mr. soon-to-be-a-minister had this weird holy roller relationship thing going, but still . . . three months. I'm just sayin' I ain't mad at ya." Taylor gave me a high five, and then walked into the bathroom without another word.

I was used to my sister always being the rebellious one, but the way she felt about God and organized religion kept me on my knees. She was never big on church stuff even though Mom was. But right after Mom died, things took an obvious turn for the worse. She told me and Aunt Dorothy that it was the church that killed Mom. All that unrealistic faith talk, together with Daddy's years of infidelity, that is. She swore right there, before we ever left the cemetery, that she'd have nothing more to do with either of them. Now Taylor could be a little overly dramatic at times, but not one of us, not even Aunt Dorothy, dared to cross her.

Yet, even though my identical twin sister was a drama queen, she was right. Everything had happened so fast. Joshua and I knew each other from the Bible college since he began taking classes there, but it wasn't until my church started partnering with his about six months ago that he seemed to notice me on a different level. First of all, he left his dad's church to join ours because he claimed he wanted to follow the intricate inner workings of a smaller church. Personally, I thought there was some kind of rift in the relationship between him and his parents. In any case, he began working diligently at Missionary, and I started to notice him. Good looking, single, and working for God.

I didn't find that combination too often. I still don't know what it was that made him interested in me, since I wasn't the glamorous type, and he certainly had his share of potential female companions. I sure was glad, though, when he sat me down one day after Sunday service and said he wanted us to see each other exclusively, to see where our relationship would go. Now that was a great day. I mean when a handsome, successful, God fearing man like Joshua Bennings asks if you're interested in courting, you shout an emphatic yes, amen, hallelujah, and hold your breath, all the while hoping he doesn't change his mind.

My cell phone rang, and I answered it quickly.

"Hello," I said.

"Hi, babe. I have great news." Joshua's voice exuded excitement.

"Really? Better than everything that has already happened tonight?"

"Well, it's not better than you agreeing to become my wife, but it's good."

"What is it?" Now I was intrigued.

"My mother and Lilah will be back in town the day after tomorrow, so we'll be able to spend time together, this time as a family." Joshua chuckled.

"That sounds great," I lied. "I can't wait."

I listened intently while he explained the change in plans. Joshua's mother had cut her trip to Chicago short so I'd be faced with spending extended amounts of time with Lilah sooner than I expected. I managed to escape the inevitable in the three months we were exclusively seeing each other, since the child had been shuffled off to visit her paternal great-grandmother.

Now that Joshua's mother had picked her up from Chicago, she'd be back in action. I'd have to smile, be friendly, and most of all, I'd have to be motherly. Don't get me wrong; it's not that I didn't want to be a part of that sweet little girl's life, but I just didn't think I had it in me anymore. I had tried once before, only to be disappointed in myself, when at the last minute, I freaked out and left town with the choir. I didn't even belong to the choir, but I knew as soon as we were scheduled to spend a weekend together, I had to get the heck out of there. So I used the excuse of the choir's spring concert, and it won me a little time. Unfortunately, this time, leaving was not an option. I'd have to stay and face my own fears. I'd have to look into her eyes, cuddle her in my arms, and have the same nightmare I always had. Of them.

Chapter Two

I woke up excited, hopped out of my carnation pink canopy bed with expectation, and looked down at my exquisitely dressed ring finger. The memory of yesterday's magnificent events was still dancing around in my head, still making me the happiest I've ever been. I grabbed my terrycloth robe and headed for the bathroom, filled with a mixture of emotions. How could I marry the man of my dreams and spend the rest of my life lying to him? Sure people did it all the time, but I wasn't other people. I had a real relationship with my Heavenly Father that I didn't want to mess up for any reason. Lord knows I'd messed up enough times before. While I showered, I decided to pray, something I did quite often. When I came out, I covered my body with shea butter lotion, then chose a cotton aquamarine dress to wear. Determined to squeeze my size fourteen body into that size thirteen dress, I took a deep breath and zipped it up before I let it out. A couple of inches were not going to stop me. Twirling myself around in front of my full length mirror, I promised myself I'd make up for my tasty indiscretions with extra workout time at the gym. Not that I was a fitness enthusiast, but my sister was, and she dragged me down there kicking and screaming anytime she noticed I was putting on a few pounds. I couldn't argue this time, not unless I wanted them to roll me down the aisle. I sucked in my stomach and put my hands on my hips. If I were going to be a chic bride, I had a lot of work to do.

Within minutes I was out of my apartment building and

on my way to work where I could escape my problems by hiding myself in service, the same thing I always did. Help the college, help the church, help the family. If only a sista could help herself. Since my car was in the shop, and I had to take the subway, I arrived at work a little early. When I walked through the front door of Brooklyn Missionary Bible College, I smelled cinnamon in the air and wondered if Dr. Harding was having a bagel with his morning coffee. As I turned down the corridor, the first person I saw was Marisol sitting at her desk. She had her usually free flowing brown hair pulled up into a bun with a butterfly pin in the center.

I guess I could say that next to my sister, Marisol was my closest friend. We were not only co-workers, but sometimes confidants. And I do emphasize sometimes. See, I didn't keep many females close to me, didn't trust them much at all. Mom taught me that way back in the day. I always seemed to work better with men anyway, and I didn't mean that the way my freaky sister would. I meant that I genuinely got along better with men, without all the drama and hater issues. Now I'm not saying that I'm special or anything, but I am saying that I don't have time for female foolishness. Some of the sisters I ran into wouldn't know common sense if it kicked them in the face. Anyway, here at work, Marisol was my girl. "Good morning." I waved cheerily, throwing my hand in her face.

"Morning, girl." Marisol waved without looking up from the papers in her hand.

I cleared my throat and kept my left hand in her face. "I said good morning."

"What's wrong with you? I . . ." Marisol looked up, right into the glare of my three-carat diamond ring.

"Nothing. Everything is right with me, very right." I tried to contain my excitement.

"Girl, no." Marisol covered her mouth in disbelief. Then she started jumping up and down, hugging me over and over again. "When did you get this?"

"Last night."

"Last night? Wow." Marisol examined the ring from top to bottom. "And you didn't call me?"

"It was so romantic, and it was like everything I've ever dreamed of."

"Ooh tell me, tell me. I want to hear every detail," Marisol squealed.

"You know I'll tell you, but not now." I lowered my voice and looked over my shoulder as a few professors walked by.

"All right, but I don't know if I can wait until then." Marisol picked up my hand and eyed my ring one last time. "Ooh, girl, this rock, this rock."

"I've got to get to my station before neither of us have jobs. Then I'll have to hock the rock for rent."

"Oh, you've got jokes today."

I snatched my hand away from her and started toward my area. "We'll talk later."

"And, you know we will. Wow." Marisol shook her head and giggled. "Congrats again."

I walked slowly, allowing myself to daydream along the way, and finally stopped at my cubicle. I glanced at the Post-It Notes that covered my bulletin board before I took the files out of my inbox and turned on my computer. I looked at the black screen, logged in, and began to type furiously. Brooklyn Missionary Bible College, with its red brick and ivory columns, was a haven for those who desired ecumenical degrees and seminology certificates. It was also a good place for general Bible study and personal spiritual development, staffed with some of the city's most prestigious PhDs. Dr. Harding was one of them, although he usually remained more humble than most. Two of the things I liked most about working at the college were first, that I got to work with ministers from all over the country, and secondly, Joshua, whose business had now become my pleasure, attended the school also. I always relished the opportunity to see him every day before his classes.

He was, undoubtedly, the best thing that had ever happened to me, besides Jesus, of course. The problem was some people didn't think so, and they did their best to find something wrong with our relationship anytime they could; his family, my family and the myriad of folk we called our church family. Most of them didn't bother me though. The only thing that truly stood in the way of my happiness was the secret I was carrying, the one that had been tearing me apart from the moment I succumbed to it, something that would disappoint everyone I knew and taint my spotless reputation in the church; something a man like Joshua could probably never understand.

Now if I could have gone back to fix it, I would have, but there was no changing that lone moment in time when Joshua looked solemnly into my eyes and expressed the painful way in which his wife had died, how what she had done was inexcusable. There was no changing that moment when I could've been honest. But I wasn't. Instead, I held his hands, kept my mouth closed, and nodded in agreement at the horror of what she'd done. Yes, I missed my opportunity, and that was in the past. It was what it was. I could only go forward and forget, at least until Joshua's phone call stopped me in my tracks.

"Hello, sweetheart," Joshua said.

"Hi. How are you?"

"Great."

"What's up?"

"I'm just working some numbers out right now, but that's not important. Listen, I know you're busy too, but I just wanted you to know I've got special plans for the five of us tonight."

"Special plans for five?"

"Honey, don't you remember that Lilah will be here soon?"

Suddenly, Joshua sounded annoyed. "Her and my mom's flight is scheduled to arrive any minute now."

"Of course. I just didn't realize they'd be up to getting together so soon after their trip." I held my breath for a moment.

"I'm sure they'll be a little tired, but I managed to talk Mom into it."

I'll bet you did. "Wonderful then."

"I can hardly wait till tonight," Joshua said.

"Neither can I." That was the first lie for the day. I was in no way ready to sit down with Pastor and First Lady Bennings while they go on and on about their fine congregation and their fine family as if everyone else outside of their circle were mere dirt. Nor was I in the mood to humiliate myself by trying to entertain the princess, Lilah. Now that was pressure.

"Look, I've got to get back to work. I'll see you later, babe."

"Bye." His words sent shivers through me. So I closed my eyes and pretended that everything was all right in my world. I smiled and decided that I needed to buy a gift for Lilah. Maybe that would help break the ice between us. Placing my phone back into my purse, I went back to work, although my heart really wasn't in it. I sat at my desk looking over the numerous files of students, past and present, who had crossed my path. Each one had a story, and some actually held a special place in my heart. Like Minister Ramon Vega who graduated two years ago, started his church a year ago, and whose ministry had ballooned to an impressive 3,000 within months. Whenever he would come through the campus, I'd just stand back, watch prayers answered and miracles manifested. He always had a timely and prophetic word, something I personally had learned to value. There was an anointing on that man that only God Himself could explain.

Then there was Missionary Annette Lewis, one of the sweetest women I had ever known. She took a series of spiritual development classes until God called her into the fields of Cambodia. I haven't seen her since, but it's her devoutness I miss the most. Nothing could stop that woman from being at the church every time the doors opened.

Yes, I guess I could say my job had meaning, just not necessarily the right meaning for me. I wanted to check out, go home and hide under the covers, not be bothered with the family façade I'd soon be engaged in. I thought surely it couldn't get any worse than this. That is, until I leaned over to throw a piece of paper into the trash can and noticed that someone had left the entertainment section of the newspaper sprawled open right behind my chair. I reached down to pick it up, figuring it was probably that little temp girl from the agency that left it there. She looked like the type that only cared about entertainment, with her blue nail polish and her glitter hair do's. As I was about to ball it up, I slowly focused in on the picture beside the first article. My fingers began to tremble when I saw his face.

Chapter Three

At first glance I wasn't really sure it was him, but after further examination, I knew it was him all right; a little blurry, but him just the same. He was sitting next to a woman with her arm draped over him. He wasn't facing the camera, but still I'd know that profile anywhere. I quickly scanned the article for details. It was a short article, highlighting a stage play which was earning critical acclaim in California. So he had achieved his dream of being an actor, I supposed. Well, good for him. At least his life didn't end that day. I ripped the page from the newspaper and crumpled it in my fist. I couldn't believe I was seeing him for the first time after all these years. My heart raced as I dumped the paper into the trash can, smothered the tears with my fingertips, and spun around in my chair. Then I took a deep breath, looked at the stack of papers in front of me, and started going through them, one by one, trying to act as if nothing had happened. I was virtually numb.

I went through the motions, but it was so hard to concentrate. No, this wasn't happening again. I wasn't going to let him break me. It had been so long ago since I'd seen his face, and although it was a fine one, I certainly didn't expect to see it again in a magazine. I sighed, deciding that I could deal with seeing him in a picture as long as I didn't have to see him in person. I quietly began to recite Psalm 37 until I was calm.

After what seemed like forever, it was time for my break. I

needed to get out of there, and to get some air. I went over to Dr. Harding's office and peeped my head in. "Dr. Harding, I'll be taking my break now."

"Very good, Sister Alex. I guess we can hold it down until you get back." Dr. Harding chuckled, but I was not amused. There was no humor in being his secretary. I thought of the crumpled page at the bottom of my trash can and knew there was little humor in my life at all. I turned and started toward the exit. I passed by Marisol on the way.

"Hey, where are you going, chica?"

"I'm going to make a quick run to the pharmacy across the street, then come back and eat my lunch." I hoped she wouldn't want to tag along.

"Wait for me then," Marisol said. "I brought my own lunch too."

Unfortunately Marisol loved company and loved to talk, so I was doomed. The two of us disappeared through the double glass doors and headed across the street to Phillip's Pharmacy. On the way, I described Joshua's proposal in detail, with all the highs and lows of true female gossip, and I also explained how I needed to pick up something special for Joshua's daughter.

"I'm going to look over here in this coloring book section. You go on without me." I waved her away. "I'll catch up eventually." I plundered through the coloring book selection, trying to choose between Dora or Barbie. Much to my dismay, this section was very near the checkout counter.

A wave of nausea crept through my stomach as I overheard a lady picking up a prescription for prenatal vitamins. I looked up at her. She couldn't have been more than three months along. I put my hand up to my mouth, not because I was really sick, but just because I was sick of reminders everywhere I went, even at this quaint little pharmacy. Some were subtle, some were obvious, but every single one was too much to bear. Reminders of the life I would have had if I hadn't sold my soul to the devil. *Lord,* deliver me.

Today, as I trudged up and down the aisles, dressed in my form fitting skirt suit, cloaked in the epitome of professionalism, I closed my eyes to shut out the images that had become my existence. I opened them to glance at my watch, carefully monitoring the minutes I spent in the store. Lunchtime was never long enough. Dr. Harding would be expecting me back soon, waiting for his precious messages and waiting to have his students' dissertations neatly filed away, none of which I particularly cared about. But I did care about getting my paycheck, if you could call it that, and today was payday. First I grabbed a coloring book and crayons for Lilah. Then I quickly gathered my shampoo, conditioner, packs of soft curlers, a Hershey's cookies and cream bar, a six pack of Diet Coke, two boxes of aspirin, because I had been having those unbearable headaches lately, and one pack of bunion remover because my shoes were doing something ungodly to my size nine feet. After I had placed everything inside my basket, I decided to make one quick stop at aisle six before checking out. I looked at my watch again and knew that I'd have to hurry if I were going to have time to eat lunch. I sighed as I went about my business, searching the shelves for the same female hygiene items I purchased every month.

Yet, I didn't know that here at this small, insignificant pharmacy, my deliverance would come walking through the door, and that the same ache that infiltrated my psyche, would actually force a change. Unfortunately, before there would be change, there would be trouble.

I slipped into the aisle quickly, fingering the various feminine product choices in this section. Suddenly, a shadow lurked behind me, and I lifted my eyes just in time to see a familiar face.

"Michelle, is that you?" I smiled as I recognized Brother

and Sister Harris's daughter. Within seconds, my expression changed. I also recognized the box that Michelle was holding, and I held my breath. Reminders.

Almost simultaneously, Michelle pushed the box behind her back. She shuffled around a nearby shelf, pretending to look at sanitary napkins instead of what I was almost certain she was hiding. After all, I had been browsing these well placed shelves every week for three whole years, ever since I started working across the street. The store was only so big, and I, being the observant, organized person that I am, knew almost every crack and crevice, every bend and tear. I knew exactly what that item, if nothing else, looked like, where it was and where it was supposed to be. If I knew anything at all, I knew where to find *that*.

"Oh, hi, Sister Alex." Michelle's right eye twitched as she spoke. She took one step backward, almost tripping over her own feet. She was definitely acting guilty.

"I thought that was you. What are you doing out of school?" I hoped that I didn't sound too meddlesome. I didn't usually make a habit of interfering with other people's affairs. Laughing to myself, I was sure that that my sister would disagree with that thought.

"Oh . . . I, uh . . . wasn't feeling well, so I didn't go today. In fact, that's really why I'm here . . . to get some cold medicine." Michelle coughed deeply with one hand, but kept the other one behind her back. Too obvious, I thought.

"I see. I work at the Bible college right across the street." I, without trying to, found myself staring at the girl. She was a plain looking teenager who wore no makeup or jewelry, who wore her shoulder length hair back in one ponytail. Her sweatshirt was the color of wet mud, and it was void of design or style. Her jeans and sneakers were both a faded out version of the same dullness she personified. She smelled like wet denim. She neither looked nor smelled anything like the dolled up minister's daughter I saw at church every week.

"I . . . I never even knew you worked around here." Michelle stuttered mildly and formed a fake smile.

"Yeah, I've been at The Missionary Bible Institute for three years. By the way, the cold medications are on aisle four. I shop here all the time, so follow me." Cautiously, I put my arm around Michelle, and led her to what she claimed she had been looking for, waiting to catch another glimpse of the box she so carefully kept out of sight.

"Cool. Working at a Bible college must be uh . . . different."

"Yes, it's an interesting job." When I turned to face Michelle again, she was no longer hiding anything behind her back. I looked at her thin, ashy hands and they were empty. Instantly, I looked down at the tiled floor, as if she had involuntarily dropped it, but she hadn't. She was apparently smarter than that.

We stood in the front of the brightly lit store, having a brief conversation about which products were the best at relieving the symptoms she described. The entire time I wondered, while we talked, if Michelle was truly in trouble, and if I'd be able to help. When Michelle had decided upon the items that she would purchase, I followed her toward the checkout counter. My palms were sweating the whole time.

The lady behind the counter pushed her long blond streaked hair out of her face, and quickly punched the keys on the cash register with her long butterfly decorated fingernails. Michelle bounced back and forth on the heels of her sneakers as her items were tallied up, still looking nervous. I continued to look busy, gathering up both items I needed and items I didn't need.

Finally, at the end of the transaction, Michelle looked over at me, trying to mask the sadness in her eyes. I saw right through her. In fact, I hoped she couldn't see right through me. For a moment I wished my short bob haircut was a longer, fuller hairstyle so I could hide my own eyes, my own knowing.

"Thanks again." Michelle waved.

"No problem. It was good to see you." I followed her to the door.

"You too," Michelle said. "Well, I'll see you in church on Sunday."

"Wait . . . Michelle, I . . ." My heart wouldn't stop racing. I wanted to tell her what I saw.

"Yes?"

"Nothing, nothing. I just figured I'd see you on Wednesday for Bible Study." I knew I was walking on water, but I jumped in anyway.

"I'm not sure. It depends on how my mom is feeling. She has been a little under the weather too."

"I understand." I watched her eyes. "I guess something is going around."

"Yeah, I guess so." Michelle dropped her gaze to the floor.

I wanted to say more, to tell the girl that she could be honest, that I understood, but my mouth wouldn't say what I told it to. "So I'll see you at church then."

"Yeah, I'll see you." Michelle practically fell out of the swinging doors, and I wanted to fall out right behind her. I was such a coward. Watching her run across the street to catch the bus, I waited with a mission in mind. The same mission I always had, to help the lost. Why did I have to always get involved? Then as soon as she boarded the bus, I began to search the area where the girl and I had passed, looking at each shelf, frantically needing confirmation. Just as I thought, my eyes caught a glimpse of an abandoned early pregnancy test on the edge of the wrong shelf, obviously thrown in a desperate attempt to not be discovered. I picked it up and read the label as if I had to prove something to myself. When I remembered where I was, I placed the box back in its correct spot. I wondered which pharmacy Michelle would go to next and if she would discover that she was really pregnant. I wondered if she would go through what I had gone through. Here I was a faithful customer, stranded behind the shelves of this little pharmacy, remembering my own mistakes and steadily losing my composure. "That poor girl," I whispered. A tear trickled down my cheek. I guess I didn't even hear the footsteps coming up behind me.

Chapter Four

"What's wrong, Alex? Are you crying?" Marisol squinted up her eyes in confusion. "Chica, what's wrong?"

"No, I'm fine. It's just these darn allergies, you know." I pulled tissue from my pocket and wiped my eyes. The last thing I needed was Marisol prying into my personal business. She was my friend, but we only talked about the present and the future, never the past. In fact, I was always careful not to let anyone get that close to me. I kept walking down the aisle of the pharmacy, hoping she would just leave me alone.

The store was fairly small, so thank goodness the aisles were short. The overhead lighting was bright, however, and I was sure it would reveal all the emotion in my face if I had to face Marisol again. So I kept walking, trying to look normal, trying to look like I wasn't hiding anything. Yet what I was hiding was internal.

"Yeah, girl, I know what you mean." Marisol started walking behind me down the aisles. "Hay fever season is no joke."

"Right. This time of year is always a little rough on me." I walked over to the counter and paid for my products.

"Me too, girl. Hey, why don't you try some Claritin?"

"I will." Yep, that was Marisol, the advice giver. I took a deep breath and walked past her. By this time she was busy reading the label for allergy medicine. "Look, I'm going to go on back before Dr. Harding has a fit."

"Okay, I'll see you in a few." Marisol was busy digging in her purse and didn't look up.

I hurried out of the store, dried my eyes, and blew my nose. I had to get a grip on my emotions because they were selling me out. When I finally caught my breath, I headed back to work across the street.

I peeked into Dr. Harding's office to let him know I was back, placed my bag down, took out the candy bar and stuffed it into my pocket. Then I sat down at my desk, gobbled down the turkey and cheese sandwich I'd brought from home, washed it down with a Diet Coke, went into the dimly lit storeroom, and shut the door behind me. I wanted to be alone before Marisol returned, before anyone needed me. I sat on a step ladder to get myself together, unable to stop thinking of Michelle and the consequences of her hidden box. My head was throbbing by now. Why couldn't I just let it go? I looked around the dusty storeroom and made up my mind at that moment that I'd talk to Michelle and find out the truth. I knew it wouldn't be easy, but I'd get her to confide in me, and then I'd help her to make the decision that I, God help me, should have made. She was young, vulnerable, and unmarried, but somewhere deep inside, I envied her. Maybe because she was carrying a life she still had a chance to protect. I ran my hand across my own stomach, which was a little pudgy, but only because of the butter pecan Haagen Daazs I had been drowning myself in lately. My womb was empty; no life. I sighed as I looked down at my ring finger, still feeling empty despite the intensity of my impending marriage. No life there either. When did my life become like death?

My phone vibrated in my pocket. Anxiously, I checked the caller ID and saw that it was Joshua. My sweet Joshua.

I sucked up my attitude. "Hi, baby," I said.

"Hi." Joshua's voice was slow and steady. "How is your day going?"

I thought about Michelle and the possible drama surrounding her. Suddenly, a chill went through me as I considered what Joshua's reaction might be if he knew about her condition.Joshua was originally from a small town in Rochester, New York and was the son of ministers, who he frequently referred to as "preaching machines." At first he was only taking general Bible study courses for personal development, but deep inside I knew he'd be a minister one day. It was only a matter of time. By day he did his banking thing, but every other waking hour he was a Bible student, reading and analyzing the Word of God. The only other thing he was passionate about was Lilah.

In fact, when he first showed up at Missionary Chapel Church, he always kept to himself, but I soon began to notice that he'd show up every time the church doors opened. Slowly I started to study him and noticed that he sat in the same position during each service, said very little, and then walked out immediately afterward. Finally, I started to notice there was a sadness in his eyes, and I guess that's what drew me to him. His eyes. I wanted to know what was behind this devoted man and his sadness. That's when I found out about his late wife, Delilah, who seemed to be a source of great pain for him. I figured her memory was just too much for him and that he left his parents' prestigious church because of it.

My throat became dry, and despite what I knew was the right thing to do, I wasn't sure I could ever tell him. "Oh, nothing special. What about yours?"

"Hectic, but never mind that, I can't wait to see you." Joshua's voice was a mellow mix of business and pleasure.

"I can't wait to see you either." I hoped my anticipation wasn't too evident as I didn't want to appear to be as desperate as I really was.

"I'll pick you up at six," he said.

"I'll see you then."

"By the way, do you remember Sister Winifred's niece, Yvonne?"

"Yes, I do. The cute one who just moved here, right?"

"Right. Well, Sister Winifred just called and asked me if I would help to show her niece around now that she's in town." Joshua sighed. "So I just wanted you to know that she might be tagging along with us at some point."

"Oh . . . no problem," I said, but I didn't really mean it. Sister Winifred was the pushiest, nosiest woman in our church, and her niece, although she seemed tolerable, was a beautiful, and outgoing young woman. Not that I was the jealous type, but a caring man like Joshua, who was now headed to the altar, didn't need any distractions either.

"Thanks. You're a saint," he said.

"I'll talk to you later," I whispered into the phone before clicking it off.

For a moment I held it near my heart, hesitant to let him go. I knew I loved him, I just wasn't sure if love was enough. Dr. Harding peeped into the storeroom. "Alex, I thought you might be in here looking for the Wiley textbooks. When you get a chance, may I see you in my office for a moment please?"

I stood up immediately and dusted off my jacket. "Yes, sir. I'll be right there." I ran out of the storeroom and checked to see that everything was in order behind my desk.

"This is probably about that raise you were waiting for." Marisol, who had just walked by, winked.

"I don't know about all of that," I said, straightening out my hair. I was curious, yet strangely ill at ease.

"Oh, come on, girl; you deserve it. You're the hardest work-er here, for sure." This was probably true, and it wasn't the worst job in the world, but I was definitely ready for increase. "We'll see." I faked a smile as I walked away. I knocked on the door to Dr. Harding's office.

"Come in," Dr. Harding said.

I entered the small room with its black metal desk and

matching file cabinets. "Please have a seat." Dr. Harding motioned toward a black vinyl chair. I sat with my hands in my lap, waiting patiently to hear what would be said.

Dr. Harding rose from his chair and came over to me. He had never stood that close to me before. I could smell the coffee on his breath. Then he put his hand on my shoulder, and I held my breath.

Dr. Harding wrinkled up his face "I've got to tell you that I think you've been wasting your time here. . . ."

Chapter Five

"Excuse me? I'm wasting my time here?" I almost lost my breath at my boss's words. I rose from my seat. All I could think of was the three years of slaving away behind and in front of my desk and the hundreds of ministry students that I'd helped in the past three years. *Wasting my time?* I knew the Lord couldn't have abandoned me.

"I'm sorry, but what I mean is that you're such a good worker and that you have so much promise, that you're wasting your time here in this position. You did such a fantastic job on our previous fundraising projects, the school newsletter, and all the events you've promoted for us this year, you could clearly become a public relations liaison for our school."

"Excuse me, public relations? I don't understand."

"Well, you already have your bachelor's degree in liberal arts, and you're an excellent public speaker, so if you'd just go back to school to take a few courses . . ."

My mind processed the information quickly, adding up my living expenses and dreams. That is the few dreams I had left.

"There would be a huge pay increase, some travel required, and quite a few other perks if you know what I mean. We'd pay for your training, and after a few months, the promotion would be yours." Dr. Harding pulled the hairs of his beard.

"Oh, I see," I said, suddenly feeling foolish and trapped. Dr. Harding sat down to explain the details of his proposal as

I carefully considered everything he was saying. When he was done, he rose from his chair.

"We'd like to sponsor your education, and we'd like you to sign a contract saying that you'll accept the position with the company upon completion of your program."

"I'm flattered that you like my work. I . . . I don't know what to say." A million thoughts ran through my head. *Holy Spirit, please give me the words to say.*

"Just say yes." Dr. Harding didn't blink.

"This is so sudden, sir."

"This isn't as sudden as you think. We've been considering this for a long time. I just needed the approval from the corporate office before I approached you."

"I'll definitely give the position serious consideration." I stood up and extended my hand. "Thank you."

"You're welcome, but let me know soon what your plans are because if you want it, we can make it happen. If not, I'm afraid we'll have to start the search for the *second* best candidate." Dr. Harding smiled, and I could sense his sincerity.

"I'll let you know as soon as I can, sir." Backing up against the door and turning the knob, I had to get out of there.

I made a narrow escape from accepting a position I clearly didn't want. I hoped my lack of interest wasn't obvious, but I doubted that very much. I was never good at pretending.

Now some might have said I was stupid for not snatching up Dr. Harding's offer, but inside, it just didn't feel right. So I guess you could say I was holding out for more, holding out for purpose. I just wasn't exactly sure what that purpose was anymore.

I did manage to get through my humdrum routines, however, I did so with Dr. Harding's offer at the back of my mind and a refusal on the tip of my tongue. But I couldn't refuse what I hadn't prayed about. After all, it wasn't like I didn't need the money.

I was thirty years old, a college graduate, and still sharing an apartment with my sister because I couldn't afford to pay rent on my own. Although I knew my financial situation would change if I could ever make it to say "I do," I didn't like who I was now. Boy did my life take a downward spiral. I scratched my head as I wondered what went wrong. I got mixed up with the wrong man, that's what happened. I compromised my integrity. I compromised my faith. And as a result, I was almost left for dead.

Ten years, and yet sometimes it seemed like yesterday. I could've been the teacher I know I was meant to be. In fact, I probably could've been teacher of the year, the best elementary school teacher there ever was, just like my mother, but I ruined it. Here I was just a lowly Bible school secretary-do girl, who by day watched everyone living their lives, while mine disintegrated into dust. Dust. That's what I felt like, as if the wind could pick me up and lift me away. Away from my present and my past. As I let loose my own disappointments, I went back to work in silence. My mind went back to Michelle and the possibility of her being a mother. "Lord, let your will be done in Michelle's life," I said to myself, as I wiped away all my hopes and dreams from my eyes. If only someone had intervened on my behalf. If only Taylor had been a snitch, it would've changed the course of my life. It seems to me that my destiny was sealed the day I was born to Mrs. Gabrielle Lauren Carter, because my mother didn't take any mess; none at all. I mean me and my sister were expected to walk a chalk line. There wasn't much room for mistakes, not in our sanctified house. Mother just wasn't trying to hear it. I'm not blaming her for my cover-ups, but I'm just saying she sure didn't make mistakes easy to live with.

I picked up my cell phone to end this wondering once and for all. I still had Sister Harris's number because she and I worked on an outreach project together a few months ago. I wanted to stop Michelle from making a bigger mistake than she'd probably already made. I had to call her parents and tell them what I saw. Despite the fact that they were clergy of the church, and despite the fact that I didn't know them very well, I was going to tell them their daughter might be pregnant. I pressed the button for contacts, then pressed the letter H for the Harrises' house and waited for someone to answer.

Chapter Six

Unfortunately, just as Sister Harris picked up the phone and I was ready to tell her everything I knew, I heard Marisol's voice. "Can I get the transcript for a Morris Johnson, please?" Marisol leaned against my beige, formica desk.

My heart almost stopped as I clicked the END button on my cell phone. I hated to hang up on Sister Harris, but duty called, and I couldn't risk Marisol overhearing anything. How Marisol managed to sneak into my cubicle without me hearing her coming was a mystery to me. If she weren't my friend, I'd think she was spying on me.

"Oh, I'm sorry," Marisol said. "I didn't know you were on the phone."

"No problem. I'll make that call later." I immediately stood up and started rummaging through the beige file cabinet. "Whose file do you need?"

I glanced over at the pile of files stacked high in my inbox. "Morris Johnson. He is a recent graduate."

"Yes, I remember him. Short? Bald?"

"Yep, that's him." Marisol threw her head back, laughing hysterically.

I didn't have time for Marisol's sense of humor. I had things on my mind, too many things. "I'll have it ready for you in a few minutes."

"Good, because he's sitting in the lobby waiting for it."

"Here you go." I handed the file to her and sat back into my chair. "Now I'll just do a printout of everything else."

Marisol took the papers from my hand and began to look through them, one at a time. "Okay, this is interesting."

"What is?" I never looked up from the computer.

"That he's from the west coast, South Beach."

"What's so interesting about that?"

"I never knew anyone from California. How about you?"

"I did once." The memory made me uncomfortable. Ahmad had been the sweetest talking thing from the West Coast. I drank in everything he was dishing out, right or wrong. I thought he was the one. He was the one all right, the one to help me destroy my future. Mama told me not to get involved with his trifling behind, but I didn't listen. I thought I was too independent, too foolish, really. It took years for me to get over him. I hadn't yet gotten over him.

"Look, I've got to get back to work now before I get fired," I said.

"By the way, what happened with Dr. Harding? Did you get that raise?"

"No, actually I was offered a promotion."

"A promotion?"

"Harding wants me to be the school's public relations liaison."

"That sounds so exciting." Marisol's eyes widened.

"It's a good opportunity, but I'm just not sure I want it."

"Are you loco, chica?" I shrugged my shoulders. "No, I'm not crazy. I'm just tired of living someone else's life. I'm thirty years old, and I've got to find my own."

"So find your life, but don't give up that job. First you get engaged and now this. You're on a real lucky streak, I'm telling ya."

"I'm blessed, and luck has nothing to do with it." I said it more to convince myself than to convince her.

At the end of the day, I punched my time card, said goodbye to my fellow employees, received a congratulatory high five from Marisol, and started the short journey to the gym where Taylor worked. As I walked through the concrete Brooklyn neighborhood to get to the train station, I noticed all the women walking along the sidewalk, either sporting swollen bellies or pushing baby strollers. Even some who weren't women at all, who didn't look old enough to raise any child. How in the world did they do it? Unwillingly, my mind went back to Michelle, who was now a mother. Another punch to my soul. When I finally arrived at the gym, Taylor greeted me at the door.

"What's up, sis? I see you decided to work out today."

"Yes, I need to relieve some stress."

"Good choice." Taylor led me to an empty treadmill. I told her briefly about my encounter with Michelle in the pharmacy.

"I hope she ain't pregnant for her sake. She's too young for that mess." Taylor set the timer and walked away.

"Yes, she is too young." I began to walk, and then within seconds, I began to run, shifting my weight back and forth on each leg, huffing and puffing as if I were trying to blow one of the houses of the three little pigs down.

A few minutes later I noticed Shayla McConell walk in, and instantly I knew there would be trouble.

"Oh no, she didn't bring her raggedy tail up in here today," Taylor said. "She's not gonna bust my groove."

"Pay her no attention." I wasn't in the mood for another one of my sister's showdowns.

"Who in the world does she think she is coming in here, flaunting her platinum wedding ring and new workout gear?" Taylor whispered to me, "She is such a pain."

"Good to see you, Taylor," Shayla said.

"What's up, Shayla?" Taylor threw her long, braided weave out of her face. "Just swinging by because I heard that this business will soon be for sale." Shayla was so tall, and she had the nerve to stick her silicone implanted breasts in Taylor's face.

"What? What do you mean for sale?" She had Taylor's attention.

"Oops, I guess nobody told you, huh? Well, good news travels fast. I heard that Ms. Arlene will be looking for a buyer before you know it." Shayla looked through her Gucci purse.

"No time soon, Shayla. That's not gonna happen." Taylor's eyes were bulging.

"You'd be surprised how fast time can fly by. Maybe I'll buy this place, fix it up, and then you can work for me." Shayla touched Taylor's shoulder with her long fake nails.

I prayed that Taylor would hold herself back.

"Not in your wildest dreams." Taylor pushed her hand off of her.

"We'll see about that. Let Ms. Arlene know I stopped by." Shayla twisted herphony self to the front door, hopefully on her way back to that dungeon of hers she liked to call a fitness center.

"Over my dead body." Taylor called out to her.She had done it again, managed to get all up under my sister's skin. Shayla looked back and grinned. "Whatever."

Shayla was the type who liked to throw stuff in a person's face any chance she could get. Ever since Taylor started working there they'd been rivals. My sister was the best at what she did. People came from all over the city to work with her because she was the ultimate fitness instructor and personal trainer. Since Shayla owned the center up thestreet, she didn't like the competition Ms. Arlene's place was giving her. The word on the street was her rich, several franchise owning husband bought it for her right after the wedding, which by the way was quite an extravaganza in and of itself. She went from tired aerobics instructor to entrepreneur extraordinaire almost overnight. Taylor had been livid ever since.

I sat on that exercise bike, pumping my legs into oblivion as I watched Shayla strut out the front door in her designer labels. Then my sister took off running into her boss's office. I could only imagine what Taylor was saying to her because The Push It Fitness Center was Taylor's whole life.

About twenty minutes later, Taylor came out of her office and walked over to me with her head bowed.

"What happened?" I knew it was nothing nice.

Her nostrils flared and her breathing became heavy. "Ms. Arlene doesn't understand. I live, eat, and breathe this center."

"What did she say?"

"She'll be retiring in about six months and selling the place. Six months ain't enough time for me." Taylor sighed.

"I'm sorry, Taylor."

"Yeah, me too. I begged for my job. I said I'd help out more, but it's just not enough . . ."

I felt sorry for her because I knew how much she, unlike me, loved her job. Being in fitness was the only thing she ever wanted to do with her life. "Don't worry. You're young and ambitious. I'm sure it will all work out for the best."

"Yeah, right." She turned on the balls of her feet and plopped down on a weight lifting bench where she rubbed her head against the chrome bars.

Her petite co-worker, Bria, came over to stand beside her. "Well, at least she's giving us plenty of notice."

"What am I going to do? It's May now, and I've only got up until November." Taylor turned to her.

"Just look for another job like I will." Bria sat down on an exercise ball and started rocking back and forth.

"But I love it here. I don't want another job." Taylor slammed her hand down against the bench. "I always thought I'd leave here when I was ready to open one of my own."

"Well, why don't you?" I was always good at motivating other people, but never myself.

"Why don't I what?"

"Open your own," Bria said, smacking her gum.

"I would but—" Taylor looked annoyed that I was interfering.

"But what?" I dug deeper because I had nothing to lose.

"I need to get my act together to be able to do that. And six months is not a lot of time." Taylor shook her head in despair.I wasn't used to seeing her broken like this.

"So get it together then. You're no punk, who is stopping you?" Bria gave her a playful punch in the arm. Taylor gave her such a venomous look that Bria stepped back.

"I'm stopping me; cause even though I want it real bad, I know I ain't ready." Taylor stood up and started to walk away.

"You've got some time." Bria looked at her fingernails.

"Probably not enough time, but I guess I'll give it my best shot."

"Now, that's the Taylor I know," I said.

When my long workout at the gym finally came to a close, I was tired, and my biceps were a little sore from the intense exercise I forced on myself. I knew I would have to work a little harder if I wanted to fit into a decent size wedding dress.Rush hour on the number four train was no picnic in the park. Unfortunately, my car spent more time in the shop than it did on the street, so there I was taking the train again. There wasn't an empty seat in sight, so I stood against the door, squeezed between two women. Not exactly my idea of how I wanted to be squeezed. The train jerked me back and forth as a dirty faced old man leaned toward my direction. I turned my cheek to him but I could still smell his garlic breath. Two more stops on the stinking train, and I'd be home where I could kick back and relax a little before my date with Joshua tonight.

When the doors opened, I walked out into the subway station, up the stairs, and finally into the fresh air. Since I was still wearing my workout gear, which was a rarity, and since

I was going out tonight, I decided to run all the way home. Needless to say, I was gasping for air before I hit the end of the block. No, I was nothing like my sister, the queen of fitness. As I turned the first corner and was about to cross the street, I looked up, but couldn't believe my eyes. I blinked my eyelids to be sure it wasn't true. No, he was not with her.

Chapter Seven

When I saw them together, my footsteps froze. I knew it had to be his wife because Taylor had bragged about stealing him from a woman that looked like her. I immediately looked for any sign of togetherness, so I could have more facts to throw at Taylor when and if I needed to. There were no signs. All I saw was a quick exchange of a child, who appeared to be Derek's son. Derek was one of the guys Taylor was currently dating, and according to her, he had one eleven-year-old son. I watched the tall, slim woman with long blond cornrows roll her neck and speed off in her Mustang. I quickly ducked behind a graffiti covered wall, breathing hard. I waited until I saw him get back into his white Honda Accord and drive down the street before I took off running again. If Taylor was the one seeing a married man, why in the world was I hiding? I couldn't believe my sister was dating married men now, separated or not. She had dropped her standards, and for what? A couple of laughs? A couple of drinks? I wondered when she would figure out that it wasn't worth it. Remembering my mother's voice urging us to never lose respect for ourselves, I clenched my teeth. She'd probably be so disappointed in us both.

When I arrived at my building I was sweating heavily, and I couldn't wait to strip out of my gray sweat suit. I walked up the front steps stairs, and once inside, I then climbed up the narrow staircase leading to my apartment. On the way up I smelled Mrs. Rosetti's homemade spaghetti sauce, which increased my hunger. Seeing old man Jenkins's scrawny cat roaming the hallway as I neared my floor made my skin crawl. The cat rubbed itself against my leg while I fished through my gym bag for the key. "You little fur ball." I pushed him away from me with my foot. Finally, I flung the door open wide and stood in the safety of my own living room. With my bag still in my hand, I sifted through the mail on the side table. Bills, bills, nothing but bills. I needed a raise. I set the mail down and proceeded to the bathroom. A good hot bath would start my evening off right. By the time my home spa experience was over and I came out of the bathroom, wearing my pink terry cloth bath robe, Taylor was already sitting on the couch. I saw her peep over at me from the corner of her eye.

"You're finally home." I didn't know what to say, given the sullen expression on her face. "Yep." Taylor's head was buried in her hands. Suddenly, as if feeling my stares, she looked up. "You know, I'm fired up. I can't believe Ms. Arlene is selling the center."

Given the mood she was in, I didn't dare mention that I had seen Derek earlier. Besides, knowing the way she dealt her player card, she probably wouldn't care anyway. "Well it won't be so bad if you can buy the center. Anything can happen in six months." I circled the couch.

"Whatever. That's easy for you to say. You've already got your job and a husband to support you."

"Oh, come on, don't give me that. You could've gone to college. That was your choice. And all you've ever wanted to do is what you're doing now, so . . . My job is dead end, and you know I don't really like it. And as for the husband part, well, I haven't walked down the aisle yet."

"What's that supposed to mean? If I didn't know any better, I'd think you were scared or something."

I turned away from Taylor so she couldn't read me. "Don't be silly. I'm just saying . . . I'm not married yet."

"Mmm. I'm just sayin' . . ."

"Oh, don't give me that look of yours. I'm going to marry Joshua. And you're going to own your own fitness center.

"Whatever you say." Taylor leaned over to open a bottle of nail polish. Ironically, I pictured Taylor dressed in her most appealing workout gear, commanding a large fitness staff. Yet, for some reason, I couldn't picture me making it to the altar. I saw myself in a white gown, and I even saw Joshua waiting, but in my dream, I never made it. Something always happened, but I never made it to say, "I do."

"I'm serious." I went on with the fantasy. "You've got resources. You'll do a business plan, get a loan, and maybe even get an investor."

Taylor's eyes grew wide. "I knew that college education of yours would pay off one day."

"Ha-ha. You'll be in business before you know it. So you see, it's not so bad." I stood up.

Taylor put her foot up on the couch and stuffed cotton between her toes. Then she slowly began to run the brush across her toenails. "All I know is that by the time Ms. Arlene has her retirement party in November, The Push It Fitness Center had better be all mine."

"Well, I believe you're just the woman to make it happen."

"I ain't gonna let that heifer, Shayla McConnell, get it." Taylor shook her fist in the air.

"I can't believe that Shayla is still antagonizing you after all this time."

"Yeah, and not only that, but she wants to make Ms. Arlene an offer. Knowing Miss Stuck Up, I'm sure it's going to be a fat offer." Taylor stopped polishing and looked up at me.

"So get a loan."

"With my credit, I doubt if they'll loan me a pen." Taylor

picked up a pen from the center table and threw it down just to demonstrate her point.

"Maybe with some credit counseling and super saving from now until then, you can push it."

"I've got no choice. There ain't no way I'm gonna sit back and just watch the best thing in my life be sold right out from under me." Taylor threw her hands into the air. "I know what you mean."

"Not without a fight that is." Taylor balled her fingers into a fist and punched a pink throw pillow.

I walked into my bedroom, took off my bathrobe and eased into an apricot colored shorts set. When I came back into the living room, Taylor's head was still bowed. This wasn't like her at all. She never let life get her down.

"By the way, I got offered a promotion." I sat on the arm of the couch.

"Oh, yeah?"

"Yes."

"You ain't tryin' to make me feel better, are you?"

"No, I'm sorry. I . . . I don't even want the job. I mean it's tempting and all, because the pay will be much better, but I don't want to be a public relations liaison." I stood up and walked into the kitchen.

Taylor followed. "What's your problem?" Taylor sucked her teeth. "At least you've got a job."

"I'd have to take more classes and travel a lot, and I'm not sure I want to do this."

"You're not still on that little teacher thing, are you?"

I didn't answer. "I'm not interested in public relations."

"Then turn down the job. It's your life. Ain't nobody stopping you."

"You're right. It's my life, and I'm messing it up." I tried to contain myself, but before I knew it, a tear had run down my cheek.

All of a sudden Taylor stood up and looked into my eyes. "That's not it at all, is it?"

"What are you talking about?"

"It's not the job you're worrying about." Taylor pointed her long fingernail at me. "It's the marriage."

I looked down at the floor and didn't say a word.

"I knew it. You ain't happy, and that's not like you; not when you're about to be Mrs. Joshua Bennings. So what is it? I know his family is not the easiest to deal with, but still . . ."

This was true. Joshua's family hadn't been the most welcoming. Oh sure, they were cordial at church functions and the occasional dinner at their huge Long Island home, but I'd never felt their genuine approval since Joshua and I had become an item. In fact, they had, a couple of times, tried to set Joshua up with more suitable women from their church; all daughters of well known pastors. Each time, Joshua had politely rebuked them, and assured me that I had his heart. Still I always wondered if at the back of his mind, he, too, felt I was beneath him. My father was no well known anything; just a common, retired sanitation worker. My mother, God rest her soul, was a first generation school teacher in the public school system. Nothing to be ashamed of, but nothing to compare to Joshua's family either. Joshua's father was not only a pastor, but he was also a third generation judge. His mother was not only a first lady, but she was also a Congresswoman. Together, they were nothing to be scoffed at, and they were united in their mission to protect their only son.

"No, it's not his parents," I said.

"Good, 'cause I don't like them anyway." Taylor stretched her gum out on her tongue, and then rolled it back into her mouth.

"You don't like anybody."

"Whatever."

"It's just that . . ." I stood up and began pacing the worn carpet.

"What is it?"

I looked into Taylor's eyes. "I've started having those dreams again."

Chapter Eight

The kitchen was nothing elaborate, just a bright yellow color we'd painted it a few years back and a simple square table with vinyl chairs. But just like during our childhood, it was our favorite meeting place. Mom was always in there cooking something good for us to eat.

"Not those same dreams you had back then?" Taylor put her hands on her hips and squinted her eyes.

"Yes, those."

I reached into the cabinet and opened a box of doughnuts. Whenever I was nervous, I liked to eat.

"But that was so long ago, Alex," Taylor said.

"Don't you think I know that? Do you think I'm having them on purpose or something? Like I planned for my life to become this big mess?"

"Well, why now?"

"It all started up again when Joshua and I started going out together. I mean he started talking about marriage and children, me being a mother to his daughter, how he wants a big family, and I guess it has all been bothering me."

"You guess?"

"It has been building up slowly, getting worse as the weeks go by," I said. "Here we are three months later, and I'm in a lot of trouble. My heart wants to marry Joshua, but my mind tells me I can't." I tossed a doughnut into my mouth.

Taylor reached over and took the box out of my hands. "Look, don't be a fool. Neither one of us ain't getting any younger. Just because I don't want to be tied down doesn't mean you shouldn't be. You believe in all that love garbage. I don't, but I believe it works for you. You'll get married. I'll be your maid of honor. I'll look stunning, try not to outshine you, and you two boring people will go off somewhere and live happily ever after or as close to it as possible."

"I hope you're right." I stuck another doughnut into my mouth.

"You know I'm right; that is if you stop sucking down doughnuts like they're fresh air." Taylor pushed the box across the small table. "Look, Josh is a little too sweet for my taste, but he's all right for you."

"Sweet?" I frowned up my face at her. "Hey, my man isn't gay."

"I didn't say he was gay, he's just a little too soft, but that's your style so—"

"I guess I'm worried that he's not over his wife and how she died."

"Well, death ain't easy. I still remember watching Mommy, praying, hoping, and shrinking down to nothing." Taylor closed her eyes as if the memory drained her. "Death is hard. I can't tell no lies about that. Give him time."

"I feel like I'm running out of time."

"When is the wedding?"

"I don't know yet, but we'll probably decide on a date tonight."

"Well, just talk to him about her. Maybe his feelings have changed now that he has you."

"I can't."

"Talk to him," Taylor said.

"I can't." I chewed, then swallowed. "I mean, I try, but he avoids the subject."

"Let me tell you what to do. Wear an enticing outfit, flatter him, and then hit him up over dinner when there is nowhere else to go." Taylor stood up. "He'll have to talk."

"Sounds worth a try." I nodded my head in agreement. "Thanks."

"Hey, you're talking to the dude master." Taylor spun around, letting her braids fly against her face.

"All right, dude master. I'll give it a try." I poured myself a glass of skim milk and sat down at the rectangular table.

"Alex."

"Yes?" I turned to face my sister.

"It ain't so bad talking to you when you're not preaching that I'm on my way to hell." Taylor laughed.

"Yeah, and when you're not telling me to meet you there." I let out a loud giggle.

My laughter was interrupted by the ringing of my cell phone. Instead of looking at the caller ID, I looked up at the clock. Maybe it was Joshua again, or worse yet, it was probably Daddy. It kept ringing as I swallowed hard.

Chapter Nine

I finally picked up the cordless phone and let out a deep breath when I heard my father's raspy voice. He had smoked cigars for forty-five years, and although, thankfully, he had given them up, the effects were still evident in his sound and in his persistent cough.

"Hi, Daddy," I said.

"Hi, Alex."

"Daddy, I can't talk right now because I'm about to go out with Joshua." I wasn't about to tell him about the engagement over the phone.

"Oh, uh . . . him."

I held the phone and sighed. "Yes, Daddy, him."

"Well, all right. I won't even ask about Taylor because I'm sure she's going out too."

"Actually Daddy, she's not. Taylor isn't..."

Taylor signaled me that she didn't want to speak and Daddy told me the same. It was hard trying to mend broken relationships and theirs was no exception. Taylor had very little to say to Daddy since Mommy died. She clearly blamed him for her death as if she died of heartache instead of cancer. No one really understood Taylor's theory but we took it all in stride, usually just staying away from her. Taylor had an attitude no one in their right mind wanted to deal with.

"I'll talk to you later, Daddy. Love you." I hung up the phone abruptly, wondering how I would break the news to him.

No, I hadn't told him about the engagement yet. I was sure he'd be upset because he thought Joshua's family was too arrogant. The one time he attended one of Pastor Bennings's services at Kingdom House of Prayer, he became offended at the man's preaching style, wardrobe, and demeanor. That was two months ago. Since then I hadn't heard anything encouraging about me being with Joshua. He didn't have anything against Joshua personally, but he believed I could find someone whose family was a little more down to earth. Time and time again I told him I wasn't in a relationship with Joshua's family, but you know fathers; he only understood what he perceived to be the best for me.

I showered and changed into a flowing, sleeveless dress. It was red, and I hoped it wasn't too bold for the occasion. "How do I look?"

"Cute, but not as cute as me." Taylor quietly left the kitchen headed toward her bedroom as the doorbell rang. I went to answer it and let Joshua in.

"You look so good, baby." He looked handsome in his beige and white pin striped suit. "So do you." I let him kiss me on the cheek, grabbed my red clutch, and we were on our way to meet his parents and daughter at Mariachis Italian Restaurant. "So have you given any thought to the date for our wedding?" Joshua asked while staring straight ahead at the road.

"Well I—"

"I was thinking next month, the third."

"Next month? But there is so much to do, so much to prepare. You know I want a good sized wedding, and that's not enough time to give everyone notice, including myself."

"Have you told your father yet?"

"Well no, but you know he was well aware of your intentions when you took an interest in me. You were very straightforward with Daddy, telling him you wanted to court me with his permission, with the intention of possible marriage." I was almost stuttering. "So that just about sums it up right there."

"Yes, but he's got to be told that the courtship is over and that the engagement is on."

"I'll tell him as soon as I get a chance to get over there."

"It has been two days. He should already know by now." Joshua's voice was cold.

"You're right. I'm sorry."

"Are you stalling?"

"Of course not."

Joshua looked over at me. "I mean, you don't want to tell your father. You're putting off our wedding indefinitely. You make me feel like you're not sure about marrying me."

"Oh, that's one of the few things I am sure of; my love and commitment to you."

"Then what's the problem?" Joshua took one hand off the wheel and put it in mine.

"What do you mean?"

"I mean, sometimes I get these feelings like . . . never mind."

"Let's do it in August, then."

"But that's three months away." Joshua parked the car.

"I'm not worth waiting three months for?" I asked, batting my eyelashes.

"I didn't say that. It's just that . . ."

I didn't let him speak. Instead, I pulled him close to me and covered his mouth with kisses.

"What was I saying again?" Joshua smiled. "We'll get married whenever you want."

It was easy to distract him now, but I wondered how long it would last. His parents and daughter were already there as we entered the restaurant.

"Hello, dear." Mrs. Bennings was svelte, stunning even. She gave me a peck on the cheek, and then grabbed my hand. "My, what a lovely little ring. I'm sure your father must be so proud."

Little? Oh, no she didn't. "It's so good to see you two again," I said, almost blinded by the glare of her dangling diamond earrings and matching bracelet.

"How are you?" Pastor Bennings said, giving me a hug with his long arms. He was an incredibly tall man with a broad chest, and my big self almost felt tiny in his presence.

"I'm blessed, thank you," I said.

"God is good all the time." Pastor Bennings laughed.

"All the time, He is good," Joshua said, pulling the chair out for his mother.

I looked down at Lilah. "Hi there, Lilah." She was absolutely gorgeous, with big chestnut brown eyes, multiple dark wavy ponytails, and dimpled cheeks like her father's. Instantly, I wondered what her mother had looked like. I had never seen a picture, not even a glimpse of the woman whose shadow I was to walk in.

"Hi." Lilah smiled. "I remember you from church."

"That's right. I'm Sister Alex," I said.

Lilah looked up into my eyes. "You sing in the choir, right?"

"Well, kind of. Actually, I sing with the praise team."

"Oh."

"How about you sit right here next to me so we can get to know each other better."

"I don't want to sit next to you. I want to sit by my grandma." Lilah poked out her lips.

"Lilah, that's not a nice thing to say." Joshua gasped in horror.

"No, that's okay. She has the right to sit wherever she wants. Go on, sweetie." I watched her pass me by and slip into a seat between her grandparents, trying to hide my embarrassment.

The four of us talked briefly about wedding planners, guest lists, and the inevitable engagement party, while Lilah entertained herself as most three-year-olds do. I smiled politely, made gracious comments to Lilah whenever the need arose, and managed to get through the evening fairly unscathed. I tried not to focus on their disapproving eyes or their condescending voices. I wanted only to be loving and kind as Jesus would have wanted me to be. That wasn't easy with the Bennings family, but I did it.

The evening seemed to be going well considering how badly I knew it could have gone. Then Mrs. Bennings insisted on raising her glass of sparkling water to make a toast. We all fixed our eyes on her and raised our glasses of fruit juices and soda. "To my precious son and his wife to be. May he be happier with this one than with that heathen of a woman he married the first time."

Chapter Ten

The next day, after I left work, I stopped at Miller's Mechanic Shop to pick up my car. Miller, an older man with a raggedy beard and rotting teeth, smiled as I paid him what I considered a reasonable price. My car wasn't much by most standards, but it beat riding the train all the time, and it had the prettiest carnation pink paint job my dad could afford. In any case, it was a college graduation present from my parents and it still ran pretty good most of the time. I smiled as I put my key into the ignition, and then I zoomed off, happily on my way.

As I drove, I contemplated Sister Bennings's comments from the night before. Would I really make a better wife for Joshua? Certainly not without telling him the truth, the whole truth. I thought about Michelle and the personal commitment I made to help her. That was just like me always getting involved in other people's problems. If only I had called back and at least left a message for Michelle's parents. No, instead I dropped that phone, and dropped the whole idea of calling, like it was on fire.

I thought about Joshua, if he would ever let me get close enough to him, if I would ever marry him. Then came the dreaded question: Could I be a proper mother to his three year old daughter? Suddenly, an unimaginable fear came to me, worse than those that came before it. What if I weren't physically capable of having children with him after what had happened to me? I began to tremble at the possibility. Another strike to my soul. There were so many, but I dismissed the thought quickly.

After entering my block, and spotting an empty parking space, I hurried to parallel park in front of my six story, stone faced apartment building. I walked through the lobby slowly, feeling the heat and the weight of the day, not even stopping to check my mailbox. Then I started the lonely walk through the dimly lit hallway and up the stairs to the third floor. When I reached my apartment, before I could turn the key in the lock, the door was pulled open.

"Oh hi, Taylor," I said to the used to be mirror image of myself.

"No time for that, girl. Come on in." Taylor pulled me by the arm.

"What?" We were like oil and water, the two of us.

"Not just what, but who?"

"I'm tired, Taylor, and I don't have time for games." I pushed past my sister, walking to the bathroom. I turned on the water and began to wash my face with Noxema.

"All right, all right, but I've got a special VIP invitation for us to attend Club Hot25 tonight—"

"Taylor—" I turned off the water.

"Wait a minute. Now I know what you're about to say, but just listen for a minute. They're gonna have a special guest tonight."

"I have Bible Study tonight." I stopped drying my face and looked Taylor right in the eyes.

"I know that, but guess who is going to be there?" Taylor followed me around the couch like a child. "One of your favorite entertainers."

"CeCe Winans?"

"Very funny. No, one of your favorite entertainers from back in the day . . . Anita Baker."

"That's nice, but you know where I stand on that. I'll be at church tonight, but I do appreciate you thinking about me."

"You mean you're not going? Don't you even care?"

"Yes, I care. And no, I'm not going. But thanks anyway. In fact, as soon as I freshen up a little, Joshua will be here to pick me up."

Taylor stormed out of the bathroom, slamming the door. Another typical confrontation with my twin. I sighed before proceeding to peel off my work clothes and hopping into the tub. My shower was brief and unsatisfying, and when I was done, I walked out into the living room, wrapped in a peach towel and feeling frustrated. Here I was battling the same spirit all over again. I knew it was spiritual warfare, but heck, my soul was weary.

"You and your Bible toting fiancé can just get the heck on for all I care." Taylor took up a pillow and threw it at me. "Go on with your hypocritical self."

I pretended to smile as the pillow hit me in the face, but on the inside, Taylor had cut me. If I had to endure one more remark from her about my faith, I didn't know what I was going to do. After all, I was already dealing with my own issues, crying out in prayer and in my sleep, waiting for God to answer. The last thing I needed was to be reminded of who I was, or wasn't in Christ. Or maybe that was the first thing I needed. I wasn't really sure anymore. One thing was sure though, that my twin sister, who should've been my best friend, was instead, a spiritual enemy.I huffed, looking at my watch and counted the seconds. Joshua couldn't get there fast enough. Couldn't I just enjoy a night at church without being bashed for it? I watched Taylor's mini skirt clad body walk through the ivory door before she left the living room.

Once I was inside my bedroom, I squeezed myself into a panty girdle, then slipped into my pink and lilac flowered sundress and my pink platform sandals as if I were a cover girl. And I was, just not the type you'd see on your typical high fashion magazine. I was just a little bigger, but better.Then I

lay across my bed, inhaling the rosemary potpourri and looking at the floral pattern on her wallpaper. I should've been
praying, pouring out my heart, but after the confrontation I
had with Taylor, I was too undone. I blinked a lone tear away
in silence.

"Lord, forgive her. Forgive me."

Finally the door bell rang. I listened as Taylor and her com-
panion, Malcolm, walked out into the hallway. By the time
they had walked down the two flights of stairs, through the
small lobby, and out of the front door, I rushed over to peep
out of the window. I could see Taylor poking out her apple
red bottom lip. Then she stomped her way down the concrete
steps, all the way to Malcolm's car, flipped her long brown
weave braids, diva style, and hopped into the passenger's seat
of his Lexus.

When Joshua arrived at the door fifteen minutes later,
there was no subtlety in the way I breathlessly flung the front
door wide open. I was ready to go, ready to vent. Joshua was
a tall, lanky man. His skin was like carved caramel. His eyes
were chestnut brown like his daughter's, and he had a wide,
dimpled smile that would instantly invite a person in. The
problem was though, that he'd usually shut them out before
they could accept the invitation. Not that he was mean or
anything, but he was definitely reserved.

"I'm glad to see you." I grabbed his hands and pulled him
inside the apartment.

"Me too, but you look upset." Joshua peeled my hands off
his and remained standing by the door.

"It's nothing. Taylor and I just got into it."

"Again?"

"Again." I flipped my naturally long eyelashes, a tactic I'd
been using for years. "What was it this time?"

"Same old, same old," I said.

"Oh, she wanted you to go out?"

I put my hands on my hips and sighed. "And not just any old 'out' of course but 'out' to a club."

"Let me guess. They're having a special guest or something?"

"Of course. She justified it this time by saying Anita Baker would be there. I don't care. I mean, I just don't get it. When is that girl going to learn?" I walked around the room picking up the scattered items Taylor had left behind. That's the way it was between her and me. I'd always have to pick up after her mess. She'd disappoint Mommy, and I'd have to straighten things out, make it better, be the perfect daughter. So she'd get all the attention, negative or not, and I'd get all the work. "When will she learn?"

"When she's ready," Joshua said.

"What am I supposed to do until she's ready?"

"Keep on praying." Joshua looked down at me and smiled.

"That's all I've been doing. Seems like something should've broke loose up in her by now."

"I know what you mean. I used to feel the same way about my cousin, Charles." Joshua shook his head. "That dude is always into something, but God works in His own time."

"You're right. I'm overreacting over nothing," I said.

"Well, I wouldn't say over nothing. It's something."

"It's something, but it's nothing new."

"Nope, definitely not new. Let's go before we're late to Bible Study." Joshua pulled up his sleeve, revealing his hairy arm, and looked at his watch.

"Hey, not so fast. Don't I get a little hello kiss first?"

I put my hand behind his head, stood on my tiptoes to line my lips up with his, moved in very close, and then quickly planted one right on his cheek.

"Oh, very funny."

"I thought so." I licked my lips and followed him outside of the apartment, giggling. I enjoyed teasing him. The lightheartedness of it helped me to forget the hidden things of my heart.

When we reached his Chevy Tahoe, he came around to my side and opened the door. He held my hand, and as he helped me inside, I felt my dress rising. I quickly pulled it down to my knees and leaned back against the front seat. I didn't want to tempt him or tempt myself. I already had enough problems to deal with.

We rode through the streets full of traffic until we arrived at The Brooklyn Missionary Chapel Church. Joshua parked his truck a few feet away from the church, and I was grateful that he didn't have to park by a meter. As we walked toward the building, we saw Sister Winifred climbing the front steps of the church.

Sister Winifred, with her pale yellow skin, bluish-gray eyes, curly gray wig, and just a hint of pale pink lipstick across her thin lips, wore her thick black rimmed glasses with the chain connected to them. She wore a tweed suit, and she carried a white vinyl purse with a big gold colored buckle on it and wore matching white vinyl shoes. She carried her extra large print Bible in her other hand, and when she noticed us coming, she frowned. She always seemed miserable.

"Good evening, Sister Winifred," I said

"Oh hello, dear. Hello, Deacon." Sister Winifred gave a fake smile, revealing all of her fake teeth. I remembered Sister Winifred when she was toothless just a few weeks before. I had to restrain myself from laughing.

Then out of nowhere came Sister Winifred's niece, her youngest brother's child, Yvonne. Yvonne was a few inches shorter than me, probably a few dress sizes smaller than me, but she was quite curvaceous, and she didn't mind showing it off. She wore a body hugging halter dress with a tight fitting blazer on top, and she wore black stilettos. Her curly red hair framed her tiny face.

"Hello, Sister Alex and Brother Joshua. Or should I say, Deacon Joshua?" Yvonne giggled hesitantly.

"How are you, Yvonne?" I leaned forward to give her a hug.

"It's good to see you again." Joshua smiled.

"Deacon Joshua, my auntie says you're going to be showing me around New York soon. That's so nice of you to offer, but I wouldn't want you to go to any trouble."

"Oh, it's no trouble at all. I'm glad to help," Joshua answered, keeping his eyes on hers. I kept my eyes on Joshua.

"Well, thank you so much. I appreciate that. It gets kind of lonely being in a new city and all."

"Yes, I'm sure it does," Joshua said, looking at her from head to toe. "When I first moved here two years ago, I was totally lost until someone showed me around."

"Anyway, thanks again. I'll be in touch." Yvonne grinned and walked away.

I didn't quite know what to think of her, the way she flounced around, fluttering her fake eyelashes and twisting her hips. I didn't know what to think of her being here at Brooklyn Missionary Chapel Church. Was she really here seeking the Lord or was there something else she was after? For some reason, I felt the Lord wasn't the only one she wanted to get close to.

Joshua and I entered the sanctuary together, although we quickly became separated by our various responsibilities. Immediately, Brother Alonzo cranked up the organ. I joined the praise team up front and began to lead the praise and worship. "I enter the holy of holies. I enter through the blood of the Lamb. . . ." We sang. Joshua placed his Bible on the front pew and took his place amongst the other deacons. The organist began to accompany our singing as we ushered in the Holy Spirit.

In a matter of minutes, all of the animosity I felt toward

Taylor earlier was washed away by God's presence. I knew that somehow, despite what I was feeling inside, everything was going to be all right. At least until the middle of service when I passed by Sister Winifred and she opened her big mouth. Sister Winifred looked over her reading glasses with her tricky eyes.

"Now, Sister Alex, I see you're wearing a big ring on that finger of yours. I hope that means the deacon is going to make an honest woman out of you." Sister Winifred sighed. "I mean, you may not be his parents' pick, and you may have put on a few pounds, but you're clean, you're good at serving, and that baby of his sho' enough needs a mama."

Chapter Eleven

No she did not. I just stood back and glared at her, couldn't even say a word. How dare that evil woman talk about me like that and to my face? Thank God the Holy Ghost held me back because I wanted to jump on that old lady. I couldn't believe that stopping to ask Joshua a simple question would prompt her to hit us up with that one. Her mouth was incredibly foul, nothing like the sweet lips Pastor was always telling us we should have. She was always minding someone else's business and hurting someone else's feelings. When was she going to stop being such a meddlesome busybody?

Joshua stood there, holding onto the back of a pew with his mouth open, looking like a hungry dog. I was annoyed that he wouldn't just respond. What a coward. Was the idea of marrying me so shameful that it warranted this reaction? He could have stood up for me. He could have told her she was wrong about his parents, but he didn't. She knew them, and he knew them. Yes, my feelings were definitely hurt. "Yes, Sister Winifred, we're engaged." I had no choice but to end it. "But I've got to get back on my post."

"Well, God bless you two." Sister Winifred started shuffling herself down the aisle.

Out of the corner of my eye, I could see that Joshua looked relieved. While I stood behind Sister Winifred, absorbing her response, Joshua quietly slipped away. He escaped this time, and he avoided me for the rest of the evening.

At the end of the Bible Study, Pastor Martin made an announcement about needing volunteers in various areas for the new Elijah Project and that we should sign up at the information desk in the lobby. I skimmed over the list as I waited for Joshua. Volunteers were needed for several of the youth departments and that was out. Food was a maybe. Nothing else really interested me at the time. I thought maybe I was burnt out. I shrugged my shoulders, made a mental note of all of the available choices, then walked outside. I promised myself I would sign up next time. I had to give it more thought and definitely some prayer.

Joshua came out minutes later. "Are you ready?"

"Yes." I didn't even look at him. Was it possible to love someone so much and yet want to strangle them at the same time?

"Did you sign up for the Elijah Project?" Joshua pulled a pen out of his pocket.

"No, not yet." I was determined not to give in.

"Why not?"

I was forced to look at him now, but I made it brief because I was still upset. "I don't know. I just haven't decided yet. I don't want to just pick something. I want it to be right. Whatever I choose, I want to belong there, to make a difference there."

"I know what you mean."

"What about you?"

"I'm going to be working with Brother Jacob, helping the homeless."

"That sounds very interesting," I said.

"Something you might be interested in?"

"No, I don't think so." I began to dig in my purse, avoiding eye contact. "I'm going to pray about it."

"Okay then, let's go." Joshua led the way to his car and opened the door for me.

Such impeccable manners, and yet he couldn't even answer a simple reasonable question. I glanced back at the church and saw Sister Winifred, her niece, and three of her grandchildren piling into their station wagon. I flinched at the embarrassment, still not believing that lady's comment. I expected him to defend my honor in the face of Sister Winifred, not just stand quietly as if he didn't even know who I was. Yes, Joshua had snuck away and gotten himself off the hook, or at least he thought he had. Even the ride home was awkward, but I didn't dare bring up the indiscrepency. I just held it in, breathed deeply, and waited until the ride was over.

When I arrived at home that evening, I threw off my church ensemble and jumped into bed, still seething with anger over Joshua's ambivalence. I called out for Taylor, but as usual, she was not home yet. Why couldn't she just calm down and stop living so fast? Every day I remembered what living the 'fast life' had taken from me. Then I started thinking about Dr. Harding's offer and the motivation I would need to get that promotion. Maybe then I could afford to move on with my life.I turned on the television and flipped from channel to channel until I settled on the ten o'clock news. After watching a few depressing segments, I began to fall asleep. I tried to fight it, to wait up for Taylor, but as it got later and later, I finally gave in to my body.

In my sleep I tossed and turned amongst the covers, waiting for Taylor to get home, hoping we could reconcile our differences, hoping no more nightmares would come in the meantime.

I woke up in the middle of the night and realized that I hadn't heard my sister come in. I rolled over and looked at the clock. It was already after two A.M. I heard a car drive up, so I stuck my head outside the window. No sign of Taylor yet. Frustrated, I went back to bed, but not without thinking of the twins again. Lately, they were always in my dreams. *I walked barefoot through the alley, away from the unbearable squish-*

ing sounds, but they followed me everywhere I went. The farther away I ran, the louder the echoes became, so I covered my ears. Since I was totally naked except for a torn surgical gown, I shivered uncontrollably. Suddenly a sheet fell over my head, blinding me. Then I tripped in the length of it and fell, tumbling and slipping on the blood drenched ground until I was completely tangled up in it. As I fumbled to get free, I felt rough hands squeezing the cloth tightly around my face, suffocating me.

"No!" I screamed. But the more I screamed, the less I could breathe.

Right before I took my last breath, I forced my eyes open, and I shuddered as a cold bead of sweat ran down my forehead. I put my hands up to my mouth as I realized it was all just another one of my nightmares. Why did I keep having them?

I reached over to grab my Bible off the nightstand, flipped to the 27th Psalm and began reading. *"The Lord is my light and my salvation; whom shall I fear? The Lord is the strength of my life; of whom shall I be afraid?"* My eyes opened wide when the yellow glaze of sunlight hit my window pane. Its light flowed through the glass and onto my floral comforter, warming the very essence of the room. I sat up straight in bed, with my heart still beating fast, wondering if my sister had made it home.

"Dear Lord, thank you for this day. Please help me to not only get through it safely, but please help me to be a decent representation of your kingdom today and every day. In the name of the Almighty Jesus. Amen."

I peeped my head out of my bedroom and heard my sister coughing, gagging, actually. I knew Taylor had to be hung over again.

I pulled off my cotton nightgown, grabbed my bathrobe, and went into the bathroom to shower. Before walking out, I stopped to look at myself in the mirror. Admiring my somewhat heart shaped face, short bob haircut, big, dark brown eyes, and big everything else, I smiled at the thought that

Taylor was my twin. My identical twin, yet there was nothing identical about us anymore. At least not since Haagen Daazs became my best friend and Satan became Taylor's.

I slapped on some lotion, slipped into a checkered skirt and white blouse, then went to Taylor's room. Taylor was sprawled across her bed dressed only in her panties and bra. Her clothes lay on the floor in a pile beside her bed. When I reached out to touch her, she rolled her body into a vulnerable lump. I knew my body could never fit into such a ball. The smell of wine and vomit threatened to make me sick. So I covered her with a blanket and left the room quietly. "How long, Lord?"

I went back to my own room and opened my Bible. When I finished reading Psalm 91, I dialed Joshua's cell phone. It rang several times before he finally answered.

"Hello."

"I thought you were busy." Hearing Joshua's voice relieved me.

"Not a chance. What's up?"

"It's Taylor," I sighed. "She's hung over again."

"I'm not surprised. Have you prayed?"

"Not yet, but that's all I do." Deep inside I knew my prayers were not in vain. But I wanted to know when the change would come. "That's all you can do." Joshua's voice was deep and hypnotizing. I held onto every word.

"I just don't know how much more of this I can take." I sighed into the phone. "I can't wait until we get married so I don't have to deal with this nonsense anymore."

"That's going to happen soon, but don't leave bitter. I'm sure you can take a whole lot more than you give yourself credit for. God made you strong." Joshua cleared his voice. "He who endures to the end, remember?"

"Right. Except right now I don't think I can endure to the end. I feel like I'm going to collapse." I let a little giggle seep through.

"You won't. Do you need me to come over?"

I threw myself across the bed and wrapped myself up in my sheets. "No. I'm just venting. I know you're busy working today. I didn't mean to bother you."

"You never bother me. Hopefully, we'll finish up early, and I can scoop you up for some grub."

"Grub sounds good, especially since I haven't even eaten breakfast yet."

"Well, I've been up since five o'clock."

"Aww, poor baby."

"Talk like that will get you everywhere," Joshua said.

"I hope so." I rolled over under the covers. Suddenly, there was a loud crash.

"What was that?"

"Don't know. I've got to go." I slammed the cordless phone down on its hook and ran from the room.

Chapter Twelve

I charged into Taylor's room. "Are you okay?"

"I'm sorry, I didn't mean to wake you up. I knocked over this lamp. Stupid thing is broken."

Taylor's room was a mess. Her bed sheets reeked of alcohol. Her dresser drawers were open and clothes were thrown everywhere. Typical Taylor. Ever since she was a little girl she wouldn't clean up after herself. Mom used to go off all the time, asking her how she expected to walk through the pearly gates of heaven and onto streets paved with gold, with a heap of dust and dirt behind her. Taylor would just laugh and go about her business until Mom started swinging that belt that is. Yep, Taylor never took much of anything seriously.

"Oh, I thought maybe you fell down or something, you know?"

"No, I don't know. Why would I be falling? I ain't drunk in case that's what you're thinking ."

"Okay." It was too early for an unnecessary confrontation.

"Maybe I'm just a little drunk, but I can stand up . . ." Taylor stumbled, "without falling down."

"Sure you can." I was tired of these games.

"What's that supposed to mean?"

"Nothing," I huffed. "I'm going back to bed."

"You do that. Just carry your goody-goody self to bed."

"Oh, so now I'm the bad person for being good?"

"No, you're just the bad person period," Taylor replied.

Taylor closed the door behind me, but I heard her stumble again.

About half an hour later I found my sister stretched out on the couch, still dressed in her little black underwear, with her ankles crossed, flipping through *Ebony* magazine as if it weren't a workday. Thank goodness, it wasn't a workday for me. She had the portable fan, which was set on the end table, blowing directly into her face. I wished I could feel so free. Irresponsibility did have its own allure. Since I was blessed with the day off, I sat down in the soft cushioned armchair across from her and popped open a can of Sprite.

Taylor lifted her eyes off the pages. "You know that's bad for you, right?"

"I know. But at least it's caffeine and alcohol free."

"Hmm. You got jokes."

"Don't worry. I'm going to eventually give up drinking sodas."

Taylor didn't bother to say a word, but I knew what she was thinking. She wasalways the twin in perfect health, physically fit. And yet I was the one who was a high risk for diabetes, high blood pressure, heart attack, and stroke. I paused to think about the numerous prescriptions my mother had filled daily. For a moment I considered the possibility of needing some of those medications myself one day. Immediately, I realized my mistake, and I opened her mouth to recant that thought.

"By His stripes, I'm healed." I shook the thought of illness from my mind. I was determined to live, to be strong and healthy.

I looked up at Taylor whose eyes were back on her magazine. Taylor never even saw my mouth move, and I was glad because she'd only mock me if she had.

"Are you going to buy a ticket to the church anniversary banquet?" I asked, anxious to change the subject away from my questionable eating habits.

"Maybe. When is it again?"

"It's on the third Sunday of this month, remember?" I pulled a stack of tickets out from my purse. "So you've got a little more than a week to get yourself together."

"I'm already together." Taylor started looking through her Coach signature purse. "Okay, how much is it?"

"Since it's a fundraiser, it's fifty dollars." I held out my hand for the money. "It will be held at the Kingdom House of Prayer's building since ours is too small for the event."

Taylor shook her head. "Y'all trying to kill a sista or something?"

"No, we're just trying to raise money for the missions fund."

"Right," Taylor said.

"It takes a lot of money to send missionaries and supplies to Africa."

"Right."

"No, really."

Taylor smirked. "I know that. Just because I didn't waste my time in college doesn't mean I'm stupid."

"Then right after the banquet, there comes The Missionary Women's Day Conference, and I know you're coming for that."

Taylor sat up straight on the couch, still holding the magazine. "What makes you so sure?"

"Because we used to have so much fun at those." I remembered the days Mom used to bring us and how we'd play happily around her skirt tail the entire time. How we loved watching the beautiful women in their fancy outfits prancing by. Then there was always something to get into, whether it was a stack of new church fans, or a pan full of homemade cookies.

"We were kids. We had fun at everything." Taylor dismissed my enthusiasm quickly. She would never show weakness.

"No, there was always something special about the women's conferences."

"Whatever," Taylor said.

I decided not to pressure her any further. "Will I see you this evening, or do you have another hot date?"

"Not tonight. I'm tired." Taylor put the magazine down. "I need a little time for myself."

"Really? I thought you couldn't survive without having a man hanging around you."

"Oh, I know you're not talking about me. What about you?" Taylor began to roll her neck, and I hated when she did that.

"What is that supposed to mean?"

"Are you kidding? You're so tight up on Joshua, he probably can't tell where he ends and you begin."

"Very funny." I stood up and opened my mouth wide in disbelief.

"Look, all I'm saying is you're all up on a brother." Taylor stood up too.

"So what? We're getting married."

"So what? Chill out. Just 'cause he's in that holy of holy school of yours don't mean you can't let him breathe. Goodness."

I growled in frustration, and then walked into the kitchen to keep myself from killing my sister. I tried to ignore Taylor's wiry voice, but it echoed in my head. Opening the refrigerator gave me a quick blast of cool air as I perused what I was about to eat for breakfast.

Maybe pancakes or waffles. Maybe pancakes and waffles with a side order of bacon and eggs. I thought about what Taylor said as I began to stir the pancake batter. Maybe I was too clingy. Maybe it was turning Joshua off. I didn't know if that were true or not, but I knew I had a more serious problem. Pancakes and problems. Problems and pancakes would go nicely together, I decided.

Today was the day I promised Sister Jackie that I'd deliver an oral presentation onthe Bible college and jobs in the ministry to her seventh grade history classes in honor of career week. Dr. Harding had jumped at the opportunity to promote his agenda and had given me the day off. Deep in my heart I always believed I'd be a teacher like my mother had been. Although I eventually gave up the idea, I had once majored in education and had considered it my calling. That is up until the day my world came crashing down around me. I hadn't been the same since. Don't get me wrong, I'd been saved, sanctified, Holy Ghost filled, and fire baptized for years now, but when I went to sleep at night, it wasn't Jesus that I saw.

I shook the past from my head and began to focus on the task at hand. I gathered my display boards, and other articles of interest, and began to load them into my car. I was anxious to get it over with, afraid that today might trigger the same old regrets. After all, here I was again, getting involved in the lives of children.

Involuntarily, my mind went back to Michelle and why I never finished the call that day. I could have stepped in right away, but I didn't. Instead, here I was afraid. "Lord, I know you haven't given me a spirit of fear, but of a sound mind. Please help me. In Jesus' name. Amen."

I reached into my briefcase and took one last glance at my planner. The upcoming church anniversary banquet, which Taylor had already purchased a ticket for, and the annual women's conference, were both events I looked forward to. I secretly hoped that one of those would warm my sister's cold heart. I hopped into my carnation pink car and headed toward the school.

As I walked down the front steps of the junior high school, I breathed a sigh of relief that my presentation had been a success. The school was an old building and its steps were steep. A group of boys wearing sagging jeans and long sleeveless T-shirts passed by, nearly knocking me over. Teenagers and their familiar noises were everywhere. I heard the sounds of girls giggling and of rap music playing in the distance. The air was full of youth and energy, which I was excited to feed upon. Before I hit the bottom step I looked up into Joshua's brown eyes. His tall lanky frame leaned against the school gate, providing the perfect aesthetic addition to the view.

"Hello, Ms. Teacher," Joshua said.

"Oh, please don't say that." I shook my head.

"Why not? I'm sure you did well today." Joshua looked into my big eyes with his sleepy looking ones.

"I did okay. The kids were happy. The principal sat in on everything, and Sister Jackie was ecstatic." I took my eyes off him and turned to the school. "What are you doing here though?"

"I got off early, and I was in the neighborhood."

"Well, it was nice of you to come down here to meet me."

"I know what a big day this is for you." A toothy grin spread across Joshua's face, and I thought I would drown in his warmth. "Why would you say that?"

"Are you kidding me? Ever since you had to substitute teach your Aunt Dorothy's Sunday School class, you've been going on and on about the experience."

"I'm sorry. I didn't realize—"

"No, it's okay. I like to see you happy." Joshua smiled. "In fact, I was beginning to think you didn't like kids up until then."

"Really? Why would you say that?"

"You never mention any. You kind of stay away from them and the whole subject of kids I guess. Even the other night with Lilah, you were very quiet."

I was caught. "I'm sorry. The other night was very stressful for me with your parents and all, and I wasn't aware that I was doing that. I love kids, actually, and I can't wait to be Lilah's stepmother. . . . I tried to hide what was rising up in me.

"I didn't mean it like that. It's just that you look a little sad sometimes when I say we'll be a family soon."

"Oh no, it's not that I'm sad. I'm just a little nervous about her . . . Lilah, I mean . . . not having a—"

"You'll make a wonderful mother."

I scrambled to change the subject. "But anyway, I won't be doing anything like this again anytime soon. My friend, Jackie, owes me big."

"Your smile tells me differently, but I'll drop it." Joshua walked me down the street to my car. "What if I pick you up for dinner at about six o'clock?"

"Sure. That sounds good. What about Lilah?"

"She'll be next door at Mrs. Johnson's house. She's great with kids. You'll love her."

"Okay then, since that's settled, where are we going?" I climbed into my car. "I'm taking you downtown to Juniors." Joshua closed the car door gently, bent down, and leaned his head in the window. "Where they have the best cheesecake in Brooklyn."

"Says who?"

"Says me," Joshua kissed me softly on the lips.

"Oh well, when you put it like that . . ." I licked my full lips and kissed him back with all the intensity I vibrated with. For a few minutes we were lost in each other's gaze until the sound of a fire truck zooming by broke the mood.

"I'll see you later, future Mrs. Bennings."

"I like the sound of that." I smiled. "I'll see you later."

"Don't make me wait too long." Joshua put his hands on mine and stared into my eyes.

If I had stayed any longer, I would have melted right there in the front seat of my car. "I promise it won't be very long now."

He let go of my hands, smiled, and turned to walk away.

I watched him disappear through the crowd as I drove out of the parking lot.

***

After a delicious steak dinner at Juniors and, of course, after indulging in Juniors's famous cheesecake for dessert, I smiled and wiped my mouth with my napkin. When I reached for my glass of Diet Coke, Joshua stroked my fingers with his. He paid the waitress, left a generous tip on the table, and led the way to the door. We strolled downtown, window shopping, discussing the usual church business and the latest conquests in Joshua's bright future in ministry. He finished my sentences, and I finished his. Everything seemed to be perfect as we walked arm in arm along Fulton Street. We passed by the many street vendors, stopping to sample a few pieces of costume jewelry. I felt so secure in his strong arms. He stopped under a street light where he tilted my chin upward and planted a soft kiss right on my ready lips. I closed my eyes, expecting more, but he had already backed away.

I looked into his eyes and caught a glimpse of sadness, that same sadness I saw when I first met him. He looked like a wounded animal back then, the vulnerable widow. How I had longed to soothe his gentle spirit, even before he took an interest in me.

I looked into those brown eyes and decided to go for it. "You know, I think we make a good team."

"Yes we do."

"And I know you'll be a good husband."

"I'll do my best."

I was getting nowhere. "Is everything okay?"

"Yes, everything is fine." Joshua returned his attention to me.

Feeling awkward, I quickly tried to fix the mood. "I mean, you have such vision." Joshua didn't respond.

"I wish I had it all together like you," I desperately grasped for words.

"Don't be ridiculous. You're very organized." Joshua looked directly into my eyes.

"No, I'm not. Mr. Harding wants me to go back to school to be a public relations liaison, but I don't want that."

"Okay, so what do you want?"

"I don't know, but I want to do something meaningful. I mean, something meaningful to me, that is." Joshua smirked.

"Well?"

"I haven't figured it out yet, but I um . . ."

"You'll figure it out."

"I know that I do better with a partner, you know, as part of a team. What about you?" I threw out the bait to see if he would take it. I wanted him to talk about his first marriage.

"What about me?"

"Do you do better when you're not operating solo? You know . . ." Joshua didn't answer. "My mom and dad were a great team, at least in their last few years together, you know, after my dad stopped roaming and came home. I can see that your parents are clearly a force to be reckoned with."

"And?"

"Marriage can be good, I guess." I secretly wondered if I were being too assertive, yet my fear wasn't enough to stop what I felt in my heart.

"Yes, I'm sure it can be, and ours will be. I won't allow it to be any other way." Joshua turned away. "Look at the time. We'd better get going." Joshua looked at his watch and started walking toward his car.

"The night is still young." I didn't want the evening to end, but I had obviously ruined it.

"Not when we've got to get up early in the morning, and I've got a couple of hours of study to get in tonight also." Joshua kept walking until he reached the location he had parked his car.

"I guess you're right." I surrendered to the tension.

During the ride home, he was so quiet and detached that I

felt like a stranger. Not the person that he had been dating for three months, the woman he had planned to marry. I hoped that I hadn't said or done anything to seriously offend him. I turned on the radio hoping that the gospel tunes would win over my own emotions, but it did not help. I prayed silently for strength. "Lord, please help me with this relationship."

That night, instead of doing my normal scripture readings, I only read one verse and almost cried myself to sleep. "What is wrong with me, Lord?"

Finally, in an attempt to get answers, I reached over and dialed Joshua's number. The phone rang and rang, but he didn't answer.

Chapter Thirteen

It was another Wednesday night Bible Study at church with the bustling crowd, scents of various perfumes and colognes all mixed up together, the shaking of sweaty hands, and the hugging of sweaty necks. Daddy and Aunt Dorothy stood around the lobby telling their usual stories about the good old days.

Aunt Dorothy grabbed me and whispered in my ear. "I'm gonna host your engagement party at my house. I've got it all worked out, chile."

"Thanks, Aunt Dorothy." I smiled, afraid to ask the specifics of what her plans were, but I was grateful. Besides, I knew Sister Benning wouldn't like it, and that reason alone made it all worthwhile. Mrs. Margaret brought in her pans of peach cobbler and apple butter, recipes she'd grown up with in Alabama. The choir pranced about in their emerald green robes. The church mothers cackled, and the deacons groaned on the opposite sides of the church. There sitting near the pulpit was the invincible Pastor Martin. He was a stocky, middle aged man with a slightly receding hairline and a thick, gray mustache.

I sang three songs with the praise team, and that was enough to take my mind off my problems with Joshua. That was enough to transport my mind to another realm where nothing else mattered but God.

Sister Martin, wearing her typical dark colored skirt suit, led the congregation in prayer, covering everyone; the sick, the homeless, the unemployed, the hungry, and generally, every disadvantaged person from the United States to Africa and back again. Finally, Pastor Martin stood behind the pulpit and preached about faith with the conviction of ten men. I drank in every word and wished Taylor was there to hear it also.

When I looked in front of me, I saw Sister Winifred sitting in the front row with her crooked legs crossed and her thin gray hair pinned up in a bun. I looked behind me and found Sister Williams smiling. She was holding her new baby. He was a round faced baby boy wrapped in a light blue knitted blanket. She clung to him proudly. I could finally see the sense of satisfaction and relief in her eyes after years of trying to conceive. I saw that the baby had big brown eyes, but I couldn't look into them. There was that pinching feeling again. Reminders.

I just kept on listening and kept on praying. "Lord, why isn't this pain over?"

Finally, I tiptoed out of her row and down the carpeted aisle. When I turned the corner, I practically fell into the restroom, taking a deep breath as I closed the door behind me. As I leaned against one of the stalls, basking in the relief I thought had come, I heard gurgling noises coming from one of the stalls.

Suddenly, Michelle came out with a napkin over her mouth.

"Oh, I didn't know anyone was in here." I wiped my eyes quickly to hide my own grief.

"Yes, I'm still not feeling very well." She smiled nervously.

"This is a hideout for all of us women." I smiled back and turned to the mirror, pretending to fix my hair.

From the mirror I could see that Michelle's eyes were a glossy red as if she had been crying. I couldn't take it anymore. I whirled around and grabbed the girl by the hand.

"Come with me." Michelle followed me out the back door into a lonely corner by the garbage bin.

"What's going on with you?" I asked her.

"Nothing. I don't know what you mean." Michelle shook her head as if she had no idea what I was talking about.

"Let's be honest, Michelle. I saw you trying to purchase a home pregnancy kit the other day. You hid it behind your back, then threw it down like I'm blind, then you come in here today with fire engine red eyes and you're throwing up all over the place. Now I may be quite a few years older than you, but I'm nobody's fool."

"Nobody is calling you a fool, Sister Alex, but—"

"I want to help you, but I can't if you don't tell me what's going on." I held onto both of Michelle's arms and shook her gently.

"Nothing, really I—" Michelle started.

"Nothing? Okay, it's my mistake then. I'm sorry for pulling you out here." I threw up my hands and turned to walk away.

"No, wait." Michelle grabbed my shoulder strap.

"Yes?"

"You're right. I do need someone to talk to. My friends are no help, and he . . ." Her words trailed off.

"You can trust me. God has a way of bringing people together."

"Oh, yeah? Where was God when I needed Him? Why wasn't he there to stop me from making such a bad mistake?"

"Sweetheart, God has been there all along, and He has been speaking to you through His Word. He says, 'My sheep hear my voice.' But He gives us all freedom of choice even if we make the wrong choices."

"I never thought I'd ruin my whole life, but I did. You're right."

"I'm right?"

"I did buy a home pregnancy test, and I'm pregnant." Michelle began to cry uncontrollably. "I'm pregnant, and I don't know what to do. I shouldn't have—"

"I know. I know, but that's all over now. All we're concerned with is you and the health of that baby you're carrying." I pointed, inconspicuously, to Michelle's stomach.

"The health isn't going to matter," Michelle said.

"Of course it does. Why wouldn't it matter?"

"Because I'm not going to carry it to term." Michelle turned her back on me. "I can't."

"What do you mean you can't? Even if you don't want to keep the baby, you can always put the baby up for adoption."

"No, I can't."

"Why not?"

"Do you see my mom out there directing the choir and my sister singing a solo? My brother is playing the drums, and my father is sitting next to Pastor Martin in the pulpit." Michelle sighed. "You know this kind of disgrace would kill them."

"No, it won't. It will hurt them, but they'll live through it, and so will you. But most importantly, this child will live through it." I grabbed Michelle by the shoulders and shook her gently. "I can't."

"What about the father? Is he willing to play an active role in the child's life?" I let go of Michelle.

"No, he doesn't want any part of it. He has his own plans. It was just a mistake." Michelle looked down at the floor. "He is the son of a family friend, and I tried to help him through a tough time he was having, and one thing led to another. I should've never . . . I should've known better."

"Don't worry about that now. Did you repent?"

"Repent?"

"Yes, for the fornication," I said.

"Oh yeah, I have . . . over and over again."

"Well, it only takes once. Then it's finished, forgotten in

God's eyes. He is just to cleanse us from all unrighteousness." An involuntary tear rolled down my face, and I wiped it away with my hand. "You don't have to commit another sin."

"Another sin?"

"Yes. Abortion is murder." I didn't dare breathe or blink. I couldn't believe I wasn't choking on my own hypocritical words. I just stared into Michelle's frightened eyes, hoping to make the kind of connection that could save two young lives.

"I never really thought about it like that. I mean, it's not like it's a real baby or anything . . . I mean, not at this stage anyway."

"Oh, it's a real baby from the time God puts it in your womb, from conception. Remember, God calls the end from the beginning, so He sees what that baby will grow up to be. He or she actually already has a destiny, a purpose. You have a purpose." I stood close to Michelle and stroked her hair.

"I never thought of that." Michelle's eyes began to swell with tears.

"I know you didn't."

For a few minutes there was just silence, the sound of broken hearts and remorse.

"I'll tell you what. You get yourself together so you can go back in before Pastor gives the benediction, and I'll meet with you later." I took a piece of paper out of my purse and wrote my number on it. "I'll help you to tell your family if you want me to."

"Oh please, would you?"

"Just promise me one thing."

"What is it?"

"That you won't do anything until you talk to me first. Promise me." I held both the girl's sweaty palms.

"I promise." Michelle wiped away the remaining tears with her sleeve.

"Good." I gave her one last hug before I turned to go back inside. Before we knew it, the door opened wide. "What in the world are you two doing out here?"

Chapter Fourteen

As soon as I heard Sister Winifred's voice, I knew there would be trouble. She had a small garbage bag in her hand, which she dropped into the garbage bin.

I passed by her, followed by a shaky Michelle. "Excuse me, ma'am. We were just leaving." I walked into the building through the lobby, into the sanctuary, then quickly down the aisle, thinking I'd die before I could get back to my seat. My breathing was sporadic. I felt Sister Winifred right on my heels. Nervous, I accidentally dropped my purse, and as I squatted down to pick it up, Sister Winifred stood right behind me. I looked up into her eyes, and she frowned up her already wrinkled face. I stood up and found my seat quickly.

Looking back at Michelle, I could see that she had returned to sit by her siblings, and was looking straight ahead as if she were in a trance. Her stress was obvious, and I wasn't sure how I would be able to help her, but I was sure that this wasn't about me. I turned around quickly and sat still in my seat, hoping Sister Winifred wouldn't question me, or worse yet, put the word out that Michelle and I were having a tearful conversation in the back of the church. Not that it was any of her business anyway, but that had never stopped her before. She was always creeping around the church, giving people a scripture on whatever it was she felt they had done wrong. Somebody needed to give her a scripture on gossiping.I didn't dare turn my head toward Sister Winifred. Instead, I fumbled around in my purse, indiscriminately flipped the pages of my

Bible, and waited for the service to be over. I crossed my legs and focused on what Pastor Martin was saying from the pulpit. My heart was heavy and I needed all the Word I could get.

When the service was over, I gathered my things and waited in the lobby for Joshua to complete his deacon duties. Aunt Dorothy came over wearing a big blue feathered hat and matching blue dress. "Alex, will you still be working with us on the anniversary banquet later on in the week?"

"Sure, no problem." Unfortunately, it was a problem. My schedule was getting fuller and fuller as the days went by. I hardly had any time for myself. There was always something to do for somebody. Yet I smiled at Aunt Dorothy and made a mental note to stay on the anniversary banquet committee.

Aunt Dorothy hugged me, and I caught one of her blue feathers right in my mouth. "I'll call you then, sweetie."

"Yes ma'am." Between the anniversary committee, The Elijah Project, and praise team rehearsals, along with the regular twice a week services, I'd be moving into the church soon if I weren't careful.A few seconds after Aunt Dorothy walked away, Yvonne came out carrying her Bible at her side. She wore a form fitting pink skirt suit. Her face was heavily painted with eyeliner, bright pink lipstick, and pink blush. She stood beside me and smiled. Then she reached into her purse and handed me an envelope. I took it from her, maintaining a puzzled look on my face. "Oh."

"Would you please give this to Deacon Joshua for me?" Yvonne smiled.

I wasn't sure what she was up to, but I didn't like it. "Sure. I'll see that he gets it."

"I'm volunteering to work alongside him and Brother Jacob in the homeless ministry. You know, for the Elijah Project?" Yvonne said.

"I see." My throat became dry and scratchy, as if I were wading across the Sahara Desert. My flesh wanted to lash out, to question her motives, but I had no earthly reason to do so. I made my emotions submit to the Holy Spirit. Still, something inside me couldn't rest. Something had stolen my peace.

Chapter Fifteen

On Friday morning, when I walked through the doors of Missionary Bible College, the first one I saw was Dr. Harding. He was tall, well built, and had a full head of white hair. Although he appeared to be deep in conversation on his cell phone, he didn't hesitate to give me last minute instructions. Before I could put down my purse, he lowered his glasses, handed me a broom and pointed to pieces of a broken coffee cup on the floor. He nodded gratefully and disappeared into his office. That was my life.

"Good morning, everyone," I said.

"Morning, Alex." Marisol leaned against the wall talking to a student with wavy brown locks that hung to the side of her head.

When I finished sweeping, I checked the inventory of office supplies. As soon as I made notes on the deliveries, checked them against purchase orders, I was able to determine what shortages I had to warn Mr. Harding of. Being the organizational whiz that I was, I loved keeping accurate, up to date records, and as a secretary, I had more than my share of work in this area.

"Alex, I need you to log in this information." Mr. Harding handed me a sheet of paper.

"Right, I know," I recited, without even looking at it. "Yes, sir."

"You always do such a good job. I hope you're still considering my offer to fund your public relations career. If you decide to accept, I'll need you to go on a short mission trip to Nairobe, Kenya to wrap up some loose ends for me."

"I'm still considering it, but you know, I . . . I'm not sure I can handle it." I smiled my biggest smile.

"With an accelerated program, you'll be ready to take your place in public relations in no time. "

"I know, and thank you. But I'm just not sure that I can go back to school right now. I've got so much going on right now. You know Deacon Joshua Bennings and I are getting married." I held out my ring finger.

"Congratulations on your engagement to Brother Joshua."

"My aunt will be throwing an intimate little engagement party for us, and I hope you can come. The invitations should be in the mail any day now." I was hoping to throw him off. Up until now he hadn't even been on the guest list.

"How nice." Dr. Harding adjusted his glasses and smiled.I was hesitant. "Again, I'm just not sure yet about the position."

"Alex, what if I extended the time you had to decide, would that help? You wouldn't have to give me an answer until the end of the summer since the official position won't become available until then anyway." Dr. Harding's eyes lit up with his idea. "There is only one catch, of course."

"What is that, sir?"

"That you go to Nairobe first. You can consider this trip a trial, a free vacation of sorts or whatever you like, but I need the work done either way."

"When is the trip?"

"The trip will be the second week of July, with or without you. We'd love to have you on board, Alex."

"That sounds really generous of you, Dr. Harding, and I will give this offer serious consideration. I'll have to—"

"No need to explain, but your being a mere secretary is such a waste of talent." Dr. Harding walked away, shaking his head. "Think about it."

I smiled as I swallowed my real dreams. Although most of my days were uneventful, they were productive. I fulfilled my duties with a certain level of dignity, and while I wasn't completely fulfilled, I did feel some measure of satisfaction. My real dreams, however, were lost in the abyss of misfortune.

When it was time for my break, I went across the street to McDonald's to eat a Big Mac combo as I contemplated the job offer again. Public relations wasn't my cup of tea. It wasn't fair that Taylor came home after a day of work, physically rejuvenated, energetic, full of passion, and full of exhilarating stories of her clients' progress. I wanted to feel connected to my clients like that, but my exhaustion and lack of enthusiasm always held me back. There was always a line I wouldn't dare cross. Unfortunately, the only thing about the offer that excited me was the chance to go to Kenya. Public relations. It wasn't a bad field. It just wasn't enough for me. I didn't know what I was supposed to do for a living, and I didn't know what I was supposed to do for God. I hated being indecisive. *Please, Lord, fill me.* Maybe this trip was what I needed to decide. Maybe I could spend the week in Kenya, away from Joshua, not only working, but also reflecting on my life and clearing my head before the wedding. The real question was could I live with myself if I married Joshua and didn't clear out the cobwebs of my past? Also if I did marry him, could we survive if he didn't face his own issues?

I picked up my cell phone and called Joshua. "Hi, Josh."

"Hi, baby," Joshua said.

I hesitated for a moment, not knowing how to tell him. "I've got news."

"Really? What's going on?"

I took a deep breath. "I'll be going to Kenya on the second week of July."

"Kenya? What are you talking about?"

"Remember that position Dr. Harding offered me?"

"Yes."

"Well, he's allowing me to test it out by doing one public relations assignment in Nairobe, Kenya." I waited anxiously for his response. "I'm hoping to be able to do some missions work also."

"I see."

"It's only for a week and um—"

"But that's too close to our wedding date," Joshua interrupted.

"It's only for a week, and believe me, your mother has this wedding under control. I'm sure everything will have been done by the time I leave."

"This is big news," Joshua said, with a hint of surrender on his voice.

"It's something I've been thinking about ever since Dr. Harding mentioned it."

"I know that, but—"

"Please don't make this harder than it already is. I need this trip." In my heart I was pleading with him because I knew I needed this.

Joshua's tone was mellow. "It is a great opportunity for you, so I'll have to be supportive even though my heart doesn't want you to go."

"I'll be back, Joshua." I paused. "I love you."

"I love you too."

When I hung up the phone, I walked over to Dr. Harding's office and knocked on his door.

"Come in," Dr. Harding said in his gruff voice.

I entered, but stood against the door. "I've been thinking about what you said."

"And?" Dr. Harding never looked up from his papers.

"And I'll go on the trip to Kenya."

Dr. Harding smiled. "Good, good. I feel this will be mutually beneficial."

"I believe so too."

"We'll talk about the travel details later." Dr. Harding finally looked up.

"Yes. Thanks again, sir." I turned to leave.

"You're welcome."

"Yes, sir." I went back to work, but this time with a smile.

By the end of the day, I had already applied online for a single entry, three month tourist visa and mailed off my passport to the Consulate General of Kenya in New York. Thankfully, I had already obtained a passport for last year's praise conference in Canada, even though my lack of funds never allowed me to make it on the trip. I also scheduled a doctor's appointment so I could be vaccinated for yellow fever. There was so much to do before my trip, but I enjoyed the anticipation.

Surprisingly, it had been a good day, and I left work hopeful about the future, ready to assist Michelle with tackling hers.After work I drove straight to the Harrises' home to meet with Michelle's parents.

Sister Harris greeted me at the door. "Please come in, Sister Alex." She led me over to an antique looking armchair. "What brings you by?"

"Well, I hope I'm not interrupting anything important because if I am, then I can come back another time." I sat down and hoped I could find an excuse to run out. How did I get involved in this anyway?

"Don't be silly. We weren't doing anything important right now."

"Nope, not a thing." Minister Harris sat down on the couch next to his wife, and suddenly I felt outnumbered. Where in the world was Michelle?

"Oh, I see. Well I've got something really important to tell you, something you should know and—"

Sister Harris smiled. "Is this about your engagement to Deacon Joshua? He's a wonderful young man."

"Congratulations. You two make a nice couple," Minister Harris said.

"Thank you. No, it's not about that." I wanted to bolt through the door as quickly as possible.

"What is this about, dear?" Sister Harris crossed her legs.

My voice was shaky. "Actually, it's about Michelle."

Minister Harris pulled his glasses down onto the tip of his nose. "Our Michelle?" Minister Harris leaned forward.

Sister Harris sat on the edge of her seat. Then Michelle walked into the room, holding a book up to her chest. I let out a big sigh of relief.

I smiled at her as she took her place in the room. "Yes, it's about Michelle."

"Well?" Sister Harris squeezed together her arched eyebrows.

"Sometimes people, even Christian people, make mistakes. If we repent, then God is merciful enough to forgive." I fumbled with my fingers as I spoke. *Help me, Lord Jesus.*

"Right," Sister Harris said.

"Mom, I've made a mistake," Michelle said.

"What kind of mistake?" Minister Harris took his glasses off altogether and stared into Michelle's eyes. I, on the other hand, just sat there feeling very awkward and un-useful.

Michelle set the book down on the coffee table. "Mom and Dad, I'm pregnant."

"Oh my goodness, no," Sister Harris said.

"Michelle Harris, what in the world were you thinking?" Minister Harris raised his voice.

Michelle dropped her head. "I'm so sorry, Daddy."

"Oh no, how could this happen?" Sister Harris put her hand to her head as if a headache had just come on.

"That's a very unfortunate and costly mistake, Michelle," Minister Harris said.

Those were the last words I heard before I asked that we

have a word of prayer. "Father, I pray that you give this family peace with what has happened. Give them wisdom in how to handle this situation. Give them forgiveness for whatever trust has been betrayed. Give them strength to stand against persecution and judgment. And finally, give them joy in loving the new addition to the family. In the matchless name of Jesus. Amen."

Then I hugged Sister Harris and Michelle, ready to give them all their privacy. Minister and Sister Harris seemed quietly devastated, yet I was still relieved to know that the healing process could finally begin. Sister Harris thanked me for coming as she walked me to the door. At least she seemed calm. I didn't dare look at Minister Harris, and he didn't even say good-bye. I felt confident that Michelle's family would soon become a strong support system after the initial shock had dissipated, of course. Then I walked to my car, opened my door, and before I could sit down, I heard Sister Harris scream.

Chapter Sixteen

Hearing Michelle's mom scream quickened my steps, but I didn't dare look back.

I felt her pain, so I prayed all the way home. The next beautiful spring day I awoke in my canopy bed to the sound of my favorite gospel station, WGSP New York. I bounced out of bed to the tune of Mary Mary's "Heaven." After a good cool shower, I was refreshed and ready to face this Saturday with my father.

I walked into the living room and looked out of the window. The huge cloudsswirled around in dark circles, holding the promise of rain. When I lifted the window slightly, I first smelled the moisture in the air, but after the raindrops began to hit the pavement, the stench of wet cement settled in.

I backed away from the window as Taylor entered the room, wearing a silk nightie and high heeled slippers. Even her not together look was together.

"Aren't you going with us to Mama's gravesite?" I asked her.

"Not today," Taylor answered.

I shook my head. "You're not going?"

"That's what I said." Taylor looked like she was in one of her moods.

"May I ask, why not?"

"You can ask, but it ain't really none of your business." Taylor rolled her eyes.

I turned and walked away from her before I had a chance to

react in the flesh. *Help me, Lord Jesus.* I wanted to give Taylor a backhand across her face for being so selfish and disrespectful, but I didn't have time to deal with her nasty attitude. Besides, Daddy was already waiting for me to pick him up, and I wanted to hit the highway before it started pouring.

Sighing, I went into the bathroom and examined myself in the full-length mirror. I sucked in my stomach, adjusted my girdle underneath my pleated skirt, wishing my thighs weren't so unruly. I fluffed my hair and used concealer to mask the dark circles under my eyes. I wasn't my best today, but I was ready. Suddenly I remembered that Joshua was taking Yvonne into Manhattan today. I didn't understand what the rush was and why it couldn't wait until next weekend, but I didn't argue. It was all Sister Winifred's idea to partner her fireball of a niece with my man. I wasn't happy about it all, but I couldn't cancel on Daddy. Even though Joshua was trustworthy, I still had a bad feeling about it.

When I walked back into the living room, complete with cotton hat and matching purse, Taylor looked me up and down.

"You look cute," Taylor complimented.

"Thanks." I bit my tongue not to say more.

"I'm sorry about before, but I just don't feel like going anywhere with that man." Taylor turned her back to me.

"That man is your father," I said.

"And?"

"Okay, I understand." I didn't understand.

"No, you don't."

"You're right, I don't, but it's your choice."

"That's right. It's my choice, and no one knows what I'm going through." Taylor turned around with tears in her eyes.

"God knows."

"There you go again with that God stuff." Taylor stormed out of the room.

"Well, it's true. I don't know, but He does." I followed my sister into her bedroom.

"Why doesn't he fix everything, then?"

"God moves in His own time. His thoughts are not our thoughts. His ways are not our ways."

"I've heard that before." Taylor dropped down onto her bed and didn't turn around.

"He is a problem solver."

"Promises are for fools."

"I'm nobody's fool." I sensed offense rising up in her.

"That's a matter of opinion."

"Such a pretty face and such an ugly mouth." I placed my hands on my broad hips. "I can't reason with you."

"Then don't."

"I guess I'll see you when we get back this afternoon." I was determined not to let my sister get to me.

"I'll be gone by then," Taylor said.

"Good." I let the door slam on the way out.

An hour later I sent Taylor a text message saying that I was sorry. Her response was: YEAH, RIGHT.

Sure enough, as soon as I returned to the apartment, Taylor was gone. Everything was quiet. No loud music, no gum smacking, no telephone gossiping. There was only Taylor's lingering exotic scent.

I dropped my purse down on the couch and went over to call Joshua on the cordless. I hadn't heard from him all day.

The phone rang twice, and then he answered.

"Hi."

"Hi," I said.

"What's going on?"

"Not much. Dad and I just got back from the cemetery."

"Oh, right. How was it? Sorry I haven't called."

"That's okay." I held my breath, hoping to get an explanation, but really hoping for more than that. "I figured you were busy."

Suddenly, I heard Yvonne's irritating laugh in the background. I felt my blood pressure rising.

"Busy is only half of it. We must've been in every store on the East and Westside. Sister Winifred told Yvonne to make sure she came home dressed like a New Yorker."

"Oh." I rolled my eyes, glad he couldn't see my expression through the phone. "How is Lilah holding up?"

"Great. Lilah loves shopping, especially since we stopped at a toy store and let her pick out a couple of things."

"Really? It sounds like fun."

"Are you kidding me? This was harder than all the banking I do at work. You know I'm not good with this shopping stuff. I should've let you show Yvonne around."

You should've. "I can imagine. I'm sorry I missed it."

"I'm sorry too. You would have probably enjoyed it, being a woman and all," Joshua said.

"Now, what's that supposed to mean?" I heard Lilah playing happily in the background.

"Nothing really," Joshua said.

I wasn't handling this whole jealousy thing too well. "Well, I see you're busy . . . shopping, so I'll just talk to you later."

"Actually, we're about to get Lilah some ice cream, and then we're leaving."

"Oh?"

"Yeah we've got to wrap it up. I've got to get ready for class, remember?"

"Oh, I remember." I was feeling more and more insecure as the seconds went by. "Look, I'll call you when I get in." Joshua's voice didn't waver.

"Okay. Bye." My heart felt like it was failing me as I contemplated our relationship and how complex it had become. I couldn't figure him out. Sometimes he was caring and attentive, and then other times he was distant and aloof. Then when I thought about the Yvonne factor, that only heated things up.

I took a quick shower, and then changed into a pair of sweatpants and a T-shirt. I lay across the living room couch, immobilized as I popped chocolate coated pretzels into my mouth.

I heard Taylor running up the stairs, taking her usual deep cleansing breaths when she reached the top of the stairs. I opened the door for her and caught Taylor searching her denim purse for her keys. "I'm surprised you're already back." Taylor came in, mouth first.

"We never planned to stay very long, just long enough to leave fresh flowers. It makes Dad feel better," I said.

Taylor walked by as I lifted myself up from the couch. Her clothes were wrinkled and wet. Her eyes looked heavy as if from sleepiness. Going straight for the kitchen, Taylor didn't stop until she made herself a chicken salad sandwich, one of my specialties. And while she was probably enjoying her moment of peace, I came in and sat down next to her.

"So what did you do today?" I tried very hard not to sound judgmental.

"Nothing much, just went out with some guy named Michael."

I imagined Taylor involved in some sleazy rendezvous instead of with the family, and it made my heart sick. "Did you get my text?"

"Yeah, I did," Taylor said. "We're cool."

"Dad asked about you."

"Really?"

"We missed you." I looked into my sister's eyes, the same eyes I saw when I looked in the mirror.

"Now it ain't even that serious. You'll get over it." Taylor took a big bite of her sandwich.

"Are you still going to the banquet with us tomorrow?" I hoped so. I couldn't stand the thought of more rejection.

"What banquet?"

I immediately gave her a reprimanding look. "Are you kidding me? The banquet at the church, the one I've been working on and talking about for months."

"Right, the church banquet. Sure. I bought a ticket, didn't I?"

"Just checking." I didn't dare challenge my sister. I remembered the text I sent to her earlier, telling her that Jesus still loves her. I just hoped with all my heart that she would accept that fact and change.

"Did you ever find out about that girl?"

I opened a box of Oreos. "You mean Michelle?"

"Yeah, her."

"Yes, she's pregnant. I helped her tell her parents."

Taylor's eyes brightened. Drama always excited her. "Ooh, I know they were mad."

"They'll be okay. I'm going to help her."

"So what else is new? You always tryin' to help everybody." Taylor sucked her teeth. "You ain't no better than the rest of us."

"I didn't say I was better." I snapped back.

Taylor pulled back our sheer curtains and peeked through the window. "Hey, it's still early, so I say we go looking for wedding dresses."

"Sure, why not." I smiled at the thought of soon being a bride.

My cell phone rang, and I saw that it was Joshua. I picked it up and smiled. Maybe he missed me after all, I thought. "Hello," I said in my most sultry voice.

"It's me again. I just wanted you to know that Mrs. Johnson just called and she has had a family emergency. I've got class tonight so . . ." He sounded very anxious.

My smile dissipated.

"I need you to babysit with Lilah."

Chapter Seventeen

Saturday evening and I was stuck with babysitting Lilah. Joshua gave me a quick peck on the cheek and dropped her off at my apartment on his way to class. It wasn't that she could intentionally cause me any real harm, but I was breaking out in a cold sweat nonetheless. She skipped in and immediately jumped onto the couch.

Taylor squatted down in front of Lilah. "Are you thirsty?" Lilah nodded.

"I'll get you something to drink then." Taylor disappeared into the kitchen.

Lilah was a beautiful, caramel toned child, her father's sweet little darling, and I wanted more than anything to be her mother. She had already lost one mother, who was probably beautiful, although her character was questionable. What kind of married woman would do that to her unborn child? I mean, didn't she care about Joshua's feelings at all? What could have possibly made her risk everything? I circled the child trying to imagine exactly what her mother was really like, and how I would measure up in comparison. Underneath my fear, I wanted to be a perfect mother, but deep inside I knew there was no such thing. I hadn't been perfect when I did what I did. My own mother had not been perfect when she raised us either. But still, I wanted my life to be what it should've been. I would've given anything to have the opportunity Delilah had.

"Lilah, what would you like to do?"

She shook her head and looked away. "I don't know." Then she jumped down from the couch.

It was obvious I didn't know what to do with her. The poor girl was stuck with me. Unworthy, insecure, future step-mama me.

Taylor came out of the kitchen with a cup of orange juice. "Here you go."

Lilah smiled. "Thank you."

"No problem," Taylor said.

I just stood there like the air had been knocked out of me, waiting for words to say, waiting for some magical clue. I took a deep breath. Just be myself. No, this was too important.

I picked up Lilah and put her on my lap. "Lilah, would you like to play a game?"

"No," she replied.

"I could read you a story." I was getting desperate.

"No." Lilah climbed off of my lap.

Instantly, I was out of suggestions, and Lilah was already squirming around like she was restless.

I was no good at this. "Hey, I know what . . ."

"What?" Taylor looked as desperate as I was. She didn't do kids at all, ever.

"Let's just do what we had originally planned to do," I said.

Taylor snapped her fingers. "Okay. . . ."

"We'll go bridal store shopping, and Lilah can help me pick out my wedding dress." I looked into Lilah's eyes. "Would you like to help me pick out my dress for the wedding?"

Lilah hunched her shoulders. "Sure."

"Good. Then we're out of here." I grabbed my purse and led Lilah by the hand. Taylor followed closely behind. So we went downtown to check out the bridal shops. After an hour and a half of searching, we finally found the perfect wedding dress for me. It was a white, full-length, traditional gown made of satin, with three quarter length sleeves, and a long train. When I stepped out of the dressing room, all eyes were on me.

"I don't wanna do this anymore," Lilah whined and rubbed her eyes." I wanna go now."

"Okay, sweetheart." I wanted to bend down to soothe her, but since I was dressed in the wedding dress of my dreams, I couldn't.

"Now that's what I'm talking 'bout, right there, girl." Taylor snapped her fingers, and I knew it was the one.

I wished my mother was here to see it.

"It's a little tight though." I held my bloated stomach in.

"We'll fix that." Taylor poked me in the stomach. I admired myself in the full length mirror and was excited that my dream was finally coming true."Little girl, how would you like to go to the park now?"

"Yay." Lilah leaped into the air.

I scooped Lilah into my arms, carried her to the car, and we were on our way.

When we left downtown, we went straight to Prospect Park. Already dressed in workout gear, I wore my usual baggy sweat pants and a plain T-shirt while Taylor wore her favorite red and white jogging suit with a matching headband.

"I don't know if this is a good idea." I dragged myself along.

"Yeah, it is. You're the one that needs to fit into a decent sized wedding dress, right?" Taylor asked.

"Easy for you to say." I put Lilah's toys down and gave her instructions on where she could play alongside the track.

"Hey, no pain, no gain. Let's hit it." Then Taylor took off running down the track like it belonged to her, like everything belonged to her. I tagged along behind her, my body an unwilling participant in this activity.

Taylor ran around the entire track several times, but I ran back and forth on one side of the track so that I could keep a sharp eye on Lilah the whole time. Out of breath and about to pass out, I stopped to take a bottle of water from my backpack. Then I noticed Shayla McConnell getting out of her brand new Mercedes Benz. I gulped down my water and used my towel to wipe the sweat from my forehead. I looked ahead at Taylor who was coming back around and hoped that there would be no mess, especially not in front of the three-year-old.

Shayla immediately began walking toward us. By the time Taylor stopped in front of me, so did Shayla. "Imagine seeing you here. What a surprise."

"Get out of my face," Taylor said.

"I haven't even begun to get in your face . . . yet." Shayla laughed.

"Just leave me alone, Shayla." Taylor turned to walk away from her.

"Leave you alone? Oh, I wouldn't dare bother you." Shayla let out a big laugh. "After all, in a few short months you'll be on my payroll."

Taylor hollered back. "Over my dead body."

"Now I don't think it's going to take all that, but I must admit that would be interesting." Shayla continued to laugh as she took off running down the track.

I had to stop Taylor from running after her. Then I pulled her to the side; away from Lilah.

"I've only got a few months to get that center. Push It has got to be mine, Alex. I just can't stand by and watch a skeezer like her buy it. Sometimes when you want something bad enough, you'll do anything to get it."

"Yeah, I know what you mean," I said.

Taylor slapped me across the back. "Come on, I'm gonna have you in super shape for your wedding."

I coughed. "Well you've only got two and a half months left so . . ."

"You ain't giving me much to work with either." Taylor shook her head. "Let's go."

We ran around again and again until I felt dizzy. Then I fell onto the grass in exhaustion. My phone rang, and it was Michelle. "Hi, how are you?"

I answered it, breathing heavily.

"I'm doing okay." Michelle's voice was cheerful. "You don't sound so good though."

"Oh, I've just been running, you know, with my sister. She's like my personal trainer."

"Oh, I see. Well, I had my first appointment today, and my mom went with me."

"Oh good," I said.

"I don't know how to thank you for helping me—"

"No need to thank me. We're all in this together. Just remember if you need anything, just ask, and I'll see what I can do."

"I will," Michelle said.

"Okay, sweetheart. I'll see you at church."

"Yeah, I'll see ya." Michelle sounded certain of herself again. She sounded like the Michelle I knew when she was a little girl; pretty, sweet, and innocent. Life had tainted her.

"Bye." I ended the call with a smile on my face, then stuck it into my backpack.

"That was Michelle, wasn't it?" Taylor had always been nosy.

"Yes, it was."

"Aren't you afraid of what Joshua will say about you helping some fornicating teenager with her illegitimate baby?"

"I don't think he'll have a problem with it," I said.

"Mr. Bishop's son? I doubt it."

"Oh, come on. He's not like that."

"I'm not sayin', I'm just sayin' . . ." Taylor smiled and hunched her shoulders.

"I'm doing what I can to help a young church sister, whatever I can, whenever I can, and nobody can have a problem with that."

"Well, go ahead with yo' bad self." Taylor did her typical model walking down the catwalk expression.

I laughed aloud until my stomach hurt. "Stop it, just stop."

"I'm just sayin' . . ." Taylor laughed too.

My phone rang again, and it was Joshua. I picked it up quickly.

"Hi, husband to be," I said, still laughing slightly.

"Hi. Is that Taylor laughing too? What's so funny?"

"It's nothing really. We just finished doing some wedding dress shopping, and now Taylor, Lilah, and I are out here on the track at Prospect Park so I can fit into one, that's all."

"Don't be silly. You're a perfect size."

"You're very sweet, and that's why I love you, but a sista is gonna lose some pounds. Just wait."

"Remember, don't make me wait too long."

"I'll be all yours in exactly two months and two weeks."

"Is that all? It seems like forever."

"I'll be your wife before you know it, baby. I'll be your wife forever." For once, I could imagine really being his. Nothing had come between us thus far.

"Oh, I almost forgot why I called."

"Yes?"

"Sister Winifred just called with some rather disturbing news, something about the little Harris girl being pregnant. Did you hear anything about that?"

Chapter Eighteen

I almost dropped my phone onto the concrete. Instead, I gripped it tighter and held on for the ride. "I uh . . . think I heard about it . . . yes." I wondered how in the world the news got out so fast.

"Well, the Harrises are devastated and rightfully so. There is talk amongst the board of ending her church activities. I don't know, but my father says—"

My heart seemed like it was pounding against my chest. "Your father? How does he know about all of this?"

"You know bad news travels fast. He is the presiding bishop, so everything goes through him."

"Right."

"I just can't believe it. Little Michelle will be having a baby."

The words came out before I could stop them. "Well, it's better than the alternative."

"You've got that right." Joshua's voice dropped, and I could still hear his sadness long after our call ended.

I walked out of the bathroom fixing my makeup. It was another Sunday, and I was doing my typical routine. I looked down at the worn blue carpet, around at the old couch with the tacky throw pillows, the nineteen inch television set with the portable antenna on top, and I knew I had to make some decisions soon. Some more cash would help. Maybe being in public relations wouldn't be so bad.

Taylor sauntered into the living room. "Morning."

"Good morning," I said.

Taylor dropped down onto the living room floor and started alternating between squat thrusts and pushups. I got the feeling she was trying to make her body surrender even if her mind wouldn't. Then I watched my sister hop up, pull a cigarette out of her pocket, light it, and start pacing the floor. There was something about staying still that seemed to make her nervous. She always liked to go, go, go, and stay gone. Never did like staying in one place too long.

Even when we were little she was the one who wanted to see places while I wanted to stay home and play house. Not her. She'd be riding her bike around the block, skating, skateboarding, or running through the park. That was her, always active, always on the go. Never could sit still long; especially not in the house. She couldn't wait to get out of school, and believe me, she barely made it out.I shook my head at the thought and waved my hand through the cloud of smoke.

"Now you know we don't smoke in this apartment." I spread my legs and folded my arms, scolding her like she was a child.

"No, *you* don't smoke in this apartment." Taylor threw her head back and laughed. "Oh, come on, I'm just kidding. Goodness."

I pulled the cigarette from her lips. "Uh-huh, put it out."

"You had to be marrying a preacher; 'cause who else would put up with yo' rules?" Taylor rolled her eyes.

I gave her a look typical of our mother and kept on walking out the front door.

By the time I stepped my foot inside the emerald green sanctuary, I knew something was different. Mother Baker, with her fire red wig, heavily made up face, and slim stature, was leaned over chunky, gray haired Mother Richards,

frowning. There were a few members of the choir whisper-
ing amongst themselves. Folks everywhere were preoccupied
or occupied, but it wasn't with the Word. I looked around for
Sister Harris or Minister Harris, but I saw neither of them. Finally, I saw Michelle slumped over on a back pew to the far
left. I wondered why she was sitting alone way back there,
so I walked over to her.

"You never sit way in the back like this. What's going on in
here?" I sat next to Michelle.

"Don't you see? The disgrace has begun." Michelle lifted
her head from her hands, and then put it back again.

"What do you mean?"

"My parents are in Pastor Martin's office talking about my
issue," Michelle said.

"Oh, I see."

"Everyone knows." Michelle lifted her head again.

"I guess the news spread like wildfire," I said. "I'm sorry,
but everyone will get over it."

"I don't know about all of that. Some people seem really
upset. It's almost as if I did something to them."

"That's just ignorance. Like I said, they'll get over it, and
they'll stop talking. No one has any right to judge you; no one
at all." I felt myself getting angry.

"I wish you'd tell them that." Michelle pointed discreetly to
a group of three women sitting near the front wearing big and
medium sized hats. They were talking out of the sides of their
mouths and looking back. Ushers were standing at the door,
looking out of the corners of their eyes.

"Hang in there. God will take care of everything." I patted
Michelle on the head, and then proceeded to take my place
for the praise service.

When Michelle walked by Sister Winifred, I was pulled
aside.

"It's not a good idea, dear, for a decent girl to be seen talk-

ing to her, you know, while she's that way. People might get
the wrong idea, you know. And then you won't be able to
snag that deacon of yours when the time is right." Sister Winifred shook her head. "I remind my niece, Yvonne, of that all
the time."

"Sister Winifred, I appreciate your concern, but I can take
care of myself very well, thank you. I'm not worried about
what you or anyone else in this church thinks about me."
I looked Sister Winifred directly in her light eyes. "Now if
you'll excuse me, I've got to get to the front with the praise
team."

I couldn't believe the nerve of that lady. I walked away
from her and said a silent prayer. As I took my place to sing,
I looked out at Joshua who came in and sat on the front row.
He smiled at me, and I smiled back. Seconds later, I saw Sister
Winifred and Yvonne sit down behind him. Yvonne leaned
forward to whisper something in Joshua's ear, and I saw him
grin. That was it for me. Forget about the spirit. I had stepped
into the flesh. I wanted to step off the stage and pull those
cute little red ringlets out of her hair. Yet I kept on singing for
the Lord until a peace fell upon me.

When the service was over, I went over to the information
desk again, knowing I had to sign up for something. I looked
over the list of various needs in the community. Michelle
walked by me with her parents. "Goodnight, Sister Alex."

"Goodnight, sweetheart. Keep your head up now," I said,
smiling at Mr. and Mrs. Harris as they passed by.

They smiled back and nodded their heads, acknowledging
me, but they didn't stop. I didn't hold it against them because I knew they were still hurt. I watched them walk out the
front door, and my heart felt heavy with compassion. What
the community really needed were programs to help young
girls like Michelle. Now, I'd sign up for that in a heartbeat.
Maybe I'd get around to asking Pastor Martin about it one

day. Maybe Sister Trudy might want to facilitate a program like that since she had teenage daughters. I sighed as I signed up to help with the sick and shut-ins. A noble cause indeed, but nothing I felt passionate about.

When I looked at my watch, I realized I only had a couple of hours to change and return to church for the banquet. I was still upset with Joshua, so I didn't wait to say good-bye, and sadly, I doubted if he would even notice I was gone.

I came in the door and found Taylor on the couch watching television. I sat next to my sister and began to briefly tell her what happened to Michelle at the church. Then I realized I didn't have much time to freshen up before I had to be back at the church again. Taylor, on the other hand, who had promised she would come to the banquet, was still dressed in jeans. "Why aren't you dressed for the anniversary banquet?"

"I know I said I'd go, and I bought a ticket and all that junk, but I changed my mind."

"What do you mean, you're not going? It's our church's forty-third anniversary."

"It's not my church, it's yours, and after hearing all that noise they've been throwin' at Michelle, I don't even want to be around those hypocrites." Taylor stood up. "I ain't going."

"Not going?"

"Nope. You can give my ticket to someone else."

Involuntarily, my eyes began to fill up with tears. "All Mom wanted was for us to be okay when she was gone. All she ever wanted was that we would both be saved." I stood up and positioned myself in the middle of the walkway, hoping to block Taylor in.

"The church was very important to her."

"That's a low blow. Now you're going to use cheap tricks to try to get me into the church. Well, no thank you." Taylor hit the wall with her fist.

"What are you saying? You know it was Mom's last request."

"I don't know about any requests except that she asked to live, and she didn't. She requested that a lot of folk pray for her, and what good did that do?"

"Don't say that," I said.

"So don't tell me about what Mom wanted. Mom wanted me to be happy, and if you're trying to guilt trip me into going, it ain't gonna work."

"You turn everything around, don't you?" My resolve was crumbling. "No, I thought it was you who did all the turning." Taylor turned her back to me. "I don't care what you say. I ain't going."

"Taylor, if you walk out that door, things will never be the same between us." I did all I could to hold back tears of anger before they broke free and began to roll down my face.

Taylor walked past me, pushing her shoulder slightly against mine, and pulling open the front door. "Things ain't been the same between us for a long time." Taylor slammed the door behind her.

I was hardly in the mood for a celebration at this point, but I pulled myself together. "The devil is a liar," I said to myself as I headed out to the banquet.

It was quite a black tie affair. Although it was Missionary's church anniversary, it was held at the Benningses' church, Kingdom House of Prayer, so that we could accommodate all the guests who would attend. Pastor Bennings prayed and gave the blessing. Pastor Martin delivered the message. Our choir sang. The Benningses' praise dancers performed. Joshua and I served as we always did, with Yvonne's taut silhouette in the background.

Chapter Nineteen

On the first day of June, when I left work, I decided to visit my sister down at the Push It Fitness Center, one of the best centers in Brooklyn, a state of the art facility with an indoor heated swimming pool, racquetball, basketball, and tennis court, along with a variety of steppers, stationery bikes, treadmills, and specialized weight lifting equipment. They were beautiful machines, and Taylor knew how to manipulate and maneuver each one. I admired her for her expertise and for the well toned body she eagerly displayed in her red spandex shorts set.

"So many surprise visitors today." Taylor rolled her eyes. "No one uses phones anymore."

I stood facing her directly. "I would have, but I just happened to be in the area. I figured we needed to talk."

"There ain't nothing we need to talk about. Now do you want a workout or what?"

"Okay, fine. I'll work out then." Despite the heated confrontations we'd had lately, I never held a grudge and neither did she, at least not with me, that is.

"Good. I'll put you over here now. Do fifteen minutes on this, then the stationery bike just to warm up. Then I'll be back to really get you started."

Taylor set the timer on the treadmill and left me to fend for myself. This promised to be interesting. Not that I was an ugly slob or anything, but I had put on quite a few extra pounds over the last couple of years. She'd tried to warn me, but I'd never listen.

Taylor and I were never the slimmest people in the world, even from the beginning. As children we were thick bodied with thick medium length brown hair and big brown eyes. We were always a little shapelier than most; what people usually called "big boned," but lately I just had a little too much meat on mine. She led me over to the weight lifting corner and started me off with three pound weights. She showed me a couple of simple exercises I could do to strengthen my arms and torso. If Taylor had any favorite place at all, it was the gym. Most people liked quiet and slowness to soothe them, but not her. She always said she liked the raw, jagged noises of the gym.

I had to admit there was something about the smell and the tingle of the sweat, the feel of my muscles contracting against the cold hard metal. Sometimes I'd get lost in the rhythm. I didn't like everything about working out, like my sister did, but it was getting better. I was determined to get in shape for my wedding.

I had a twin, who was supposed to be a mirror image of me, not a mockery of me. "I don't know if I ever told you this, but this place is pretty nice," I said.

"Yeah, and it costs a lot to run too." Taylor smirked.

"I'll bet."

"Ms. Arlene said if I could come up with a decent down payment, she'd consider an offer from me. She says I'm the best, and she'd like me to take over when she retires."

"That's great."

Taylor snapped her fingers. "Just remember that I'm gonna own this center one day."

"Well, God bless you."

"Look at me." Taylor twirled around in perfect form. "I'm already blessed." After a moment of silence, she said, "I'm sorry about the banquet."

"It's all right." I turned my back to her so she wouldn't see the disappointment in my eyes. "Don't worry about it."

"How was it?"

"It was nice."

"With your stuffy future in-laws, Pastor and First Lady Bennings, hosting it, I doubt that, but anyway."

"They're not so bad." I tried my best to stay calm and not to get offended.

"You're right. They're not so bad." Taylor laughed. "They're worse."

I laughed too, because I was tired of fighting.

Chapter Twenty

After I left the gym, I went to praise team rehearsal for an hour, and then drove to the neighborhood supermarket to pick up a few groceries. Eventually, I ended up in the kitchen making yet another meal. I was a good cook, not a fancy one or anything like that, but I could really work miracles with the basics.

I dipped the chicken into the already seasoned flour and dropped them carefully into the heated pan of oil. Fried chicken was one of Taylor's favorites. She was always nagging me about such greasy foods, but she wouldn't come near the kitchen to save her life. No, Taylor figured she was just too cute for that.

I, on the other hand, was the domesticated one, always hoping to hook a hungry husband one day. And now, I was finally engaged. I opened the oven door to check on my biscuits and wiped my flour covered hands down my apron. I knew my mom, who was a great cook herself, would have been so proud of me.

Taylor bounced into the room cheerfully. "What's up?"

"I'm glad you're here. You can help." I handed Taylor a dish cloth.

"Sure, what can I do?"

"The dishes, maybe."

"Dishes? Oh no, you know I don't do dishes." Taylor put the dish cloth back on the sink.

"No cooking. No dishes. What do you do?"

"Let's see. I'm good at running things." Taylor looked over at the pan of chicken. "Now that's not good for you."

"Your criticism isn't good for me either, but that never stopped you before." I smirked.

"Jokes, I've got no time for jokes. I've got to get ready for my hot date tonight." Taylor winked as she strutted out of the kitchen.

That was Taylor, totally vain and self-absorbed, but I loved her anyway. Ever since we hit puberty, both Taylor's hormones and her self esteem seemed to blow up out of proportion. The only one she seemed to love more than herself was our mom. Mom was Taylor's idol back then; mine too, although I was more of a Daddy's girl myself. Taylor got ready for her date, but she didn't really look excited about it. She had been dating Derek for six whole weeks now, off and on, and that was a pretty good record for her. Taylor's relationships usually didn't linger on too long. I knew she didn't have the faintest idea how to hold a relationship together. Sometimes I wasn't too sure how to hold one together either. She always preferred to call her relationships mutual understandings, connected by a mutual attraction, as if it were some kind of voluntary meeting of adult minds. "Nothing serious; just having fun," she'd say.

"Going out with Derek again?" I said, looking up from my book. "Yeah."

"Interesting. It must be serious."

"Why would you say that?"

"Well, you two have been an item for a while, haven't you?" I turned my chicken in the pan as I looked into my sister's face.

"You know me. I'm just kicking it until I get bored because boredom is never an option for a diva like me. Men are just a disposable means of entertainment. And just because I haven't kicked him to the curb yet, that doesn't mean he's putting a ring on my finger or nothing." Taylor wiggled the manicured fingers on her left hand.

"I didn't say that."

"I've got no plans to be locked down while some lame mate literally drains the life out of me."

"Wow, I never knew your opinion of marriage was so negative."

"I'm not against marriage for others. Just for me. I'm not going out like Mom did." Taylor adjusted her skirt and stockings.

"Is that what you think, that Mom's marriage killed her?"

"You know it wasn't the happiest one."

"But that doesn't mean she died unhappy." I was sorry that my sister felt that way. I didn't want our mother's memory to be desecrated.

"I didn't say that."

"But you meant it."

"You don't know what I mean. I'm just saying I don't want to be drowning in my wedding dress with my trip down the aisle as my last happy day."

"Mom was happy. She loved the Lord, and then in her later years, after she and Dad reconciled . . . well, I know she loved him too."

"Maybe she did."

"She did. Mom put Dad's infidelity behind her a long time ago, and she was happy before she died."

"Come on now. Dad was not around for years. How do you know Mom was happy before she died?"

"Because I was there, and because Mom told us she was." I put my cooking fork down and searched my sister's face, desperately trying to find common ground. "You know she was happy."

"I don't know anything except she got sick, and they put her in the ground. That's all I know. Daddy comes back what . . .

maybe a year and a half before she's gone, and everything is supposed to be all right. I'm having a hard time putting it all behind me. And I never want to be tied to any man."

"It's your choice, but God made marriage a good thing."

"Whatever. I promise to dance at your wedding then, okay?" Taylor sucked her teeth and walked out of the room.

I guess neither one of us believed in fairytale endings anymore. Saddened by the realization that both our ideas about life were tainted, I began to pray. "Lord, please intervene in our lives. Please save my sister, return her to you. Take away all the bitterness she feels. Wipe away the disillusionment, and let it not be a hindrance to the softening of her heart. Dear Lord, strengthen mine also so that I may face the future and once and for all, forget my past. In the mighty name of Jesus. Amen."

Later that evening I started out to meet Joshua at his apartment. He was cooking dinner for me for the first time in our now four month relationship. I drove downtown alongside the other cars, buses, and taxi cabs until I pulled into the narrow street where the building's parking lot was located. I stepped out of my car, walked through the corridor, and into the co-operative apartment building attached to it. I dialed his apartment, and after he spoke to me on the intercom, he buzzed me in. I signed in at the security desk and took the elevator to the eighth floor.

I knocked, and he came to the door wearing a short sleeved silk shirt and black slacks. He gave me a quick kiss on the lips and invited me in.

"I'm glad you're doing the cooking tonight."

"That's right." Joshua held up his potholder covered hand. "Tonight your stomach is in my hands."

"Be gentle," I said.

"Most definitely." Joshua smiled as he walked toward the kitchen.

I paused to check out my appearance in front of his mirror covered wall. I was stunning, despite the hips I wished I could master and a much too heavy chest. I did like my shapely legs in stilettos though, and examined them one at a time. Then I sat down on his burgundy leather sectional and looked around the room, admiring his taste in art. He had quite an extensive collection of paintings all around the room. There was a tall African sculpture in the corner. Then I stood up and went out onto the balcony where I could see the Brooklyn Bridge and all of the city lights. I couldn't wait until this beautiful apartment would really be mine, when Joshua would truly be mine. It seemed almost too good to be true. When I heard Joshua calling my name, I went back inside, and we enjoyed the simple spaghetti and salad dinner that he had prepared. "I never really thanked you for taking care of Lilah the other day. I was in a bind; thanks." Joshua buttered his Italian bread.

"You don't have to thank me." I took a sip of my fruit punch. "She's a beautiful girl."

"You're going to make a beautiful stepmother."

"I don't know about all that. Joshua I . . ." I wanted to tell him everything, about my past, about my fears, but my tongue wouldn't form the words.

"You don't have to say anything. You'll be all the mother Lilah will ever need."

We ate until we were full and content.

"Thank you for this wonderful evening." I fiddled with the small flower in my hair.

"Thank you for making it wonderful." Joshua took my hand over the table.

"No, I mean everything was really nice. The meal, the candles, the conversation, everything." I could hardly believe how perfect everything was.

"Well, I wanted this to be very special. You're always cook-

ing for me. I wanted to return the favor." Joshua started to
clear the table. The candles continued to flicker.

"That in itself was a bold move. I appreciate it." I stood up
to help him.

"Oh, no. I've got it." Joshua took the plate from my hand.
"Tonight I'll handle everything."

I excused myself and went to use the bathroom. When I
returned, Joshua beckoned me over to the couch. He gave me
a choice of movies we could watch, and I chose a romantic
comedy. We laughed and cuddled, but the night was growing
shorter.

"Wow, look at the time." Joshua scrambled around the
couch looking for the remote control. "I can't seem to find
the remote."

"I know that's the end of the world for you, being a man."

"The comedy continues." Joshua smiled as he walked over
to the television to eject the disk from the DVD player. "That
was a long movie." I stood up to stretch my arms and legs.
"Funny, but long."

Joshua didn't answer. Suddenly I felt him walk up behind
me. I felt his breath on my neck before he touched my shoulder. I thought I would sink to the floor if he squeezed any
gentler. I turned around to face him as we stood barely inches
apart, his lips hungrily found mine. I happily responded with
needy kisses of my own. After a few minutes in his passionate embrace, I caught my breath and pulled myself out of his
arms. For a moment, we studied each other's eyes.

"I'd better walk you downstairs, Sister Alex."

"I think you're right, Brother Joshua." I took a deep breath
before I stood up.

"Alex . . . I . . ."

"Yes?"

"Never mind. Let's go."

I gathered my purse and jacket, wondering what it was he

really wanted to say. He held the door open for me, and then we entered the elevator. His eyes met mine, but no words were spoken, leaving much to the imagination.

Once we were in the lobby, Joshua gave me a quick kiss on the lips and escorted me to my car.

"I'll see you tomorrow." Joshua said before closing my car door.

"Yes, you will." I waved good-bye before I rolled up my window.

I watched him standing there staring at the car as I drove away. Tonight made me believe that he could actually be mine one day. That is until I looked into my rearview mirror, saw him answering his cell phone, and knew in my heart that it was Yvonne.

Chapter Twenty-one

I drove Taylor, myself, and my father to the engagement party in my four door Pontiac Sunfire. Lil' Pink, I called it, because of its bright carnation pink color. Everyone knew that it was my favorite color. Taylor didn't have her own car because she thought it was a waste of good money. She said she'd always have a man, and he'd always have a car. Besides, she was saving her money to open her own fitness center one day. So I was always stuck chauffeuring her around between dates.

Joshua, Malcolm, and Marisol were meeting us at the party, along with Joshua's parents and Lilah. Aunt Dorothy's house was the biggest one on the block. It was a split level house covered in beige and tan stones. There was a carport and a curved driveway that allowed visitors to drive in and out in a circle. So we pulled up behind Joshua's car and anxiously ran in to greet everyone.

I felt beautiful in my powder blue sundress with matching platform sandals and the small flower stuck in my shiny bob. I hugged Joshua first, spoke to the few other guests, hugged Lilah, and then hugged Aunt Dorothy, although I couldn't get my arms all the way around her. "Thanks for the party, but you didn't have to—"

"Don't mention it, sweetheart. You deserve it. And everyone else, well, they just come along with the package." Aunt Dorothy was always honest if nothing else. She would speak her mind in a heartbeat and leave you gasping for air.

I swatted her with my purse. "You're such a mess."

"Girl, take it back, 'cause the good Lord can't bless no mess."

"You haven't changed a bit in all these years," I said.

Aunt Dorothy smiled. "I'll take that as a good thing."

"Better than that. It's a God thing." I patted my Aunt Dorothy gently on the back.

Aunt Dorothy touched her face. "You look just like your mother when she was your age."

"Really?" I wished I could see Mom's face at that moment.

"Oh, yes," Aunt Dorothy said. "You and Taylor both, of course."

"I miss her so much." I leaned my head on my aunt's shoulder.

"So do I. She was my only sister. God rest her soul."

"Just like Taylor is mine," I said.

"Like it or not, it's the truth." Aunt Dorothy smiled. "And you two ought to be close."

"Just because we're twins doesn't mean it works out that way." I curled up my lips.

"I can see that, but it's a real shame though." Aunt Dorothy shifted her wig. "You two used to be inseparable."

"We were kids."

"Sometimes kids know more than adults." Aunt Dorothy pointed to Taylor as she walked out the front door.

Talking to Aunt Dorothy made me remember Mom and how she was always getting on us about stuff. She'd frown up her round face, and it was always "Alex this" or "Taylor that." I guess she never had much patience for mothering, especially not for mothering twins, which was odd considering the numerous awards she won for working with kids. Don't get me wrong, she'd have us wearing cute matching outfits, matching hairdos, and she'd hover lovingly around us, but when we'd mess up, it was like the end of the world. She never did say half as much to Taylor, though, when she messed up. Sometimes it was almost like she condoned her behavior with the way she shook her head, smiling and saying "Taylor, chile, you're something, really something." I always wondered about that. When we were ten and Taylor was missing in Macy's Department Store, it was me who got in trouble for not keeping an eye out for her. When we were fourteen and she failed three classes in freshman year, I got blamed for not helping her study, and when we were twenty-one and Taylor stopped coming to church, I know Mom wanted to blame me for that too. Although she never could get the words out, I could see it in her eyes.

I'll never forget that first Sunday after Taylor's eighteenth birthday when she made her shocking "no more church every Sunday for me" announcement. Mom was busy ushering that day, and I was right on her heels. Most of the time she would pass me without even looking my way. Then without warning, she'd look at me as if she had seen a ghost. I knew what that look meant. She had caught a glimpse of my twin.

I blinked away the tears as I continued walking down the plush carpeted aisles. I watched Mom float through the crowds in her favorite first Sunday dress, which was white with pale pink sequins. She was a vision.

Daddy sat in the middle row flipping through the pages of the Bible, trying to dissect the words that had eluded him for so many years. I sat down next to him, and he squeezed my hand as if he knew the pain that I was feeling. Maybe he felt some too. If he did, he didn't show it. He just grinned at me and turned back to the Bible.

Mom went about her business during the service and never looked back at either of us. It was just me and Daddy, secretly fighting for a place in her heart.

"Excuse me." I went out behind Taylor and found her standing up against the mailbox. She was wearing a tight, red haltered jumpsuit, and she had her weave braids pulled back in a ponytail.

"It's too late for the postman."

"It's too stuffy in there for me." Taylor pulled out a cigarette and lit it.

"You'd rather be out and about, right?"

"You got that right." Taylor stuck the cigarette in her mouth and inhaled.

"I thought you weren't going to smoke in the house." I tried to mask my disappointment.

"I know. I only do it sometimes when I get stressed out." Taylor puffed the smoke into my face.

"I see. So you'd rather be out here destroying your lungs than inside at your own sister's engagement party." I coughed, and then stepped back, waving the smoke away with my hands.

"Whatever. I just can't kick it with a bunch of senior citizens."

"Oh, come on. The only seniors are Dad, Aunt Dorothy, and Sister Trudy."

"And that's one too many," Taylor spat out.

"Oh, come on, you can't be serious."

"Like a heart attack." Taylor inhaled again.

"A little wisdom won't hurt us."

Taylor picked up her foot and began to fiddle with her stilettos as if her feet were hurting. "Won't hurt you. I'm not trying to hear anything they have to say, bless their aging hearts."

"That's so mean."

"I'm sorry. I know this is your engagement party, but I'm just having a really bad day, that's all. Please go on without me." Taylor put her foot down and started to examine her fingernails. "I don't know why Aunt Dorothy would plan to have a party on a Thursday evening of all days. Doesn't she know that people work?"

I wondered where her selfishness would end.

"It's not that bad. You know Auntie works a double shift on Saturdays, so you know it had to be held on a weekday."

"I know, but this ain't my type of party." Taylor rolled her mascara drenched eyes. "My kind of party doesn't even get started till 'bout midnight."

"Aunt Dorothy went through a lot of trouble to throw me this little party, so the least you can do is be nice about it."

"Oh, I'll be nice." Taylor put on a fake smile, revealing one gold tooth in the front of her mouth. I couldn't believe my sister, who had the same conservative upbringing as me, had turned out to be so ghetto.

The door opened, and Aunt Dorothy called Taylor and me inside for dinner. I noticed that the Benningses had arrived fashionably late, of course, and were propped against a wall as if they were afraid to sit down. They gave me their standard hug before we all sat down at the table. Dad led us in prayer, and Aunt Dorothy did the serving. We ate potato salad, barbecue short ribs, baked macaroni and cheese, collard greens, black-eyed peas, and rice with gravy. Then everyone watched as Joshua and I sliced the chocolate fudge ice cream cake. Dad made a short speech on how happy he was for me, and then snapped a few pictures with his digital camera. Pastor Bennings prayed over our future union, and we mingled in a state of pseudo happiness, each of us afraid that at any moment, any one of us could blow.

When I looked over at Joshua, he was carrying Lilah on his shoulders. I smiled at her, and she turned her head. Something inside me stirred, and for a moment, I was far away from the celebration. Only a few weeks to the wedding, yet I wondered how long I could go on with this façade? I worked the room, laughing and talking in my usual friendly way. Then I found Lilah at the other side of the room, leaning over a dish of shrimp puffs. She looked up at me and smiled with her eyes. I picked up a fork and offered her a shrimp puff from the dish. "Would you like one?"

"Yes, please," Lilah said.

I watched as she put it playfully into her mouth, daydreaming about what it would be like to have a child of my own. As I admired her, I noticed that her brown eyes were getting puffy and watery. Within seconds, Lilah's face started breaking out in hives. Her lips and tongue were swollen. I stood there in utter disbelief as her condition deteriorated before my eyes. Then Lilah started to cry uncontrollably.

I picked her up and brought her over to Joshua.

He grabbed Lilah from my arms and began to comfort her with his words and his touch. "What happened to her?"

"I don't know. All I did was give her a shrimp puff," I said.

Needless to say, she was allergic to shrimp. How was I supposed to know that? The Benningses gathered around Lilah, moving frantically. Joshua called 911 while Aunt Dorothy, who was a registered nurse, made Lilah lie down on the antique couch with her feet elevated slightly above the height of her chest. The other guests became anxious. Mrs. Bennings turned to Joshua and whispered, "I just don't understand why she'd offer the child anything without checking with us first."

"I'm sorry. I'm so sorry." I kept saying over and over again until it echoed in my brain. My head swirled as I watched the paramedics take Lilah out on a stretcher. "Joshua, I—"

But he had disappeared inside the ambulance. His parents followed closely behind in their Lexus. I stood in the doorway of Aunt Dorothy's house, praying that Lilah would be all right.

Chapter Twenty-two

I followed them to the hospital, and then lingered in the distance. Nothing could've made me feel worse. I had made Joshua's little angel sick. We hardly made eye contact at the beginning. He filled out the appropriate papers, whispered something to his parents, nodded at me, and disappeared behind the double doors.

Immediately, I began to pace the floor.

"Don't worry, dear, it's not entirely your fault. We should've been watching her more closely," Mrs. Bennings said.

I put my hands over my face. "Thanks, but I feel so bad."

"Mirriam, please. You're upsetting the child." Pastor Bennings waved his hand as if to quiet his wife, but there was no stopping her.

"Nonsense, she's a grown woman. She's strong. I'm quite sure she is capable of handling this. She'll be a wife and mother soon, so she'll have to be strong." Mrs. Bennings smirked.

"I never knew that Lilah had allergies." I shook my head repeatedly.

"Right. I see Joshua hasn't even covered the basics with you yet," Mrs. Bennings huffed. "And the wedding is when again?"

I knew where this was going. It was Alex bashing time, and I wasn't going to be a willing participant. I gave a closed tooth grin and glided out of the room. I wasn't about to lose my religion for the likes of Mrs. Mirriam Bennings.

Two hours later Joshua emerged with a smiling Lilah. "Go

give your grandparents a hug," Joshua said. "You gave us all quite a scare."

Mrs. Bennings bent over to scoop Lilah up.

"I'm sorry I scared you, Grandma." Lilah threw her arms around her grandmother's neck.

"Oh, Grandma's little pumpkin. It's not your fault." Mrs. Bennings looked over at Joshua and me from the corner of her eye. "We were supposed to protect you."

"Stay away from the shrimp dishes, young lady," Pastor Bennings said.

"They gave her a shot of ephedrine to reduce the swelling, and she has a prescription for antihistamine also." Joshua looked at his daughter. "Thank God she's okay."

Mrs. Bennings smiled. "Indeed."I left at two o'clock that morning feeling terribly drained.

When the alarm clock buzzed, I opened my big, dark brown eyes to a brand new summer day. As I reached over to turn off the alarm, I could feel the sun streaming in from my window onto my bare arm. It was Friday. I was grateful that I had been able to put my engagement party disaster behind me and that Joshua had forgiven me for what had happened to Lilah. It had been a long night.I heard my sister singing in the living room, shook my head, and turned over in my bed. Suddenly, I remembered the promise she made to me about attending the Annual Women's Day program. When I first asked her if she wanted to attend the church function, I really expected her to throw something at me. However, as I began to explain more about the event's focus being the empowerment of women, I managed to convince her. Aunt Dorothy also reminded her of how much fun she and I used to have at these kinds of events. A smile grew on my lips as I thought about my sister being back in the house of the Lord.Unable to sleep any longer, I crept onto my bedroom floor. I peeped out into the living room and saw Taylor doing her routine leg curls and ab crunches on her exercise mat. I shook my head because that girl was absolutely relentless. I slipped by her and headed straight for the kitchen. "Good morning."

"Morning." Taylor mumbled, then jumped up and followed me into the kitchen.

"You want some?" I held up a package of frozen waffles.

"Nope." She took a granola bar and a sports shake from the cabinet.

"Oh, so it's like that?"

Taylor snapped her fingers. "Yep, it's like that."

"So you're ready for the women's program today?"

"I guess so. I ain't got nothing to lose anyway," Taylor said. "Even though I'm probably just wasting my time."

"Well, we'll see about that. Women's empowerment should be very interesting."

Taylor sucked her teeth and left the kitchen. "Maybe."

Later on that evening, as we rode together in my car, we strained to recall moments from our childhood when more than just our faces were alike. I could tell Taylor was probably a little nervous because she started squirming in her seat as soon as we pulled up in front of the church. It had been a long time since Taylor had gone to church; not since Mom died. Not that she was hanging out at the altar before our mom died, but at least back then she had a reason to visit on occasion. Mom wouldn't have had it any other way. Now that she was gone, Taylor had no reason. In fact, now that Mom was gone, it was almost as if she were soulless.

I looked up at the tall brick building, with its provincial steeple and stained glass windows. The sunlight intensified its beauty. Taylor looked good in her peach colored slacks with a split up the legs and a sleek low cut blouse, while I wore one of my simple sundresses. We saw a few groups of ladies standing together talking and hugging. My eyes searched for Aunt Dorothy's face through the crowd, but I didn't see her yet. I did, however, see Mrs. Winifred, and I cringed inside my own skin. She was wearing a big bronze colored hat with feathers on it, and a bronze colored dress with sequins. There was the red haired hottie standing next to her, and I struggled to maintain my composure.

"Well, well, well. What do we have here?" Mrs. Winifred put her bony hand on her hip. "Ms. Carter, the other Ms. Carter that is. What a pleasant surprise."

"I wish I could say the same." Taylor responded right before I pulled her away.

We narrowly escaped the stares and open arms of those who were so surprised to see her. Some people asked where she had been, and others just whispered or made funny faces. Church folk were something to see.

Mrs. Arnez, an older Spanish woman, greeted us at the French doors and ushered us into the sanctuary. She handed us each a program, and I glanced at the theme in bold letters: THE INNER BEAUTY OF WOMEN. I tried to point this out to Taylor, but she just pushed my hand away, obviously fueled by skepticism.

Taylor whispered, "What can a bunch of church mothers teach me about beauty?"

As we walked down the aisle, we saw Aunt Dorothy. She was wearing a long blue sequined dress and a big matching hat. She put her wrinkled hands around our necks as if we were children and squeezed my sister and me together. She smelled like spearmint. Then she pointed her big finger and told us to move closer to the front. Sister Patrice, one of the younger ushers, led us to our seats.

We finally sat down somewhere in the middle section of pews, and I looked ahead at the altar, the emerald colored pulpit and matching chairs, and the colorful floral arrangement. I remembered that the last time Taylor set foot in this church was for Mom's funeral, and I closed my eyes, hoping to blink away the memory. Believing that maybe my sister had the same memory, I reached over and squeezed Taylor's hand.

"I've got to go up now." I patted her on the shoulder before I walked away.

"No problem," Taylor said.

I went to the front and assembled myself with the praise team. We sang, "With Long Life He Will Satisfy Me," and "Lord, You're Awesome," two songs I was almost sure that Taylor had never heard before. Some things had changed since she had been there last. Finally they sang, "Behold the Lamb," and as I looked out into the audience, she appeared to be listening attentively.

By the time I sat down, I was praising God on the outside, crying for my sister's heart on the inside. We sat through prayer, several selections from the choir, and a special message from Dr. Sonia McDowell, a minister and national women's advocate.

She was a petite woman, much shorter than I would have expected, but she seemed strong and self assured. She wore a gray pin striped skirt suit and a gray pin striped hat over her medium length bob. Although she must have been in her late forties, her skin seemed to sparkle under the lights. She had a small body, but she made up for it with her big voice. She not only preached about the inner beauty of women, but she demonstrated it, walking up and down from the platform, back and forth from behind the pulpit with a style and grace even Cleopatra would admire.

At times she ran across the platform like she was on fire, telling about her personal experiences with relationships, telling about her former self-destructive ways, telling about a spirit of condemnation. The funny thing was, some of her old ways sounded a lot like my sister's present ways. And some even sounded like my own. I listened and absorbed what I could as a shame came over me. I could relate to her struggle, and yet, she testified that the Lord had helped her. Taylor leaned over close to me. "I wonder why the Lord never helped me."

We sang, we laughed, we clapped, and the crowd roared as we were taken on a journey inside ourselves, a place I was certain Taylor hadn't been in awhile. Maybe never.

When the program was over, we walked out together. "That was good, wasn't it?" I said to my sister.

"Yeah, it was." Taylor put her hand up to wipe her eye. "I hate to admit it, but there was something special about this service."

"We've got workshops going on here tomorrow too, you know."

"Workshops?"

"In health and nutrition, beauty tips, family, career management, etc."

"Sure, that's my thing," Taylor said.

"Okay. Then we'll come again tomorrow," I said.

"If I don't have anything better to do."

"Of course," I said, careful not to pressure her too much. Suddenly, Taylor began to pat her eyes with tissue. I could tell she was holding back and I hoped with every breath, that she would come and surrender her life to the Lord. That would make it a perfect day.People were beginning to crowd the sidewalk as they were dismissed from the church. We waved goodbye to Aunt Dorothy and started the trek to my car parked up the street.

As I neared my car, we heard footsteps coming up behind us. Maybe someone at the church needed me for something. Someone was always needing something. I turned around quickly and stared into a familiar face. Every nerve inside me stood on end. "What in heaven's name are you doing here?"

Chapter Twenty-three

He was a vision. Ahmad was still one of the most beautiful men I had ever seen. His hazel eyes, skin the color of a sun-drenched peach, and his medium brown, naturally highlighted ringlets hung about his broad shoulders. His physique was still firm, except now, every inch of him seemed to be defined, like he had spent every waking hour in the gym. Biceps and triceps were overwhelming my senses. Time had only enhanced him. The picture in the paper had certainly not done him any justice.

"Alex." Ahmad looked directly into my eyes and stirred a million memories at once.

"Ahmad, what in the world are you doing here?" I found myself shaken.

"I'm in New York on business, and I came looking for you. I told this one lady at the church, who I didn't recognize, that I was an old friend of yours, and next thing I know, two other ladies were pointing me in this direction."

"You shouldn't be here, at all," I said.

"I'm sorry if I startled you. I just—"

"I don't believe this mess." Taylor frowned up her face. "What do you want after all these years?"

"Good to see you too, Taylor." Ahmad turned to face Taylor, then turned back to me again.

"Look, don't play with me, okay?" Taylor put her hands on her hips.

"What do you want?" I insisted. No one had time to play childish games.

"Look, I don't want to cause any trouble." Ahmad threw up his hands in mock surrender. "I just want to talk to you."

"Talk?" I found that hard to believe, considering the circumstances.

Ahmad looked around him and whispered, "Yes, talk. I need to . . . talk to you . . . in private."

"Private?" I still couldn't believe this was happening.

"I don't believe this mess," Taylor repeated.

"Please." Ahmad put his hand on my shoulder, and I thought I'd faint. A flood of memories came to my mind, some good, some bad, and some ugly. I looked around to see if anyone was looking. Then I took his hand off of me.

"Look, I can't do this." I put my hands up to my mouth, overcome with emotions.

"Do what? All I'm asking for is a few minutes, maybe at that coffee shop around the corner, the one we used to go to." Ahmad wouldn't give up. Same Ahmad.

"I know the one, but . . ." I couldn't believe he was standing here before me begging me to go and talk with him. What I wouldn't have given to hear those words ten years ago.

"Look, she ain't going with you nowhere, so you can just–" Taylor got up in his face.

"No, Taylor, it's okay. I'll go." I pulled her back.

"What, are you crazy? You're going with this dude?" Taylor was clearly ready to fight for me.

"Please, Taylor . . . I'm just going around the corner for a few minutes. Take my keys, and go on without me." My eyes pleaded with Taylor.

"I'll bring her home," Ahmad said.

"No, I'll take a cab home." I handed Taylor the car keys. "I'll be okay."

"Are you sure?" Taylor looked like she wanted to go off on him instead.

"I'm sure." I started walking away. "I won't be long. Go on."

I looked behind me to make sure no one was watching me, then I disappeared with the man, in whose hands, I'd once placed my life.

Chapter Twenty-four

When we arrived at the coffee shop together, we sat at a corner booth in the back. I was nervous about being there, and mostly about being seen there with him. He seemed comfortable enough though. He leaned back in his seat, ordered two lattes and even loosened the collar on his designer looking shirt.

"What is this all about?" I didn't know what to think or how to feel.

"About? Can't two old friends get together and talk?"

"First of all, we were never friends, and secondly, I doubt if we have anything to talk about. Now get to the point before I leave you sitting here by yourself."

"Ooh, so cold."

I crossed my legs. "I learned well."

"Touché." Ahmad leaned toward me. "I missed you, that's all."

I looked behind me. "You must be talking about someone else, because I know you don't expect me to believe that junk. Look, it has been a long time, and let's just leave it at that. I'm engaged now and—"

A waitress served our two drinks.

"Will there be anything else, sir?" she asked.

"No, thanks. That's it," Ahmad said to the waitress.

He waited until she had left the table, and then he reacted to my last comment. "Engaged?"

"Yes, engaged." I flashed the ring. "Does that surprise you?

I mean that I would go on with my life. It took me a long time, I'll admit, but I have gone on with my life. Now I suggest you continue to go on with yours. Now if you'll excuse me, I . . ." I started to stand up, but he grabbed my hand, and I sat back down.

"I'm sorry I shouldn't have come up on you like this. It's just that I knew I'd be in town for a couple of days. I'm here auditioning for a part in a play."

"I'm glad the acting thing is working out for you," I said in my typical who cares tone of voice.

"I've had a little luck with it recently, yeah."

"So?"

"I've got a flight out in the morning, and I guess I needed to see you."

"See me for what?"

"Closure."

"Closure? Now that's a joke. What do you think I needed ten years ago when you left me, when you carried your trifling behind back to Los Angeles without even giving me a thought."

Ahmad licked his lips. "Oh, I thought about you."

"I never got a phone call or a letter. Why are you here? What do you want from me?"

"I don't want to hurt you."

"Well, it's too late for that. Maybe if you just leave now, crawl back into whatever hole you slid out of, I'll be okay again."

"You sound so bitter."

"You think so?"

"Yes. I know I left you in an awkward position. I was a fool back then."

"I'm not going to argue with that, but what's done is done. You can't turn back the clock. Neither can I." I couldn't believe I was actually having this conversation, the one I had rehearsed a thousand times, and yet it never sounded quite like this in my mind. It never felt exactly like this either. No joy, no relief; just pain.

"I know, but I sometimes wonder what would have happened if we had stayed together."

"We?"

"Yes, if I had stayed, and if we had—"

I couldn't believe his arrogance. "Don't go there. I have a good life now."

"Without me?"

"With Jesus. And definitely without you." I stood up, grabbed my purse and Bible, and started walking toward the door.

Ahmad took my arm and whirled me around. "I've always loved you, you know."

"Don't." Tears began to well up in my eyes. "You don't even know what love is."

"And you do?"

"I know it's not what we had. I know that love is what I have now with my fiancé." I pulled my arm away.

"Your fiancé. Okay, I see."

"I'm sorry, but I have to go, and please don't ever contact me again."

"Now that's a little harsh, don't you think? I mean, after all we've been through together, I'd think I'd at least get an invitation to the wedding." Ahmad chuckled.

"Not a chance." I stood up and pushed my chair in. "And have a good flight back to L.A."

"Goodnight and take care," Ahmad said.

I left him drinking by himself, walked back to the church, shuffled through the crowd, and caught a cab back to my apartment. I didn't know it at the time, but someone was watching me the entire time.

Chapter Twenty-five

I hopped out of the cab and ran upstairs to my apartment, quietly closing the door behind me. As soon as I walked through the door, I heard Taylor's stereo playing in her room, so I ran to my room and barricaded myself in it. There was no doubt about the fact that I was devastated. I picked up my Bible with the carnation pink leather cover, and started reading Psalm 37 ferociously, as if nothing else mattered. I read it again and again until I was calm. The pain was still there, though, and I couldn't block out his face, his smile, or the memory of that terrible day. I couldn't escape the notion that I'd never make it down the aisle, never become Joshua's wife, not with all the deception I had going on around me.

Just then Taylor knocked on my bedroom door.

"Come in." That was all I could say.

She was all over me. "Why did you go with him?"

"I don't know." I began walking around the room, stripping out of my clothes. Taylor followed me.

"Don't tell me you still have feelings for that fool." She came right up close to my face.

"No, of course not. I just had to. I mean, I felt compelled to. I don't know. I'm all confused now, and I know confusion is of the devil." I picked up my clothes and placed them into my hamper.

"Yep, that's what Mom always used to say. I'm not trying to interfere, but I don't think it's a good idea for you to go sneaking around with yo' baby's daddy behind yo' fiancé's back."

I wanted to hit her right in the face, but the Spirit wouldn't let the flesh rise up. "I'm not sneaking around."

"Yeah, but you ain't broadcasting it either, are you?"

"I'll never see him again." A tear rolled down my cheek. "I just felt like I had to see him that one last time."

"I mean, we just had your engagement party last night," Taylor reiterated.

"I know."

Taylor stared at me. "Did it help?"

"Not really."

"Told ya. It was a waste of time. He was a waste of time. Ya better listen to the dude master. Leave that good for nothing dude alone. He's nothing but trouble, and ya know the good Deacon Josh ain't gonna approve."

"There is nothing going on to disapprove of. It was a one-time thing. He's on his way back to California, and believe me, nobody else knows about it except you and me."

"All right, I hope you know what you're doing. Just remember that I'm the playa around here." Taylor flung her braids in my face. "You're just a wannabe."

"You're impossible." I threw a throw pillow at her.

Taylor laughed and threw it back before she went into the kitchen. Then she poked her head back in. "No really though, be careful. You wouldn't want Joshua to find out about Ahmad. Believe me, he ain't worth it."

Chapter Twenty-six

The next morning I woke up ready for the workshops and interactive sessions of the women's conference, but Taylor was already gone. It was Saturday, and she had promised the night before that she would come and give it a chance. I called her, but she didn't answer her cell phone. Then I waited for her until I could wait no longer. After the conference was over, Joshua met me at the church to help everyone with the clean up. He stacked chairs, packed boxes, and followed me home.

"Thanks for everything." I hugged Joshua and pat him on the back.

"No problem." Joshua took my hand. "I'm just sorry your sister never showed up."

"So am I, I'm not really surprised though." I led Joshua into the kitchen. "Let's go have some dessert." I served Joshua a slice of sweet potato pie, and I sat down beside him with a slice for myself.

"At least she came yesterday," Joshua said.

"She did, and I really thought that since she enjoyed listening to the guest speaker yesterday, that she'd come to the workshops today, that she'd—"

"I already know what you were thinking."

"You do?"

Joshua swallowed his last piece of pie. "Don't worry."

"I'm worrying." I had already finished mine and was washing my dish.

Joshua stood up to wash his also. "I'm sure God is working on her heart just like we've been believing for."

"I guess this gathering today wasn't on her priority list." I batted my naturally long eyelashes, hoping to intensify my already vulnerable look.

"Keep your spirit intact. I'll see you tomorrow." Joshua lifted up my chin and kissed me full on the lips.

"I'm going home now before I get myself into trouble." Joshua put the dish towel down and kissed me on the forehead. He left the kitchen and headed straight for the door.

I followed him, and practically pushed him through the door even though I really wanted to let him stay a little longer. I knew better than to tempt myself. Never again.

"Goodnight and thanks again." I blew him a kiss.

"Goodnight." Joshua showed all of his white teeth before he started down the stairs.

I took a long hot bubble bath, and then settled in under my covers. I reopened myBible to Isaiah and read until I fell asleep.

I was awakened by the sound of raindrops beating against the window pane. As I got out of bed, pulled back my floral curtains, and looked through the window, I noticed the street seemed emptier than usual. There were few cars on the street and few people stirring, except for Michael, one of the neighborhood boys who sometimes helped me carry up my groceries. He had headphones on his ears, and he was dribbling a basketball down the sidewalk. It was eleven o'clock P.M. and Taylor still wasn't home. Frustrated, I hopped back into bed and pulled the covers over my head. "Lord, I'm tired of fighting, tired of waiting. I give up on Taylor."

Later when the phone rang, I opened my eyes and peeked over at the clock. It was five minutes past midnight. I rolled over on my stomach to answer it. I knew it couldn't be anything good. Whatever or whoever it was, I felt in my spirit that I was totally unprepared for it.

"Hello." I yawned and quickly covered my mouth.

"Alex." Dad was crying.

"Dad, what is it?"

Chapter Twenty-seven

"Your sister has been in a wreck." Dad sounded like he was gasping for air. "She's at Brooklyn Hospital."From that moment, everything seemed to spin out of control. "But—"

"The hospital found my cell number in her wallet, and they called me."

"Oh my goodness. I'll be over to pick you up in a few minutes." I slammed down the cordless phone, jumped into a pair of jeans and a T-shirt, grabbed my purse, and ran, without stopping, down the five flights of stairs to my car. I drove to Dad's house, crying all the way. Then I loaded him and his cane into the car, and we made our way across town to Brooklyn Hospital.

The entire time, my mind was racing, thinking back to when we were little girls, dressing alike, acting alike. Twins. We had the greatest bond as sisters, but lately it had almost drained away. The tears kept flowing until my dad handed me a tissue. I kept one hand on the wheel and used the other hand to blow my runny nose.

Taylor was always headstrong. Mom would push and she would pull. It was a regular tug of war all the time. I, of course, was the peacemaker, forever trying to patch up whatever my sister tore up. Mom always tried to scare Taylor with scriptures and warnings of hell, but she was a daredevil in every sense of the word. The more adamant Mom was about being a good girl and going to heaven, the more Taylor seemed to want to go the other way. Sometimes she'd get into it with

Mom and just wait outside on the stoop for Daddy to come home, as if Daddy could rescue her from Mom's mouth. But she just kept waiting, and Daddy never came; day after day, year after year, until finally she gave up hope that he'd ever come back. By the time Daddy finally did come back, she'd already learned how to survive Mom's rantings and ravings. In fact, she'd already learned how to survive without him.

Twins. An hour ago I had given up on her, and now I wondered if things would ever be the same between us again.

After we arrived at the hospital, Daddy gave his consent for emergency surgery, and then we waited. We prayed, and then waited some more.

Sunday morning was the first day of broken dreams when my sister finally forced her swollen eyelids open. I was sure she could feel the pull of the bandaged gash above her eyebrow. Daddy and I were just happy that she was conscious again. However, when the doctor came in to examine her, she realized that she didn't have any sensation at all below the waist. No matter how hard she tried to make her legs bend and her toes wiggle, she was powerless over them. Finally, she labeled them useless stumps beneath her sheets and asked for an explanation.

"You see there has been damage to the chain of nerve cells from the brain through the spinal cord out to the muscle. This reduces the brain's ability to control muscle movements." The doctor wrote on her chart.

"So what exactly does that mean, Doc?" Taylor looked like she was hanging on every word. Daddy and I just looked at each other. The doctor had already warned us about the severity of her injuries and about the strong probability of paralysis before we ever entered the room.

The doctor continued writing. "I'm afraid that this reduced efficiency or loss of communication prevents any willed movements, and this lack of control you're experiencing now is called paralysis."

"Paralysis? So I'm paralyzed, permanently?" Taylor shifted her upper body slightly.

"Now that's hard to say. Strength can be restored to a paralyzed muscle with changes in muscle tone," the doctor said.

Tears ran down Taylor's face. "Changes in muscle tone? I'm a personal trainer, and I've never heard of that."

"Well, you wouldn't. The medical procedures are somewhat different than those you use for beauty and fitness. Nerve regeneration is one way that strength can return to—"

"Doctor, are you saying I might stay like this forever?" At the height of Taylor's disappointment, she screamed, moaned, and cursed all the doctors. No one and nothing could comfort her, nothing she, cried out, "Except death." She rolled around in the sheets, in agony as we watched her wrestle with her own regrets and limitations.

She blinked her eyes in disbelief, and she cried until a crust of tears formed around her big, dark eyes. In fact, she wailed until the hospital staff gave her sedatives to calm her down.

I knew she thought her life was over. That much was certain. "I was young and independent. Now I have to depend on people to help me." Taylor turned her head to the side. "I was beautiful. Now my advantage is gone. No one will want me. I'll never have a husband or kids of my own."

"That's not necessarily true," I said.

"Isn't it? I'll never be a fitness instructor or personal trainer again." Taylor looked into my eyes. "My life is over."

I shook my head in utter disbelief. "Don't say that."

"Why not? It's true." Yes, it was a day of broken dreams.

She looked up at the white hospital room ceiling and cried. "Lord, why can't I feel my legs? Will I ever walk again?"

A nurse walked by the room and peeked in at her. "Good morning, Ms. Carter," she said.

"Yeah, it's morning, but I don't know what's so good about it," Taylor snapped.

The nurse then closed the door quietly and went about her business. Taylor, on the other hand, could go nowhere, so she slipped back down underneath her cover, letting the feelings of hopelessness become her soul mate.

"God is here for you, Taylor," I said.

"You know I don't want to hear it. Why should I cry out to a God who has never answered me before, a God who never answered me when my mother was dying? Why should I believe He'll answer me now?"

"God is a problem solver." I stayed close to her bedside.

"And I have a big problem, all because of some worthless brother I met late one night as I got funky on the dance floor." Tears ran down Taylor's face, and she wiped them with the back of her arm.

"Taylor I—"

"You're probably satisfied now, right?"

"No, of course not. Why would you say something like that?"

"Because you were always warning me about the devil's lifestyle, telling me that one day it would catch up with me, but I never expected it to happen this soon. Do you have to be right all the time? I mean, ever since we were kids you were always the right one, the good one."

She was right. I had always tried to be the good one, but still I always seemed to come up short. "Come on now, don't say that. God loves you just like He loves me."

Taylor covered her face with her sheet, trying to block out my words.

Ever since she had the accident a week ago, I spent my free time at the hospital, trying to make Taylor comfortable, trying to make myself feel less guilty. Hadn't I just told the Lord I had given up on my sister the night of her accident? Here I was giving up on praying for her, and there she was needing me and my prayers more than she ever had.

Mr. Harding had been nice enough to give me a week off, with pay, to spend with my sister. The problem was she made it clear that she didn't want to spend time with me. I could've understood why if she'd read my mind a few days ago, but I was sincere about wanting to help her now. Still she claimed she didn't want any help from anyone, so all I could do was wait.

She lay in her hospital bed under cold, sterile sheets, shivering and staring at the empty walls. She whimpered about how her life took such a terrible turn for the worse, and she began to break off her fingernails one by one. Then she ran her fingers through the tangled roots of her hair. She no longer had her braids in, and some of her ends were split. A touch up would've done wonders for her, but she wasn't even interested. My sister, former diva extraordinaire, didn't care about her appearance anymore. She didn't care about anything.

At the end of the week, while I was visiting, Taylor was assigned a physical therapist. He was a tall, chocolate skinned brother with a low haircut and a squared jaw. He smelled as if he were wearing some kind of expensive, musky odor cologne, but I didn't recognize the particular brand. That was Taylor's forte, not mine. She was the one who made it her business to recognize men's colognes and after shave lotions. Men used to be her hobby.

"Hi, I'm Keith Bryant." He extended his hand.

"Yeah," Taylor said.

"Hi, I'm Alex Carter, and this is my sister, Taylor." I shook his hand.

"Well, I can certainly see that you two are sisters." Keith smiled. "It is good to meet you both."

"Don't be telling him my name. I don't know him, and I don't want to know him." Taylor turned her face away from him.

"I'm here to help you." Keith began examining her chart.

"Really? How can you help me?" Taylor still wouldn't face him.

"I can work to relieve the pain and restore functional mobility." Keith bent his muscular arm back and forth to illustrate his point.

"Didn't they tell you I'm paralyzed?" Taylor's voice was low.

Keith sat down on a stool. "I know that, but I've had much success as—"

"Look, I don't care about you or your success, and I know you don't care about me. You don't even know me," Taylor spat out.

"Well, I'd like to change that if you'll give me half a chance." Keith squeezed his eyebrows together.

"I don't have time for games. I'm never gonna walk again, and that's the bottom line. Now just go away and leave me alone." Taylor pulled the covers up over her head.

Keith looked at me with regret in his eyes. "I'm sorry you feel this way. I'll leave now, Ms. Carter, but I'll be back."

"Whatever," Taylor said.

"I'm so sorry for her behavior. I–" I started.

"No, I understand. No apology necessary." Keith smiled and walked out the door.

I knew that if Taylor had met him before her accident, they probably would have gone out together. Back then she could've had any man she wanted. Now she didn't want any man.

After about an hour, Keith returned.

"Oh, you again." Taylor turned her face away from him.

"Yes, it's me again." Keith walked over to the window and opened the blinds, revealing a sunlight she wasn't ready to face.

"Don't you ever give up?" Taylor was clearly annoyed.

"Nope." Keith seemed to pay her attitude no attention.

"Great." Taylor sighed."This is my job, Miss. It's not personal. I'm not here to harass you." Keith looked at me, and I hunched my shoulders.

"That ain't what I say. Go on do your stinkin' job then." Taylor was determined to give everyone a hard time. That part hadn't changed.

"Thanks." Keith sat down in the nearest chair. "Now, may I call you Taylor, or do you prefer Ms. Carter?"

"Who cares?" Taylor yelled out.

"Good to meet you then, Taylor." Keith went on with his routine.

Taylor didn't answer.

"As I said before, my name is Keith, Keith Anderson, and I've been a physical therapist here for the past ten years." Keith spoke slowly and clearly so that we could understand every word. I appreciated that, because whenever I was nervous, I tended to miss things.

"Ten years? You don't look old enough to have ten years as a professional under your belt," I said.

"Well, that's flattering, but I assure you, I've been working in the field that long." Keith showed me his pearly white teeth.

"You must've seen a lot of awful stuff, huh?" Taylor couldn't seem to resist asking.

"I have, and nothing shocks me." Keith took up her chart and started reading it.

"That's what you say." Taylor sucked her teeth.

"I love challenges," Keith informed her.

"Is that what you think this is, a challenge? This ain't no game. This is my life you know, and it's over." Taylor was obviously losing patience.

"Please, Taylor, I didn't mean to upset you. My job is to either prevent or limit any permanent disability resulting from your injury." Keith came close to Taylor and lifted the sheet just a little.

"Prevent or limit? I'm paralyzed from the waist down. There is no coming back from that. I'm an aerobics instructor and personal trainer who needs to walk and move and dance. Like I said before, my life is over." Taylor couldn't hold back the tears any longer, and neither could I.

"An aerobics instructor. That explains what good shape you're in." Keith never looked up from the chart.

"You call this good?" Taylor sniffled, and then blew her nose.

"I mean your weight and body fat content. All of that will help you in your recovery." Keith seemed confident and unmoved by our display of emotions.

"Recovery?" Taylor rolled her eyes. "I already told you there ain't no coming back from this."

"Let's see now, your surgery was successful, and the doctor said— " Keith put her chart down.

"I don't care what the doctor said. I don't trust doctors anyway," Taylor said.

"Really?" Keith seemed to be intrigued by her attitude.

"I'm sorry-" I started.

"Doctors told me my mom's cancer was in remission. They told me she'd live, but she didn't. So you see, it's hopeless, no matter what they say. And no matter what you say." Taylor dried her eyes with a tissue.

"I'm sorry about your mother. But there is no reason you can't recover." Keith stood firm.

"Don't be sorry. They already told me I ain't gonna ever walk again," Taylor said.

"Doctors don't know everything." I added my opinion, hoping it would somehow make a difference, but doubting it.

"You can say that again." Keith agreed with me. "There comes a time when you've got to trust the Lord to—"

"Oh no, don't tell me you're one of those people too." Taylor rolled her eyes as if this was some kind of conspiracy.

"I beg your pardon. One of those people?" Keith didn't understand what he was up against.

"A Christian," Taylor said.

"Born again." Keith smiled and touched his heart.

"Yeah, that's the worst kind." Taylor turned her face away from his smile.

"Me too." I told him, hoping to form some kind of alliance in the battle to save my sister's soul.

"I can see I've got my work cut out for me here," Keith said.

"So have I," I whispered.

"You've got nothing cut out for you here. I don't want any parts of your so-called Christianity. I've already got my sister on my back twenty-four-seven. " Taylor took a deep breath. "Just do your little job, and get the heck out of my room."

Chapter Twenty-eight

The following Sunday I walked into the church with my spiritual armor on. I tiptoed across the emerald green carpet, spoke to everyone and made my way toward the front. I looked at the faces of the same crowd who were giving Michelle such a hard time, branding her with a scarlet letter. I didn't know what else to do about it, so I decided I would keep on praying.Michelle and her family were constantly on my mind, how she would be able to finish school, how she and her family were getting along, how she would give birth, and how she would face other unforeseen struggles. I wished I could go back ten years and have the courage to make the right choice like Michelle did. I couldn't help but to wonder if I had had a mentor, if things would have been different.

I went over to the front pew and knelt down on my knees to pray.

"Dear most merciful God, I thank you for being sovereign and holy. I thank you for lifting me up as I lift you up. But Father, I've already asked you to take away all fear and doubt, to make a way for me to fulfill my purpose. I've already asked for you to save and heal my sister. I've already asked for you to bless Michelle and her family in whatever ways they need to be blessed. And I've already asked that your will be done concerning myself and Deacon Joshua. So Father, I'm thanking you in advance for taking care of these matters, for using me to help all these people and to help myself as your precious Word manifests in our lives. In Jesus' name. Amen."

By the time I stood up, I felt the Holy Ghost moving in my heart and tears welling up in my eyes. I lifted my hands into the air. "Hallelujah." I smiled as signs of my emotion rolled down both cheeks. The other members of the praise team and I began to sing, "There is a sweet anointing in this sanctuary... God is here."

Finally, we were able to sit down amongst the congregation when it was time for the choir to sing. I sat next to Aunt Dorothy and opened my Bible to I Peter 4:12 as I was instructed to. I glanced behind me, but I didn't see Michelle or her family. Minister Harris wasn't seated with the other ministers. Pastor Martin preached a stirring message about overcoming spiritual battles. When he was done, he reminded everyone about the Elijah Project and that everyone should already be signed up for something.

I was glad I had already taken care of that even though I still wasn't sure if I had chosen the right thing. Choices weren't easy these days. They never were. I leaned back in my seat and looked over at Joshua who was sitting with the deacons. He winked at me, and I smiled at him. Sister Motley's one-year-old son scooted out of her arms and almost into mine. He seemed to be fascinated with my dangling earrings. At that moment my eyes caught Joshua's, and I knew he was reading my reaction. So I playfully hugged the child, and then placed him back into his mother's arms. I counted to myself and took a deep breath. Another blow to the chest. At the end of service, while I was waiting for Joshua, Yvonne came up to me, wearing a short periwinkle skirt suit and a hot pink blouse with just a hint of cleavage.

"Hi, Alex."

"Hi, Yvonne."

Suddenly, she leaned in close to my ear. Her hoop earrings dangled against my face, and I could smell the scent of Calvin Klein's Obsession. "You know Deacon Joshua is some man you've got there. If I were you, I'd hold onto him tight."

Chapter Twenty-nine

Okay, outside the church, those were fighting words, and I couldn't wait to tell Taylor what Yvonne had said. Knowing my sister, she'd want to snatch her up, but I wouldn't let that happen, although it was tempting. On the way home from church I told Joshua about Yvonne's comments, and he brushed it off like he usually did, as if I were just being paranoid. Despite what Joshua thought, I knew Yvonne was a serious problem, along with the many other problems I had.

Once I was finally home, I climbed up the metal fire escape to the roof, as I had often done it the past, to think. It was rare when I had a chance to do that anymore.

I liked to meditate on the stars, God's awesome creation. I could see them so clearly from up there, and my heart longed to be up there with them in the sky, up so high, rejoicing and dancing around in all their sparkling splendor.

I thought about my engagement to Joshua, and Dr. Harding's proposal, and yet I still didn't feel full. "Oh Lord, am I supposed to go back to school to be a public relations liaison?" Maybe that's why I'm suffering inside, feeling incomplete. Since I was whole in God, I knew I shouldn't feel like I was missing something, unless of course, I wasn't doing God's will. Maybe this trip to Kenya was exactly what I needed.

I looked down in time to see Mrs. Rodriguez coming inside with her two grandchildren, Jose and Carmen. The older one was eight, and the younger one was six. They had the cutest violet eyes and thick, wavy black hair. I would see them leaving out for school every morning, and sometimes I'd see them playing on the stoop in the evening, but whenever I saw them, they seemed happy. The innocence of childhood was amazing. I remembered mine with Taylor.

We used to be the sweetest little twins, with matching dresses, purses, and ribbons. Everything was the same, our hair, our smiles, our minds. Or at least that's what people thought.

But although we always looked the same, we were always different. I knew my sister wasn't like me when Taylor, on our eighth birthday, left me sitting at the lunch table by myself so she could go flutter her eyelashes and her pompoms at Jack Johnson from the fifth grade table. That was the first clue.

Then there were more subtle things, like the way she disappeared from the room anytime the subject of housework came up, leaving me with the bag to hold. Second clue.

And my all time favorite was the way she consciously smacked her gum, cracked her knuckles, and hiked up her dress at church despite Mom's constant reprimands. Third clue, and it was clear. We were twins in looks only.

I decided to call Joshua, but there was no answer, so I left a message on his voice mail. Ten minutes later Joshua returned my call.

"Hi, are you okay?" he asked.

"I was just thinking about Taylor and feeling a little sad."

"That's understandable."

"Not too long ago I couldn't wait to move away from her because she was getting on my last nerve, and now this happens, and it changes everything." I began to sniffle and took out a tissue to blow my nose.

"It's not your fault that—"

"I know that. I'm just praying about her situation."

"So am I."

I decided to go out on a limb. "I've also been praying about Michelle's situation. I really want to help her."

"Oh, right. Minister Harris's daughter?"

"Right. You remember her problem, don't you?"

"Of course I remember. She's pregnant, and Sister Martin mentioned something about how sweet you've been. You're an angel, and I love you for that." Joshua sounded so serious, with his deep voice reverberating in my ears.

My heart beat faster. "I wouldn't say that I'm an angel."

"Well, I'd say so. To help out a wild teenager like that, you'd have to be."

"Why would you say that she's wild?" I raised my eyebrows.

"Look at the condition she's in," Joshua said. "You don't get that way by being innocent."

Now I was ticked off. "Michelle is a very nice girl."

"Don't get me wrong, I'm sure she is. I just know she has done some not so nice things."

I held the phone, without moving, without breathing. I wanted to defend the girl, to tell him about my own experience, my own loss, but the words wouldn't come. They betrayed me once again.

"Alex?"

"I'm here. I'm just thinking." I was thinking about how self-righteous he sounded.

"Listen, don't worry about Taylor. God will work that out. He is a healer." Joshua paused. "And don't worry about that little girl. I'm sure her parents will come around and be there for her despite what she has done. You probably don't need to get involved in a situation like that anyway. I mean, what would people think?"

"What would people think? I'm not worried about what people think. Now you're beginning to sound like Mrs. Winifred."

"Well, Yvonne told—"

My heart began to beat fast. "Hold on a minute. I'm sure I don't want to hear what she has to say either."

"This Michelle girl is just—"

"I'm sorry, but I've got to go."

"Alex—"

I sighed before I clicked off the phone and stuck it inside my pocket. Telling him my secret was not going to be easy, if not impossible.

Chapter Thirty

It was almost the end of June, and Taylor had been hospitalized for three weeks. Joshua and I met in the hospital lobby. We held hands as we took the elevator up to the sixth floor. When we walked into Taylor's room, I caught her banging her head on the bed rails until her nose bled. Like she didn't have good sense.

"Stop that. You must've lost your mind," I called out.

Then Joshua ran over to let down the side rails. I grabbed a bed sheet and pinched her bleeding nose.

Blood was everywhere, staining the sheets.

"What's wrong with you, girl?" I asked.

"Nothing," Taylor said.

I grabbed a towel and began to help. "Nothing?"

"Just having a nosebleed," she replied.

Joshua walked closer to the bed. "Do you want me to get a nurse for you or something?"

Taylor looked at him up and down. "I ain't even in the mood for no ministerwannabe, Deacon."

"You'll be okay, Taylor. Give it time," Joshua said.

"Time? I don't want time. I just want to die." Taylor rolled her eyes.

"You don't mean that," I said.

"Don't tell me what I don't mean," Taylor snapped.

Joshua walked toward the door. "I'll give you two a chance to talk, but I'll be praying for you."

Joshua gave me a sympathetic look and left the room.

"Have you seen Malcolm since the accident?" I was curious as to whether or not any of her male suitors were still around at all.

"Malcolm who?" Taylor sucked her teeth. "I haven't seen that no good for nothing since I had my accident with Derek."

I wasn't sure what to say. "That's too bad. I figured you could use some more company."

"I've had company. Derek's widow came here," Taylor said.

"What?" I could hardly believe what I was hearing.

"Yeah, she came here upset about me seeing her husband," Taylor said.

"I see." I could see the hurt in Taylor's eyes.

"No, you don't see. She was gone long before I came on the scene. Besides, I don't have to explain anything to you or anyone for that matter."

"I didn't mean—"

"Look, the man was drunk. He had too many of his usual rounds of rum and Coke, and then I let him get behind the wheel. Now the man is dead. His wife doesn't matter." Taylor wiped away a tear that tried to escape. "There's nothing else to talk about."

"Taylor, I know this is hard for you, but—"

"You don't know anything. Look at you Miss Life All Perfect."

"My life is far from perfect."

"Doesn't look that way to me. You can walk, can't you?"

"Taylor—"

"You've got a job, don't you? And what about that fiancé of yours who worships the ground you walk on? You'll be married in just a couple of months. That's three things more than what I have. My life is in the toilet." Taylor frowned up as if she felt the sting of her own words.

"Now don't say that. You'll get better, and then you'll be able to work again."

"Right. I'll work again, but doing what? I'll never be able to run, bend, or exercise again. I won't be able to be a personal trainer or work in fitness ever again. And look at me; no one is going to want me like this."

"Taylor, you're just as beautiful as you always were."

"But I'm in a wheelchair, and what good is so called beauty if I can't even move."

"You'll be able to move again. I've been praying for you."

"Save it. I don't want your prayers, or the deacon's." Taylor rolled her eyes.

"Remember how everyone prayed for Mom? But it didn't stop her from going into the ground, now did it?"

"God can heal you," I said.

"Sure, He can."

I wanted to shake her so she would understand. "I mean it." I wanted her to believe.

Taylor turned her head away from me. "Just go."

"I'll go, but I'm not going to stop praying. I'll just have to have enough faith for both of us." I didn't want to sound patronizing, but it was the truth.

"Get out," Taylor threw a plastic cup in my direction as I barely escaped.

Once I was on the other side of the door, I said a little prayer.

"Lord, please help Taylor to know that you're real. Please give her peace in the midst of this trial, and finally, by your stripes we are healed. Please restore my sister's body to work as it did before in Jesus' name. Amen."

When Joshua turned the corner of the corridor, I fell into his arms, and he comforted me before we left the hospital.

Joshua and I both drove our cars back to Missionary Bible College. He went to class while I went to Dr. Harding's office. I stopped by to see Dr. Harding about my upcoming trip.

We spoke at length about the missionaries from my church who would be there and the mission assignments they would be handling as well. Then he handed me a file full of information I would need for the public relations assignment. Of course I didn't share any of my personal reasons for wanting to go. Instead, we discussed the application I had filed for my visa, the language, and other business matters. The conversation we had should have been between the two of us, but I didn't know that someone else was listening.

The next day as I was about to escape for my lunch break, I ran into Marisol in the lobby.

"Hey, hold up for a minute, girl." Marisol came running toward me. Are you trying to avoid me or something?"

We hadn't really talked since the night of my engagement party. "No, I just have a lot on my mind."

"Okay, but you can still wait for me, right?"

"Right."

"You're going to lunch, aren't you?"

"Actually, I was going to skip lunch."

"Skip lunch? Now that doesn't sound like you. What's going on?"

"I've just got a lot going on, that's all." I shook my head. "I'm going to Kenya on the mission trip, for a week," I said.

"What? Are you crazy?"

I knew she would think that way. "What?"

"You mean you're going away and leaving your fiancé here by himself for a whole week and only three weeks before your wedding?"

"Yeah, we need some time apart. I've got some stuff to sort out, and you know . . ."

"You're not having second thoughts, are you?"

"No, I've never wanted anything more than to be Mrs. Joshua Bennings. It's just that—"

"Come on now, you should be happy." Marisol gave me a

playful punch in the arm. "I'm going to take you out for lunch today. Let's go."

"Thanks."

The next thing I knew we were sitting in the corner seats of the nearest diner. It was a dark, greasy little place, and we both ordered burgers, fries, and a Coke.

"Girl, this should be the happiest time in your life. You're getting married the first of August."

Right, only a month to go." I sighed."You've got a new job offer." Marisol shook her head. "I don't see the problem."

"Yeah, a job offer that I don't really want."

"Why don't you just teach then? You told me you used to want to."

"That's all in the past. I can't deal with children anymore." I stuttered as the words fought to make their way out.

"Is that why you gave up, because you think you can't deal with kids anymore?"

I felt a rush of tears building behind my eyelids. When I looked up, it was as if Marisol was peering into my soul.

"Alex, is there something you want to tell me?"

Chapter Thirty-one

I tried not to look startled at Marisol's question even though she was staring at me. People all around us were eating and talking, minding their own business, yet I felt like all their eyes were on me, like I was center stage. I turned my back to her. "No, it's nothing. I'm just confused about what I want to do with my life, that's all."

"Are you sure? We've been working together for a couple of years now, and I consider us as friends. You've been acting really strange lately, and I believe there is more you're not telling me."

I took a bite of my burger and hoped that my full mouth would camouflage my expression. "I don't know what you're talking about."

Marisol looked sincere. "You've been very sad, and I think it's deeper than what you're saying."

"Maybe you know me too well." I turned around to face her. "Too bad I didn't have a friend like you when I was back in college."

"Oh come on, I know you had to have friends back then." Marisol dipped two of her fries in ketchup and stuck them in her mouth.

"No, I had acquaintances. I separated from my real friends after high school. Taylor was around though. She was my only real friend."

"It happens. Good friends are hard to find." Suddenly, I knew I was going to tell her what I had never told anyone.

Except Taylor. No matter what damage to my reputation, I was going to share what had been eating me up inside for all these years.

"If I had you there with me ten years ago, I know I wouldn't have destroyed my life."

"What are you talking about?"

"I've never told anyone this . . . except my sister. Promise me that you won't tell another living soul."

"Yeah, yeah, I promise." Marisol continued to steadily chew her food. "Geez. What's all this about, anyway?"

I checked my surroundings to make sure no one I knew was around, then I dropped my volume. "Ten years ago, in a lonely night in my dorm, I realized I was pregnant."

"You were?"

"Shhh. Yes." I didn't look into her eyes; instead, I stared at my hands. "I found out that I was pregnant by a man I thought I loved at the time, who didn't love me."

"That's a shame, but that ain't no crime, chica."

"I told him, and he panicked. He accused me of trying to trap him, trying to ruin his life. Then he told me he was transferring to another college to pursue his acting career."

"You're kidding?"

"No, I'm not. He told me to have an abortion. In fact he gave me money."

"What a piece of—"

"I took the money because I was stupid then. But I made him promise he'd meet me that day at least. So we could go through it together. And I thought . . . he'd change his mind. You know, happily ever after. Naïve, huh?" My face was still. "He disappeared the same day I went to the clinic."

"Oh, no." Marisol reached across the table and put her hand on mine. "I'm so sorry, chica."

"I waited for him a long time. I told him to meet me there, that if he cared at all, he would meet me there and stop me before it was too late. Or that he'd at least come to support me." Tears rolled down my face.

"But he didn't come?"

"No, he didn't. I never saw him again. Except in my dreams, that is. Sometimes he's in my dreams. I mean, nightmares."

"Oh Alex, I'm so sorry."

"No, it's okay." I clasped my hands together in my lap. "There's more."

"I'm sorry. Go on."

The wounds were being unraveled. I began to shiver. "I . . . I killed them."

"Them?"

"Yes, I killed two babies. Two." I fought to hold back the tears. "They found out that it was not just one, but two, and I didn't even know until it was too late."

"Twins?"

"Yes, twins. I would've had twins like my sister and I."

"Wow. That must've been way hard."

"It was. And then to make things worse, I nearly bled to death a few days later."

"Oh my goodness."

"My sister found me losing consciousness one day, and luckily, my parents were out of town so—"

"So?"

"It was a really bad infection. I would've died if Taylor hadn't found me."

"So that's why you didn't want to be around kids? That's why you changed your major?"

I nodded my head. "Not right away, but after awhile, I couldn't forget. I couldn't shut them out, and every time I was around kids I . . . it hurt too much. I felt too unworthy."

"You've never forgiven yourself, have you?"

"I guess not." I bowed my head. "No, I haven't."

"I know I don't have to tell you, of all people, about the cleansing blood of Jesus."

"No, you don't."

"Yet you've never received His forgiveness."

After hearing the truth of her words, I broke down and cried in her arms like I was a little baby and like she was my mother. She moved over to my side of the booth and rubbed my back gently.

"It's over now. The nightmare is over now. "

"No, it's not over." I couldn't believe I was saying these words. "I saw him again, and the nightmare is just beginning."

Chapter Thirty-two

After leaving the diner with Marisol, I told Dr. Harding that I wasn't feeling well and asked if I could leave work early. Indeed, I didn't feel well. Then I took the long way home, stopping by the local elementary school. Summer school was in session. The students were lined up, single file in the schoolyard, waiting to be dismissed as their teachers lingered about chatting. I pulled over to watch this interaction between teacher and student. Then I imagined myself in their position. In my heart I knew I could make miracles in the classroom just like my mother had.

Mom was a whiz in the classroom, just like she was at home; organized and resilient. She stood six feet tall, two hundred and fifty five pounds, and believe me, she commanded respect. Folk at the church and at school called her Mom because that's just how she was, always mothering somebody. She would get in a person's face and not back down until she had their attention, until they learned something or earned something, depending on the situation. She taught Sunday School, Bible Study, and Vacation Bible School, daring kids to call the Lord's name in vain. Oh, Sister Gabrielle Carter was nothing to be played with when it came to the things of God. And Taylor and I idolized her, each of us in our own way. Suddenly the children's images began to blur. When I blinked, I realized I had to move, so I turned the key in the ignition. The stupid car wouldn't crank. I tried again, and it still wouldn't. So I stepped out of the car and opened the hood. That was something Daddy had taught me to do ever since I first learned to drive. I didn't see anything wrong at first glance, but then, I wasn't a mechanic. I checked the dipstick for oil, and then I checked the reservoir for antifreeze. I wasn't low on anything. There was neither smoke nor a burning smell. So I closed the hood and got back into the car and tried again. I thought that maybe the battery was dead. I looked around for help. Finally, I noticed an older gentleman standing nearby, probably waiting to pick up his grandchild.

"Excuse me, sir, but I think I might need a jump."

"Sure, I've got some cables," he said.

"Great. I really appreciate it."

Within minutes, I watched him go to his trunk, connect the jumper cables from his battery to mine, and yet, my car still wouldn't start.

"Sorry, I couldn't help more." He took his equipment and closed my hood, then his.

"Don't worry about it. I'll be okay." But today I wasn't so sure.

"It may be the alternator. You know how these things go." He walked toward the children who were now being dismissed.

"Yes, unfortunately, I do." I sighed. "Thank you."

I stood there in the middle of the sidewalk with hands on my hips, trying to figure out exactly what to do next. The summer heat was beating down on my forehead. I decided to look under the hood again, not that I knew what I was looking for, but it was better than just standing around feeling stupid. After a few seconds of plundering around, I decided to call a tow truck. Suddenly I saw a shadow towering over me.

Chapter Thirty-three

The mysterious figure turned out to be Ahmad. After realizing that it was him, my mouth hurried to catch up with my mind.

I looked up into his hazel eyes. "Oh, it's you."

"Do you need any help?"

I didn't know what to say. "Well, actually—"

"Let's see now." He began to look under the hood. The sun shone brightly against my bright pink Sunfire, almost blinding me at times. I attempted to block it with my purse while Ahmad seemed to lose himself in the intricacies of my engine.

With my hand on my hip, I leaned toward him. "Are you stalking me?"

"I beg your pardon." Ahmad stopped checking the car and started to check me out.

"It's just that you came down to the church the other day, and now you're here. I thought you left town. I thought you went back to California where you belong."

"I did leave, but now I'm back." He ducked beneath the hood again.

"What?"

"Well, actually I'm back because I've been called back for a part I want."

"So does that mean you've got the part?" I hoped he had done poorly on his audition. Then he would have no choice but to pack up and go back to California.

"Why the sudden interest in my theatrical success?" Ahmad showed his perfectly white teeth. "I don't know yet."

Ahmad and I were all wrong for each other from the very beginning. Everyone knew it, I guess, except me. I was too caught up in his winning smile and smooth moves, moves that proved to be a little too sexy for me to handle. He was majoring in theatre arts with a minor in music, and he was the most exciting person around. Taylor didn't like him instantly. She said he was too shady even for her to deal with, and she dealt with all kinds. I, taken in by his charisma and fine physique, ignored her words and everyone else's. Despite rumors of his unfaithfulness around the campus and a never ending string of disagreements we had, I clung to the fact that he wanted me, that he loved me. Now where I got that idea from, I don't know. He never actually said he did, but there was something about the way he held me close to his hard chest, something that made me vulnerable. Maybe it was youth, maybe inexperience, but I fell into an Ahmad slump I couldn't easily get out of.

I sighed. "But you can't stay here."

"Why not? Maybe it's fate."

"It's not." I watched him cautiously until he found the problem with a wire and corrected it. He hopped inside my car, started it up and left it running.

"This is only a temporary solution. You've got to get it fixed at a shop. But this should be enough to get you and the car home."

"This junk just came out of the shop a few weeks ago." I punched the hood. "Thanks."

"You're welcome," he said, walking back to his own car.

I hopped into my car and took off without hesitation. Something inside me wouldn't let me linger.

The next day, since my car was in the shop again, I climbed onto the bus and pushed my change into the fare box. I was back on the bus. The bustling crowds, the noise, and the putrid smells were all the same. I squeezed by the people standing up in the front and tried to find a seat nearest to the driver. There were none left, so I ended up standing between two men, one who winked at me and the other who found it necessary to rub his arm against mine. I couldn't wait to get my car out of the shop. In the meanwhile, I was sentenced to this cultural affliction called public transportation.

When I reached my stop, I rang the bell and made my way to the back door.I stepped down, careful as not to trip, and turned the corner quickly. One block up the street I saw my dad's small house. I was home.

I used my key to enter the front door and immediately called out to my father. He came out from the kitchen slowly, walking with his cane, and he hugged me.

"I'm glad you came by."

"Me too, Dad." I sat down on the lumpy old sofa and remembered Mom sitting in that exact spot days before she died. "How are you?"

"I'm doing pretty good." Dad chuckled. "You look raggedy though."

"I'm sure I do. I've had a rough morning."

"Oh?"

"I've just come from work," I said.

"Are you going to see your sister today?"

"Probably not. I need a break."

"Say no more. She gave me a hard time last time I went. I'm going to take a break for a couple of days too. My pressure is up and the last thing I need is to have it out with your sister."

"I know what you mean."

"I don't know what your mom and I were thinking having twins." Dad laughed and I could see that his teeth were missing.

"Dad, where are your teeth?"

"I don't need them right now. They're uncomfortable."

"Dad, I don't know what to do about Taylor. Just when I thought there was a chance of her turning to God, this accident pushes her even farther away."

"Maybe it has, but then maybe it hasn't. You never know how God will be able to use a thing." Dad smiled in his usual way. "His thoughts are not our thoughts, and His ways are not our ways."

"You sound like Mom." I looked over at her picture on the center table.

"Your mother was a wise woman." Dad had a faraway look in his eye.

"I know, but I feel so sorry for Taylor. They're going to try a new method on her."

"What kind of new method?"

I vividly remembered the conversation I had with the doctor as he described the efficiency of this new method. He explained how it helped victims of spinal chord lesion or paraplegia or other diseases affecting the central nervous system. I tried to grasp what he was telling me, but I was never really good at science. As he went on and on about passive exercise versus active exercise and the intensity of each, I must admit I was totally lost.

"Something about a dynamic therapy device called Giger MD. It's supposed to help people with her kind of injury."

"Good," Dad said.

"I just can't stop feeling sorry for her." Dad reached over me to get a bowl of cashews on the side table. "You should. She has been through a lot."

"She's so lost."

"And what about you?" Dad looked directly at me. "Aren't you lost, baby girl?"

"What do you mean?"

"You've been running yourself, not away from God, maybe, but away from His purpose."

"Purpose? I don't know what you're talking about."

"Didn't you tell me a few months ago that you were thinking about going back to school to become a teacher, saying that you should've become one sooner?" Dad cracked open the cashews with the nutcracker and ate them one at a time.

"Yes, but—"

"And don't you want to be a teacher?"

"I don't know. I don't really know what I want." I leaned back against a knitted blanket. "I don't know what happened. You used to know exactly what you wanted. You were very much like your mother." Dad pushed his reading glasses down on his nose as if he were studying me.

"I know I'm comfortable at my job. I like the people, and I do my work well but—"

"But what?"

"But I want to do more." I grabbed a flowered throw pillow, one my mother had sewn with her own hands.

"So you want a promotion?

"Yes. No. I want to teach. I want to work with children but—"

"But you won't do what is necessary to achieve this?"

"It's not that, it's just that I'd have to go through the whole school thing all over again." I hated lying to my father, but I couldn't possibly break his heart by telling him the truth.

"So what? Are you afraid of failure?"

"I'm not afraid. I'm just not sure I want to change my life right now."

Mom would never have accepted that excuse. She would have rebuked me right then and there. She was that kind of woman, a no-nonsense Christian who believed that God's Word was the final authority no matter what. She did a pretty good job of instilling that in me, but I don't know where Taylor was during these lessons. Probably somewhere clowning, as usual.

Dad had a solemn look on his face. "Not even if it's God's will?"

"How do I know it's God's will? He might be happy with me being a secretary or a public relations liaison."

"But I know you're not happy. You want to teach like your mother. I always thought you would." Dad swirled his tongue around in his mouth, something he did whenever he didn't have his teeth in.

"So did I."

"You pray about it, and He'll reveal the answer to you."

"I will."

"Just don't close Him out," Dad crunched on the cashews.

"I won't. I promise." I wasn't sure where this promise would take me, butI made it, and I would keep it.

I went into the kitchen to fix my dad and me some dinner; looked into the refrigerator and cabinets only to be disappointed. I had almost forgotten that Dad was retired, now living on a fixed income. I managed to find a few miscellaneous items I could work with. I opened up two cans of corned beef and proceeded to put them into a hot frying pan. Then I sliced an onion and mixed the pieces in with corned beef. I boiled rice and opened a can of asparagus. Then I poured two glasses of apple juice and served it on the small round oak table. "Come on. Dinner is ready."

Dad walked in and sat down at the table. "I'm going to have to bring you some groceries."

"Don't worry about that. I'm hardly home anyway. Between helping out at the church, and then at the community center, I won't have time to eat them."

"Well, we'll just have to see about that. I'm going shopping anyway." I opened the refrigerator again and continued rummaging through it.

"How are the wedding plans coming?"

"Everything is fine. Josh is fine." I confiscated a few rotten apples and an almost finished quart of sour milk.

"You don't look happy for someone who will be getting married in a couple of weeks."

I didn't like where this conversation was going. "Daddy."

"Don't Daddy me. I know my girls, and you're not happy. Did those Benningses insult you, baby, 'cause I'll—"

"Joshua's parents have not insulted me, Dad."

"All right. Don't forget about your promise though."

"Believe me, I can't." *Lord, help me.*

By the time I left my dad's house, I felt drained. I was walking up the street to the bus stop when I heard that same familiar, yet annoying voice.

"Hello, Miss."

I turned around to face his almost hypnotizing eyes.

"Oh, it's you again."

"I was hoping for a better reaction than that."

I put one hand on my hip. "I'm sorry, but that's all I've got."

"A beautiful young woman like you shouldn't be walking these streets alone."

"Please. My car is in the shop, remember? So I'm taking the bus."

"That's no problem. I'm parked right over there." He pointed to a shiny looking Honda Accord that was parked across the street. "I can give you a drop wherever you need to be."

"No thanks. I don't need a ride."

"Oh come on, Alex. I'm not a stranger, and I did help you get your car started when you were stranded in the middle of nowhere."

"You're right, and I thanked you for that already. I don't owe you anything else."

"I can be your knight in shining armor if you let me."

He managed to make me blush with that one. He certainly had a way with his words, always did.

"Thanks anyway, but that ship has sailed." I continued walking until I reached the bus stop. The bus was coming, so I didn't even have time to see his reaction. I just boarded the bus and never looked back. Even as the bus rolled away, I wondered, now that Ahmad seemed determined to stay in New York, what I was going to do.

Chapter Thirty-four

The past few weeks had gone by slowly with Taylor making minimal physical progress and even less spiritual progress. Her attitude up to this point had been unbearable. On the day she was released from the hospital, my father and I pushed Taylor's wheelchair up the handicapped ramp, something we never imagined we would need to use, then we used the freight elevator to get upstairs, something we had to get special permission from the building's superintendent to use. Thank goodness the landlord promised we could move to a first floor apartment at the first availability. Taylor had started to receive disability benefits which helped with her bills, but she was ungrateful for that also. She complained about her tight quarters, complained about the stupid treadmill that was in her room and complained about the temperature day and night. I cooked, cleaned, ironed her clothes, and bathed her whenever I was home. It wasn't just housecleaning I was doing, but it was soul cleaning, trying to escape my guilt. How could I have ever said I was giving up on my own sister? During the day when I was at work, the home health aide took my place. Once a week, the van came to get Taylor for visits to the rehabilitation center. The other two times a week, Keith came to the apartment, determined to increase core strength coordination and muscle tone. He conducted tests, evaluated her strengths and weaknesses, and developed treatments to improve her physical strength, stamina, and manual dexterity. I became deeply involved with Keith's goals for Taylor's physical therapy, but the most important one for me was to provide positive psychological effects for the patient. Her injuries had not just affected the physical, but had damaged her thinking as well. Every day was a test, but I kept on praying. I kept on believing.

Joshua and I sat on the blue flowered couch, watching television and trying to drown out the obscenities Taylor hollered from her bedroom. Joshua put his arm around me, and I felt warm and secure. I wanted to drink this moment in and shut out all the other misery. "I'm sorry about all of this." I turned the volume up a notch.

"Don't be sorry. This isn't your fault. Taylor will come around." Joshua kept his eyes glued on the television program.

"Yes, but when? And will I have lost my sanity by then?"

"I hope not." Joshua gave me a playful punch in the arm.

I worked so hard at home, at work, and at church, I hardly got to see Joshua anymore. Our relationship suffered because of it. The only time I saw him was during church on Sunday and Bible Study on Wednesday nights. Even then sometimes I was too tired to go and sometimes I would fall asleep during the sermon, but I kept on pressing, determined that one day it would be better. I didn't know exactly how, but I knew that one day it would. I put my hands in Joshua's strong ones. He looked at me and smiled before turning his attention back to the show.

"Aleeeex," Taylor yelled as if the building was on fire.

"I'm coming, I'm coming." I hopped off of the couch and went running into Taylor's bedroom.

Minutes later I returned with a cup in my hand, intending to plop back down beside Joshua, but he was already standing by the door, putting on his baseball cap.

"Oh no, please don't leave. I—"

"It's okay. I'll see you Wednesday night, all right?" Joshua yawned before turning the knob.

"At Bible Study?"

"Right." Joshua gave me a peck on the cheek and left without another word.

I went to my bedroom, packed a bag for my trip to Africa, turned off all of the lights, sat in the dark, and cried because of how uncertain my life had become.

Chapter Thirty-five

It was July fourth, and just a few days before my trip, when Joshua and I went to Coney Island. The humidity was almost unbearable, and yet the crowds were still packing in. Lilah was spending the day with Joshua's parents, but he assured me that the next time we came back to this amusement park, we'd all be together as a family. Of course, I gave the usual smile and tried to ignore the warning signals in my spirit.

Joshua and I stuffed ourselves with all beef hotdogs, fries, Coca-Colas, popcorn, and cotton candy. We played pinball, skeet ball, and a racing game. Joshua played one of the batting games and won an oversized stuffed bear for me. We rode the Himalaya, enjoying the speed and the music as we whirled around forward and then backward. Then we rode the rickety Cyclone Roller Coaster and held onto each other as our bodies slammed back and forth against the hard metal seat and the bar in front of them. We were shaken up by the time the ride ended.

Finally, we left the amusement area and walked down to the beach to watch the fireworks light up the sky. We held hands as we walked along the seashore. When we grew tired, we took a bench seat on the boardwalk and watched the timeless waves of the ocean roll by. Joshua turned to me. "I can't believe you're leaving me next week."

"It's just for a week."

"But I thought you didn't even want the job."

"I don't. I mean, I'm not sure, but I want to try it."

"I don't want you to go." Joshua hugged me tight. "I'm going to miss you."

"I'm going to miss you too, but I have to do this." I pulled away from his embrace. It was hard enough for me to leave without him adding pressure to the situation.

"I know."

"It's more of a spiritual journey for me, I guess. I'm more excited about the missions than the public relations, but . . ."

Joshua sighed. "It sounds interesting."

"You could say that."

"But why three weeks before our wedding?"

"I'm sorry, but Dr. Harding needs this done now. Believe me, I've stalled as long as I could."

"You're right about that." I looked up. "That's a beautiful sky."

"Yes, it is. But not as beautiful as you."

"You really know how to make me feel special." I blushed at hearing his words.

"You're special, so it comes naturally. You know, I never thought I'd marry again."

"Really?"

"Yes, I'm glad I met you." Joshua took my hands in his strong ones.

This was my big chance, and I wasn't going to blow it. "I'm glad too, but what about Delilah?"

"What about her?"

"I mean, you never say anything about her. I've never seen a picture, nothing. I'm not sure that's healthy."

Joshua's back stiffened. "Healthy? Oh. You're a doctor now?"

"No, I'm just trying to be a friend."

"I don't hold hands with my friends." Joshua pulled his hands away from me.

"You know what I mean. If we're going to be married,

we've got to be friends too." I pushed my hair behind my ears.

"Look, we've been seeing each other for three months, then engaged for almost another three months, and yet I don't feel any closer to you than I did five months ago. It's like you've shut me out."

"I don't mean to. It's just that I—"

"I know you lost your first wife, and I know that—"

"I don't want to talk about that." Joshua turned his face away from me.

Now I was offended. "Do you talk about it with Yvonne?"

"What? Where is all this coming from? Yvonne has nothing to do with us. She has been very helpful to me and Brother Jacob with the homeless shelter project."

"I'll bet."

"I know you're not jealous of Yvonne."

"Why shouldn't I be? She's always in your face. She made it clear to me on more than one occasion that she thinks you're the greatest, and on top of that, ever since Taylor's accident, I hardly get to see you anymore." I stood up.

"That's not my fault. In a couple of weeks we'll be married, and that's all that's important." Joshua stood up too and started walking away. "Now, let's just go."

The ride home was exceptionally quiet. We rode through the busy streets, dashing between cars, and nearly dying at each stop light.

"Why won't you talk to me?" I pleaded.

"We talk all the time."

"Oh, well hallelujah for that then."

"Look, the past is painful, and the future is uncertain." Joshua never took his eyes off the road.

"But God knows your future, and He can give you a word of direction if you'll let Him."

"I know you're not preaching to me." Joshua pulled up in front of my building. "He is in control of my life."

"I don't think so. How can we ever go forward if we can't ever talk about your wife?"

"She's gone. She has nothing to do with you." Joshua sounded angrier than I had ever heard him sound before. I could see the lines of frustration in his face, even in his profile.

"That's what I used to think at first, but she does if she stands between us."

"She's not between us."

"She is if I can't reach you. She's between us every time I look into your eyes and they're vacant, every time I reach for you and you're not completely with me, every time I imagine our lives a month or a year from now and I draw a blank. I know she stands between us."

"I'm sorry you feel that way." Joshua glanced over at me. "But you don't understand."

"You're right. I don't. Make me understand. I want to know what hurts you. I want to help." I reached for his shoulder but he pulled away.

Joshua parallel parked and got out of the car. "You can't. No one can."

"Jesus can." I opened my own door and started walking toward the front steps.

"I know that. That's why I stay on my face in prayer." Joshua followed closely behind.

"But can you come up for air? Can you come up long enough to talk to me?" I was almost in tears as I unlocked the front door.

Joshua came up close to me. "Now you sound like that heathen sister of yours." I couldn't believe that he said that, but there was no turning back.

"Oh, really? Maybe I'm a heathen too then. We are twins, right?"

Chapter Thirty-six

Joshua

I drove the long way home, circling Prospect Park, East Flatbush, and Crown Heights before heading to my apartment downtown. My car bounced over potholes. People shouted, honked their horns, blasted their car stereos, and even gave me the bird, but I hardly noticed.

On the way home I wondered why women always had to push me to the brink. Why did they have to know what was on my mind? Why couldn't they just be satisfied with now? I never promised Alex anything; nothing more than marriage. That's all, and that's enough. Why should she expect or think she had a right to anything more?

I mean, who did she think she was, picking on me? I had been a perfect gentleman, even on those rough days when my flesh cried out for flesh. I had done my part and treated her well. Why did she have to push the issue and ruin everything? I didn't want to open up old wounds that were barely closed. I didn't want to remember Delilah.

Sure Alex was beautiful inside and out, and sure we would be married, but could I really have a life again after what Delilah had done? Could I really open up and trust a woman again? Delilah had hurt me more than I ever thought any human being could be hurt by someone he or she loved. She had taken my own flesh and blood away from me, the ultimate betrayal, and she had paid with her life. Marriage I could do, but what I didn't know was if I could ever give a woman my whole heart again.

Then she kept bringing up Yvonne. I mean, sure Yvonne was cute, with her tight little body, but I ain't going out like that anymore. I'm a child of God. I gave up that kind of woman a long time ago. Not to say that Yvonne was fast or anything, but she sure didn't look slow. Yeah, she fed the ego, but that was it. A favor to Sister Winifred and a good deed in general was as far as it went. I was nobody's fool. Why couldn't Alex let that go?

In any case, if I let the best thing that ever happened to me walk out of my life, I knew I needed counseling. So the very next day I went down to the church.

Pastor Martin's office was medium sized, with a mahogany desk and matching bookcase. A hanging fern graced the window, and the room was filled with many other potted plants, compliments of his wife, Sister Martin.

I entered quickly so as not to waste the time of such a busy man. As soon as Pastor Martin was seated I began to explain my dilemma to him.

Pastor Martin leaned back in his leather chair and wrinkled his mustache.

"You see, Pastor, Alex is a wonderful woman, and I don't want to hurt her, but I—"

Pastor Martin looked grieved. "I hope you haven't already done anything to hurt her.

"I don't know. I've said some harsh things to her."

"Why have you treated her this way if you care about her?"

"It's just that my wife, Delilah, was a sneaky, manipulative, and self-centered woman, and she died on the operating table . . . aborting our second child." I felt the lump in my throat as I held back my tears.

"That's a real tragedy."

"I didn't even know she was pregnant until I got the call from some obscure clinic on the other side of town, saying

that she was dead. It happened right before our second anniversary. My daughter wasn't even a year old yet.

"I'm sorry, son. I know that was a bitter pill to swallow."

"I had waited for so long to find her – who I thought was
the perfect woman, and then before I knew it, she had betrayed me, and then she was gone." I put my face in my hands.
"I never even got an explanation."

"What a tragedy."

"I can only assume that her career meant more to her than
me or her own flesh and blood. Anyway, after she died, I
left Syracuse and moved out here to Brooklyn. I had to get
away."

"You got away, but did you ever get over it?"

"I don't think I can ever get over it." I balled my fingers
into fists. "I left my parents' church so I wouldn't have to
hear about it all the time or see it in my mother's I told you
so eyes."

"I'm sorry to hear that it's been so rough for you."

"I pray so I can go on."

Pastor Martin rotated back and forth in his chair. "And
you're going on, but have you prayed to go forward? God can
heal your heart so you can do more than just exist, but so you
can make progress."

In my heart I was so angry with Delilah for leaving me, for
stealing my child away and with God for letting it all happen.
The tears were coming fast, but I held them in. I couldn't let
anyone see me cry. I was a man. "The future is so uncertain.
That's what I've learned from all of this."

"But when you serve the Almighty, your blessings are certain."

When we first got married, I used to consider Delilah to
be a blessing, before she showed me her true colors, before I
knew how power hungry she was. Next thing I knew she went
from demure acting little Delilah to a loud mouthed Jezebel.

She was a local politician, but she worked all the time, and all I got from her were complaints. She wanted more money. She wanted more control. Apparently the last thing she wanted was more kids. I don't even know why she agreed to have Lilah. Maybe that was supposed to shut me up.

"I never saw any of it coming. Sometimes I think I wasn't a good enough husband, or maybe she never loved me," I said.

"Please stop, Joshua. We may never know what was in Delilah's heart, but you're torturing yourself speculating about it."

I stood up and slammed my hand down on Pastor Martin's desk. "But what she did was so wrong. I just can't believe it sometimes."

"Listen, you've got to decide to live. You have every right as a believer. The Lord wants you to be happy."

"You're right. I know but—"

"Now I've seen you go around helping people for a lot of years since you came to our church, and now it's time to help yourself." Pastor Martin leaned forward in his chair. "Sister Alex is a treasure."

"I know."

"If you love her, maybe it's time to consider living again. You're engaged now and you wouldn't want to lose her."

I thought about what Pastor Martin was saying, and my heart felt so heavy with grief and doubt that I could not answer. Alex was going away to Kenya soon, and sometimes it felt like she was hiding something from me too. Since it was already July fifth and the wedding was August first, I needed to know what that was.

Chapter Thirty-seven

It was a beautiful summer day in the city, with only three weeks to go before the wedding. The invitations had been sent out. The caterer, the florist, the live band, the decorator, the photographer, and everything had been perfectly planned, thanks to my mother-in-law to be. How she managed to find time between her busy church activities and her duties as a congresswoman baffled me. She had taken on the role of wedding planner and decided every meticulous detail. Yet nothing was right between the bride and the groom. We hadn't spoken in a few days, and the vision of me walking down the aisle was beginning to fade.

As I was on my way home from work, I decided to stop at the corner store for a six pack of Diet Coke, scotch tape, and a roll of paper towels. When I came out of the *bodega*, I saw Joshua and Yvonne together. He was holding the door of his car open for her. She was wearing a skin tight pair of jeans and a pretty, red, low cut blouse with matching platform shoes. I felt like the wind had been knocked out of me. They were laughing and talking. Yvonne leaned on his shoulder before he opened the car door for her. Even though my heart didn't want to believe it, I didn't put anything past brothers these days. Not where sisters were concerned, especially not sisters like Sister Winifred's neice, Yvonne. She looked like she was notorious for man stealing, and she'd had her eye on him from day one.

Immediately, my eyes filled with tears. I was so angry I couldn't think. How dare he? For a moment my mind snapped, and I almost forgot who I was in Christ. I wanted to go upside her little red head. Thankfully, the Holy Spirit brought me back to who I was. Besides, being arrested for assault would not be a proper testimony for the kingdom. So I sucked in all the rage I felt, slammed the car door shut and was about to take off like I was in the Indianapolis 500.

At the precise moment, I turned to take a last glance, and he spotted me.

"Alex." Joshua ran toward my car.

I didn't answer. I just kept going.

"We're just . . ." Joshua yelled across the intersection.

"Sure." I had never been the jealous type, but Satan had been playing tricks on me lately. Since things weren't right between me and Joshua, I assumed there was someone between me and Joshua. I initially thought it was the memory of his late wife, Delilah. Now that I knew that it was Yvonne. It made sense. Another woman. A loose woman.

Driving home, I began to pray, "Lord, maybe that's what I deserve for not being honest with Joshua, but after the way he talked to me on Independence Day, things are still not right. Please help me to understand. Give me wisdom on how to handle the mess I've made of this relationship. In Jesus' name. Amen."

Before I knew it, I had pulled up in front of my building. As soon as I walked through the door of my apartment, I started to tell Taylor about what happened. No matter what we went through, she was still my girl.

"Can you believe I just saw Joshua with Yvonne? She was all over him," I fussed.

Taylor rolled herself over to me in her wheelchair. "Maybe there is an explanation, but I don't want to hear it right now."

"I don't blame you for being angry because men are trifling like that." Taylor snapped her fingers. I just can't believe he'd fall for Yvonne after all we've meant to each other, or after all he has meant to me."

"Look, I told you men are dogs. Don't get all worked up over it. They're not worth it; none of them are."

"I can't believe I just stood there looking like a fool and didn't do anything. I couldn't even move at first."

"But at least you had someone who cared about you." Taylor stuck out her bottom lip like a spoiled child. "I ain't got nobody."

"What do you mean you've got no one? You've got me."

"I don't mean that. I mean you had a shot at being happy, and I'm not joining your pity party."

"What?"

"I've got my own problems." Taylor turned her face toward the wall, and I could see the tears forming in the corners of her eyes.

"Can I help?"

"No, not unless you've got serious dollars. I've got this business deadline to meet. I only have three more months."

"Anything is possible with God."

Taylor ignored my comment. "I'm doing my best with getting information, but it doesn't seem to be coming together fast enough. I mean, Keith has been trying to help me, but my time is coming to an end."

"It'll work out. Just keep trying."

"That's what Keith says, but look at all these rejections so far." Taylor threw a handful of papers into the air. "Time after time, and no one has accepted my proposal. All the credit apps have been turned down."

"Have you tried personal lines of credit?"

"You mean like credit cards?"

"Yes, and even personal loans. Check it out."

"Cool," Taylor seemed to perk up.

"A lot of entrepreneurs have had to start that way when they couldn't secure an official business loan. Sometimes you've got to finance the dream personally when no one else believes in you." I remembered hearing that piece of advice from a local talk show host.

"Never thought of it like that."

"Believe me, when all else fails, you believe in you." If only I could take my own advice and believe in myself, my problems would be solved.

I pushed the door of my bedroom open wide, kicked off my shoes in the doorway, and threw my favorite purse across the room. I checked my phone for messages from Joshua. There were none. There was only a message from Sister Trudy telling me about an emergency member's meeting at the church tomorrow. I wondered what that was all about, but I was in no mood to dwell on it.

I jumped into the shower, believing that would calm me down. All I felt, however, was pressure, like I was being squeezed between a wall, not knowing if I'd come out alive. I didn't know if I should give up on the time Joshua and I had spent together and start again, or go back and fight. I contemplated whether or not I'd accept rejection or maintain defeat, knowing that for now he had chosen another over me.

I checked my phone again when I came out of the shower. Still no call from Joshua. I asked Taylor if she wanted to go out to dinner, but she said she didn't feel up to it. So I decided to go out to dinner by myself, something I didn't usually like to do, but I was desperate. I drove downtown, found a quaint little seafood restaurant, and sat at a table in the back to sulk. I ordered a shrimp platter, complete with a salad and baked potato. I was busy spreading butter onto my potato, minding my own business, when I looked up into the eyes of Ahmad.

"Alex, imagine seeing you here." Ahmad licked his lips like he was hungry. "I know a brother didn't let his beautiful woman eat out alone."

"Ahmad, please. Not now." I wasn't in the mood for his foolishness. "All right, all right. I see I've struck a nerve. I promise not to get on your nerves again if you let me sit down."

It wasn't my intention to agree with this handsome man from my past, but despite my better sensibilities, in my most vulnerable state, I let my lips utter the unthinkable. "Sure, why not?" I was still angry with Joshua.

I didn't know why Ahmad was here, back in my life, but not quite in my life. He was making my heart beat faster, bringing back precious memories of my youth. Not that I was a senior citizen now, but I was noticeably older. Not him. He just grew smoother with age. I wondered what the real reason was for him being here, running into me. Or was he stalking me? Maybe he had been thinking of me all along. Nah. No way had he been thinking of me while he flounced around L.A. looking for his big break. He put his hands on the table, and I noticed how strong looking they were. Long, well manicured fingers. I remembered his hands and how they had once been all over my body. I blinked away the thought quickly. *Lord Jesus, deliver me from my own mind.* I found myself watching his lips as he spoke, listening to each word as if I were out of my own body. He licked his lips as he ate and chewed gently. He had the most sensual looking lips, ones that could just drink a woman in. Then all of a sudden I found myself lost in his eyes, not because I was feeling him or anything, but because those pools of hazel took me to another time and place, the time before the storm.

Ahmad leaned in close. "So you're happy with the deacon?"

"Yes, I'm very happy." He was so close to me, I could smell the aftershave lotion on his face. I pushed myself back in my chair.

"Well, you don't look happy tonight."

I yawned. "I'm just a little tired. It has been a long day, that's all."

"I didn't know a church boy would be your type."

"There is a lot you don't know about me." I sat up straight at the table. "I've changed."

"So I see."

"No you don't see. I'm a different person now since I've given my life to the Lord."

"You sound like your mother, now."

"I'll take that as a compliment." I paused. "She was a good woman."

He took my hand. "Yes, she was. I'm sorry I missed her funeral."

"Right." I wasn't really sure how to answer that.

He had missed everything. The crying and screaming I did right after I left the clinic that day. The depression shortly after and the relapse I had a week later when the infection set in.

Mom was out of town for the weekend, so I had gone home. I didn't want my misery to become the center of attention on campus. I called Taylor as soon as I got home, but she was out on a hot date, so I was home alone. First the cramps came fiercely. Then the hot flashes and the nausea. Soon I found myself sweating and bleeding profusely. I knelt down to pray, too weak to hold myself up. I was too afraid to call anyone. I fixed myself a cup of tea, but the cramps came faster and stronger, cutting off my already sporadic breathing. I wheezed and clenched my teeth until I dropped down to the floor in a pool of my own blood.

The next thing I knew I was waking up at the hospital hooked up to intravenous tubes. Taylor had found me and taken me to the hospital just in time.

I couldn't figure Ahmad out but I wanted to. What did he want? What made him tick? I wasn't sure, but for some odd reason, I wanted to know. I needed to know. This man had done everything evil to me that was humanly possible, and yet here I was sitting with him, eating, and prying into his mind.

"Your sister hates me, doesn't she?"

"Pretty much, yes." I let myself laugh at that one.

"I could tell by the way she didn't want you to talk to me."

"Well, she's just being protective. It's a twin thing."

"Oh."

"You wouldn't understand."

"I think I can." He winked at me. "She hates me."

"Well, she doesn't care for you at all, no. She thinks you're heartless and trifling."

"And what do you think?"

"I don't know what to think. I don't know why you're here or why I'm even talking to you either." I smirked. "But I must say in the past you've been heartless and trifling."

"I see."

"No offense," I said.

"None taken."

My legs were shaking underneath the table, maybe from guilt. I kept eating without looking up at him again. That was dangerous territory. I had forgiven him a long time ago, but I never expected to see him again in person. I never expected he would resurface in my life. Not when I was trying to disassociate myself with the past. Disassociate myself from myself.

I excused myself to the restroom and tried to call Joshua.

"Hello," she said.

"Hello."

Upon hearing Yvonne's voice, I hung up. I was livid. How dare she answer his phone? Who did Yvonne think she was? Where was Joshua anyway? I was tired of his arrogance, of doing things his way while all the while he was pretending to be Mr. Holy Righteous. Didn't he care that he was hurting me? He was supposed to be my future husband, and there he had been with another woman draped comfortably around his arm. I think not. It was over with this game playing man. Then my anger bubbled over. I fixed the makeup around my eyes, reapplied my lipstick and went back out to the table. *Two can play this game.* At first I felt miserable being there with Ahmad, but after a good healthy dose of sirloin steak and a couple of rounds of iced tea, I felt pretty good. After all, Joshua had been taking me for granted. We hadn't been out together in days, and he clearly had Yvonne wrapped around his little finger. I wasn't sure exactly where our relationship stood. As I looked into Ahmad's hazel eyes, there was so much confusion in my heart; I almost wanted to forget about Joshua. Yet with a wedding just weeks away, I knew I couldn't.

After dinner, despite my telling him not to, Ahmad insisted on walking me to my car. Then came the awkward moment as I unlocked my door, trying to avoid what I feared was coming next. I could feel Ahmad leaning in close, heavily breathing on my neck.

Chapter Thirty-eight

Before I could block it, Ahmad spun me around under the street lights and planted a wet kiss on me. I tried to pull away from him, but his arms overpowered me, holding me closely against his firm chest like the old days. Surprisingly, it was nothing like I remembered.

"What am I doing?" I managed to break from him.

"What's wrong?"

I felt sick in my stomach. "Everything."

"What?"

"I shouldn't have. I mean you shouldn't be here."

"I thought we had a good time," Ahmad said.

"I did, but it has to end here. I've got too much at stake." I let out a deep sigh. "I'm sorry."

He reached for me with his large hands, but I moved to avoid his touch. "I see."

"I didn't see. But I'm seeing clearly now. I can't disappoint the Lord."

"I'm sure the Lord will understand." Ahmad smiled, obviously indicating that he found humor in what I was saying.

"No, I can't disappoint Him anymore than I already have. Goodnight." I pushed him away with one hand and opened the door of my car with the other. Then I started it up and pulled away without even looking back.

I drove home, crying the whole time. Once inside my apartment, I slumped down to the floor. "Lord, please forgive me for my shortcomings, for betraying Joshua, for allowing myself to be tempted. Keep me in the spirit, Lord so I won't fulfill the lust of the flesh. In Jesus' name. Amen."

Taylor rolled herself out in her wheelchair. "So where have you been?"

"Out to eat."

"Alone?"

"Does it matter?"

"Not to me, but to your fiancé, it might." Taylor came closer and began sniffing the air. "Is that Ahmad's cologne I smell on you?"

"Yes, but it's not what you think."

Taylor didn't blink. "Who cares what I think?"

"I mean we ran into each other."

"Ran into each other just like that?" Taylor folded her arms and gave me a skeptical head roll.

"Yes, just like that. He's on an assignment, so he's here in New York, and he won't leave. It's a play he's doing or something, and it should be over soon, hopefully."

"Really?"

"Really."

"I feel bad enough, you know. First Joshua with Yvonne, and . . . I–"

"Look, I don't think Joshua is messing with that girl. I mean she's probably just all up on a brother, you know."

"But you said—"

Taylor threw her hands up. "Yeah, I know what I said, but well, maybe I was wrong."

"Excuse me." I knew I had to be hearing things. My sister never admitted she was wrong.

"Keith came by earlier, and we talked and—"

"So you've been telling your physical therapist my business?"

"He's not just my physical therapist. He's my friend, and he keeps it real with me."

"So you're telling your new friend my business?"

"Calm down. Ain't nobody thinking about your business. Keith just helped me to realize all men aren't the same."

"Oh, so you're sweet on Keith?"

"No, I'm not. I'm just sayin' Keith is a half way decent guy, so maybe Josh is a half way decent guy too. Maybe it wasn't how it looked when you saw him with Yvonne." Taylor threw up her hands as she left the room. "I'm just sayin'."

At that moment the door bell rang, and I ran over to answer it, secretly hoping with everything in me that it was Joshua.

Chapter Thirty-nine

Unfortunately, it wasn't Joshua. It was Michelle. I opened the door for her, and Michelle came in. She wore a denim maternity shirt and her stomach was about the size of a volleyball. When I hugged her, she smelled like cocoa butter. "Hi, Michelle. What brings you by today?"

"I just had to pick up a few things in the area, and I wanted to stop by before the meeting."

"Come in and sit down." I looked toward the couch.

"No, thanks. I won't be long."

"How have you been feeling?"

"Much better thanks to you." Michelle smiled. "I'll be seven months soon."

"Wow. Almost there, huh?"

"Yep. I'll just be glad when this is all over so my life can get back to how it was." Michelle looked at her stomach. "Well, sort of how it was."

"I understand."

"I mean, I want people to stop staring at me."

"I know what you mean, but it will get better." I touched Michelle's round stomach. "How about school?"

"It's going fine. I go to a special program for young mothers in the afternoons."

"Good. I'm glad it's all working out for you."

"Sister Alex?"

"Yes, Michelle?"

"I just wanted to say thanks again. You really saved my life and my baby's life." Michelle rubbed her round stomach with her swollen hands.

I nodded. "You're welcome. I was only doing what God told me to do for a change."

"Satan has already tried to destroy me. My faith is all I have left, and to tell you the truth, that's wearing thin."

I leaned forward to pat her on the back. "Your faith is all that matters. When it gets low, go to your Bible and fill up on the Word of God."

Michelle smiled. "That's what my dad always says."

"Now what is this meeting at the church all about anyway?"

"I don't know exactly, but it's something about me and my family."

"I just checked my messages a little while ago, and Sister Trudy left me a voice-mail."

Michelle faced the door. "All I know is that we've all got to be at the church tomorrow afternoon; all members of the church."

"Well, I'll be there. Will you need a ride?" I opened the door for Michelle.

"No, thanks. I'll be riding with my parents. I just wanted to talk to you before . . ." Her voice trailed.

"Everything is going to be all right, I promise." I gave her a hug. "I'll see you there." I blinked away the tears that threatened to overtake me as Michelle walked out the door. "Give me strength, Lord."

As Michelle was leaving, I heard my phone ringing. I ran over to my purse and grabbed my cell phone.

"Oh hi, Daddy." I didn't feel like hearing any parental lectures tonight.

"Well you don't have to sound so happy to hear from me," Daddy said.

"I don't mean it like that. It's just that . . . I'm a little tired right now." I yawned into the phone for dramatic effect.

"I see." Daddy coughed for a minute. "I just wanted to know if the church called you."

"About the meeting?"

"Then they did call?"

I sighed as I imagined what controversy awaited me. "Yes. Sister Trudy left a message."

"They're calling all the members to meet Saturday at noon."

"Right, but what's going on?"

"I don't know exactly, but it has something to do with the Harrises."

"The Harrises? Michelle was just here a little while ago."

"Yes, Pastor called the meeting himself, so I don't know." There was concern in Daddy's voice just as I was sure he could probably hear concern in mine.

"Well, thanks for letting me know, Daddy, and yes, I'll be there." I sighed. "You know I'll be leaving on Sunday for my trip."

"I still don't understand why you have to go now."

I paused before answering. "I don't have to go, Daddy, but I want to go. It's only for a few days."

"Yes, but by the time you get back, you'll only have two weeks before your wedding. It doesn't make any sense."

"Don't worry, Daddy. Everything for the wedding has already been done."

Daddy put on his serious voice. "You are planning to come back, aren't you?"

I must admit that I had to think about that one for a minute. Running away from my problems seemed like a pretty good idea at this point. "Of course I'm coming back, Daddy. I'm just doing Dr. Harding a little favor and giving myself a break at the same time. Everything is ready for the wedding. Everything is just fine."

"But are you fine?" Daddy paused. "You haven't been acting like yourself lately."

"I'm okay. I just need a little break from everything."

"I know you've been under a lot of pressure with your sister and all. Then there is that family."

"Daddy." Oh no, not the Bennings lecture again.

"I'm sorry, baby. But it's the truth. I don't like the way those uppity folks treat you."

"Yes, I have been under a lot of stress. But Josh's family doesn't treat me that badly." I looked over at Taylor sitting in her wheelchair. I hated to have to leave her, but I needed to preserve my sanity, to seriously consider that public relations position, and to prepare to marry the man of my dreams by burying my past forever. Maybe I'd be able to leave that part of me in Africa.

"They don't treat you that badly?"

"Daddy, don't start."

"All right, all right. I'm sorry. I just want the best for you."

"Joshua is the best for me." I said this to appease my father because lately I wasn't too sure.

"I guess there's nothing else to say except I'll see you tomorrow then."

"Goodnight, Daddy."

"Goodnight."

But I didn't sleep well. All night I had dreams about Joshua and the meeting at the church the next day.

As soon as I walked into the church building with my father, my spirit did not feel at ease. I wondered what this emergency meeting called by the pastor was really all about. Whatever it was concerning, I knew that I'd not be fighting against mere flesh and blood, but against powers and principalities and wickedness in high places.

My father gathered around the other deacons in the lobby. Aunt Dorothy handed me a paper before I walked into the sanctuary.

"Hi, Aunt Dorothy. What's this?" I asked.

"Hi, sweetie. You're not going to like this at all," she replied.

I looked at the paper and saw that it was a signed petition to remove Minister and Sister Harris from their positions in the ministry. I couldn't believe what I was reading. At the top of the list was Sister Winifred's name. I wasn't at all surprised.

"You've got to be kidding, right?" I wasn't surprised that the trouble maker was involved in this too. Typical.

"I wish I were. They want the Harrises to resign and for the children to step down from the music ministry also."

"Aunt Dorothy, I'll be right back." I walked away, knowing I needed to pray in secret. At that moment, I looked up and saw Ahmad walking in the front door. He stood in the lobby, looking around. *What in the world is he doing here? Has he lost his mind?* Immediately, I went out to confront him.

"What are you doing here?" My heart began to race at the realization that he was here at church. "Why are you still following me?"

"Don't flatter yourself. I'm not even here for you this time. I ran into Sister Winifred a little earlier, and she asked me to run an errand for her, that's all. Is that all right with you, Sister Carter?" Ahmad's voice was bitter.

I guided him into a small prayer room beside the sanctuary. "No, that's not all right with me. I want you out and gone, back to California or wherever else you came from."

"What in heaven's name is your problem with me?"

"What do you mean?"

"You're sending me mixed signals. First you won't talk to me, then you're nice to me. Then you're pushing me away again. I don't get it. I don't get you."

"You don't have to get me. You just have to get out."

"Do you hate me that much that you would deny me being in the house of the Lord?"

"No, that's just it. You're not here for the Lord. And I don't hate you at all. I've tried, believe me I've tried to hate you for years. All those years I rubbed my empty womb and cried because my babies were gone, I wanted to hate you."

"What? Babies?"

"Yes, babies. They were twins. I didn't know until it was too late, but I should've known, they were twins, our twins."

"Hey, I didn't know." Ahmad threw up his hand. "I'm sorry."

"You knew about the one and still you threw me away without a second thought. But I don't hate you. I can't hate anyone."

"So that kiss the other night meant something to you?"

It was at this moment that I noticed the sound of heavy breathing.

Chapter Forty

When I turned around, I stared into the faces of Sister Winifred and Joshua. They were both staring at me and Ahmad with their mouths hanging open, as if they had heard everything, or at least too much.

"Joshua, I—" I reached out to him.

"No, don't." Joshua pushed my hand away and began walking away.

"Please let me explain."

"It's too late for that now. Thanks to Sister Winifred, who led me in here, I've heard enough. I've heard it all."

"Joshua, please—"

"Now I understand why you weren't happy, why you were stalling. You didn't love me. It was this guy all along."

"You've got it all wrong." I turned to Ahmad. "Would you please leave?"

Ahmad left with a smirk on his face. Sister Winifred followed him out of the room.

"I do? You lied to me. You knew what I've been through with Delilah, and you still lied to me."

"No no no."

"My parents were right." Joshua shook his head.

I reached out for him. "You don't understand."

"Don't understand?" Joshua pulled away from me.

"I'm sorry. I wanted to tell you, but I just didn't know how."

"Didn't know how? Like Delilah didn't know how to tell

me she was pregnant, that she didn't want to be a mother to my baby." Joshua was careful not to raise his voice, although he was visibly upset.

"Joshua, I am not Delilah." I tried to grab his sleeve, but a cuff link popped off.

"Aren't you?" Joshua said. "Don't worry, you can have this player. Go and be with him."

"No, Joshua, please."

"Give me my ring. The wedding is off." I removed the ring, and he snatched it out of my hand. He left the room, slamming the door behind him. Then my whole world came crashing down around me, and I went down with it. I slid down to the floor and stayed there sobbing.

Sister Winifred peeped her head in through the door. "Girl, you need to be ashamed of yourself. I remember that hooligan from when you brought him to church way back when. I know your mama taught you better manners and home training than this, God rest her soul. So we shouldn't be where we are now." Sister Winifred shook her bony finger at me.

"You were spying on me?"

"No, I wasn't spying on you. I don't know what you're talking about. I'm not the one doing something wrong, sneaking around behind my fiancé's back. It's a disgrace. No wonder you're always with that Michelle girl. You know what they say about birds of a feather . . ."

"Birds of a feather, huh?" It seemed like everything in me wanted to rise up to slap that lady in the face, but the Spirit wouldn't let me.

It's not about you, Alex. I picked myself off the floor, dried my eyes, and suddenly, I knew what I had to do.

Chapter Forty-one

As I walked back into the sanctuary, heads turned and people whispered. I didn't even bother to camouflage my tear streaked face. I was fed up. I had enough of these self-righteous, sanctimonious, so-called church folks. I had more than enough.

Aunt Dorothy met me at the back. "What's going on with you? Joshua came in looking all upset. Sister Winifred is mumbling about something. And didn't I see that old boyfriend of yours at the church a little while ago?"

"Yes, Auntie." Still in shock over what had just transpired, I could barely talk.

Aunt Dorothy looked at me and frowned. "What blew him in?"

"We'll talk about it later, Auntie. Right now I'm concerned with Michelle and her family."

"It's just not right what they're trying to do to those people." Aunt Dorothy shook her head.

"Anybody can see that, but what are we going to do about it?" I grabbed her hand.

"I don't know what we can do about it." Aunt Dorothy sighed. "The wheels are already in motion.

"But someone has to speak on their behalf. Even if they're too humble or ashamed to do it, I'm not," I said.

"Baby, this isn't your battle," Aunt Dorothy said.

"Oh yes, it is. I'm tired of running and hiding. This is very much my battle."

"What do you mean?"

"Aunt Dorothy, I don't mean to hurt you or Daddy but I've got to come forward.I've got to come clean for the sake of Michelle and her family, for the sake of the church, and for righteousness' sake."

"Girl, I don't know what in the world you're talking about now." Aunt Dorothy looked very confused.

"No you don't, but you will." I hugged my Aunt Dorothy before going forward.

I walked up to the first row and sat down.

The sanctuary was already buzzing with gossip and heated conversations. A few minutes later, Pastor Martin entered the room, and everyone scattered to their seats. He stood, not with his normal Sunday morning authoritarian demeanor, but he stood with a solemn look instead.

Sister Trudy opened up the meeting. Then one by one, people were allowed to state their complaints and opinions about the indecency of Michelle singing in the choir as an un-wed teenager, and the indecency of her parents continuing to be leaders in the church when they obviously could not even control their own daughter.

Then it was my turn. I came up to the front and took a deep breath.

"So we are ready to put the entire Harris family out of the church? Or at least out of the public eye. Why? Is it really because of sin? Isn't the church a place to overcome your sin? Or does everyone have to be already perfect to come here? I say that Michelle is not the only one who has sinned in this church. Are we punishing her because of the actual fornica-tion that is implied here, or are we simply punishing her be-cause she got caught?"

The audience began to mumble and whisper. I looked out at the back and saw Joshua standing against the back wall.

"But we can't just condone this kind of thing; having her and her situation on display," Sister Winifred said.

"No one is asking you to condone sin, but pregnancy isn't a sin. The sin is in the past. Don't we all have sins from the past? What if someone were holding them against you? Would you all have preferred that she was on some kind of birth control like so many of your own children are? Isn't that a blatant endorsement for pre-marital sex? Are we punishing Michelle because her sin is visible and ours aren't?" I took a deep breath and continued. "Or would you have preferred that she had an abortion and pretended like nothing ever happened like so many God-fearing Christian folk have? Don't act like you don't know. Statistics say that one out of six women who claim to be born again Christians has had an abortion. It's just a silent thing, a hidden thing. I know because I lived through one." It was all coming out now, ready or not.

The congregation became silent.

"Yes, me. And I never told anyone about it until now. But Jesus paid for what I've done just like He paid for all of our sins. No one is blameless here. Would you all have rather that Michelle lost her baby or killed her baby? Then we wouldn't have to be standing here today talking about an illegitimate pregnancy. Would that have been easier? Would it have soothed all your consciences? Okay, so she's pregnant, but have any of you taken the time to find out if she has repented for her sin, if she is right with the Lord? Just because she made a mistake does not make her a harlot," I said. "And then again, even if she were, and she's not, harlots have souls too."

"Now, just a minute, no one said—" Sister Winifred started.

"But that's how she has been treated. And not just her, but everyone that has been in her position for as long as I can remember. They've all been treated the same, and slowly but surely, they're shamed away from the church. What makes this sin so much worse than all the others; stealing, lying, fighting, cheating, backbiting, etc.? I'll tell you what it is, the fact that we can see it. We can see it every day growing in her belly, a reminder of what she has done. But what if we all had constant reminders of what we have done? Would we like it? Just because no one can see our sin doesn't make it any less real. God sees everything. There is no great or small sin. So while you're all looking down on the Harris family in outrage, I say, as Jesus said, 'Let he who is without sin, cast the first stone.' That alone should clear everyone out. We all make mistakes. Some of our mistakes are costlier than others, but we all make them. So let's not pretend that we are too good or perfect to understand."

"I understand what you're saying. But what about our reputation in the community?" Sister Trudy steadied herself as she spoke.

"Reputation? Her parents have always been exceptional leaders in this community, and they've done nothing except to be loving parents. They've done no wrong, and they should not be on trial here. It is not for us to judge. Remember, if we can't forgive Michelle, then Jesus can't and won't forgive us." I couldn't stop now.

Everyone shuffled around in their seats. Pastor Martin started off the clapping and everyone else joined in. Michelle ran to the front and hugged me.

"I never imagined that church folk could cause so much pain," Michelle whispered.

"I'm sorry, but the hardest part is over now." I felt extremely close to the girl. I also felt that I had finally let God use me in the capacity that He wanted, without my fear or pride getting in the way.

Soon some people in the audience were standing, clapping. Others remained in their seats mumbling to each other.

Pastor Brown came forward and hugged me. He also hugged Michelle. Then he took the microphone and stood in the pulpit. "I was actually going to reprimand the immature and ungodly behavior I've been witnessing these past couple of weeks, ever since sister Michelle started to show. After such an eloquent sermon by Sister Alex, it is obvious what the answer must be and that is to do what Jesus would do. Thank God for the messenger because now I don't have to say a thing except, 'let he who is without sin cast the first stone.' This meeting is dismissed."

"Let he who is without sin cast the first stone." I repeated those words in my head. The same stones that were hitting the Harris family, and especially, Michelle, were the same stones I feared ten years ago. The stones had caused me to take the lives of my children, innocent fetuses. They would probably have been identical twins like me and my sister. I closed my eyes as the memory became all too vivid.

After the procedure, I had layed on the table, stiff and cold, almost lifeless except for my rapid heartbeat.

They had sucked out my children with a hollow plastic tube with a vacuum. It was ten to twenty-nine times more powerful than an average vacuum, information I didn't know at the time. All I felt was the pressure of hands pulling and tugging. All I heard was talking and grinding. Then there was just silence. Blood and silence. Then I saw a dismembered body being stored in a bottle. But as if that wasn't horrendous enough, I realized there was a second bottle. There had been another. Twins. I had been carrying twins. I never considered the possibility of twins, never even considered the one a real baby. But by the time I found out, something inside me wanted to rise up from the table and lash out at them for not telling me. Unfortunately, I was too weak, too groggy, and it was too late. In and out I drifted with the intensity of the medication.

I forced my eyes open and looked out into the congregation. My father and aunt were standing too. I went back to my seat with my head held down. "Dad . . . I—"

"That was a long time ago. I'm sorry you felt like you couldn't come to me. But I am so proud of you, now." My dad took off his glasses to dry his eyes.

"Child, so am I." Aunt Dorothy gave me a sympathetic smile.

"I've got to go now, Daddy." I hugged him. "You know I've got a lot to do. My flight is tomorrow."

"I love you, Alex." Daddy kissed my forehead, and then we walked outside, arm in arm, followed by Aunt Dorothy.

"I love you too, Daddy." I wiped the tears from my face. "By the way, the wedding is off."

Daddy frowned. "Off?"

"Yes, it's off, and no, it's not Joshua's fault." I kissed Aunt Dorothy on the cheek. "I don't want to talk about it." Aunt Dorothy shook her head. "Oh, I'm sorry, baby."

I tried to fake a smile. "It's okay. I'm okay."

Daddy pulled away from me. "I knew those Benningses were up to no good."

"Daddy." The last thing I needed was to have my father upset.

"I don't care what you say; I know it's the Benningses's fault," Daddy said.

"Daddy, please stop," I said.

"All right, but I don't like it at all." Daddy pounded his fist against the church bricks.

We shared a group hug. "I have to go now. You both take care of yourselves until I get back."

"You take care of yourself, child." Aunt Dorothy said.

"I will." I walked over to my car and didn't look back. "Lord, thank you for freeing me with the truth. Now I know I'm ready to face whatever comes next."

"Alex?" Aunt Dorothy yelled out as I was driving away, but there was no turning back. I blew her a kiss, and I was gone.

I drove straight home and spent the rest of the day packing and cancelling wedding plans. I hardly talked to Taylor except to tell her to take care of herself while I was gone. I was too hurt to have long, mushy conversations.

"It's only for a week," Taylor said.

"Right." I didn't really know anymore. The wedding was off. What did I have to rush back for?

I spent the evening in my room while Taylor had her physical therapy session with Keith. Hearing them talking happily, reminded me of my broken relationship with Joshua, and I cried until I was empty. Then I filled myself by reading the Word of God.

My phone kept ringing. Daddy and Aunt Dorothy kept calling, but I didn't want to talk to anyone. I read my Bible until I drifted into sleep.

The next day I arrived at the airport early, parked, unloaded my two suitcases, and went inside to check my luggage. Before I reached the security lines, I felt a tap on my shoulder.

Chapter Forty-two

I hoped that it was Joshua, coming to rescue me, to tell me he loved me, to tell me that the wedding was still on, but it wasn't. When I turned around, it was Keith, Taylor's physical therapist, standing in front of me.

"I didn't mean to sneak up on you. I was trying to catch you before you made your flight."

No this dude was not invading my personal space at a time like this. "Excuse me?"

"I called your father, and he said you were on your way to JFK. I tried calling but—"

"Yeah, my phone is off. What's going on? Is something wrong with my sister?"

"No, there is something very right with her." Keith smiled.

"Oh, so it's like that?"

"Yes." I looked him up and down. "So what can I do for you?"

"She looks up to you, and I've messed up my chance with her."

"Wait a minute, slow down." I looked around to find a seat.

Keith sat down next to me. "I like Taylor, but she's so hard to get through to. I think I've got her figured out though, but I wanted to know if you think she'll give me another chance."

"Another chance? What have you done to her?"

"Nothing. It's just that we were talking, and all of a sudden she said she'd like to visit my church with me."

"So?"

"So . . . I told her I don't have a church home."

"Keith."

"Yeah, I know, but I just never got it together when I moved and—"

"You mean you used that as an excuse."

"Whatever. Anyway, I never figured that would be the one thing standing in the way of . . ." Keith looked down at the floor. "She called me a hypocrite for claiming to love God and not even having a church home."

"Look, if my sister is asking you about church at all, it's because you must be turning her onto it. And if she called you a hypocrite, she meant it. So get yourself together because you know right from wrong."

"Yeah."

"The last time Taylor mentioned church to me was the first day of the Women's Conference, before her accident, and I actually thought she was close to receiving the Lord. But things didn't work out that way."

"She has been very bitter about everything, but do you think I have a shot with her at all?"

Now I was annoyed. I had my own problems, serious ones. "You came all the way down here to ask me that?"

"I had to know before you went away."

It's not about you, Alex. I looked directly into Keith's eyes.

"I'm so sorry about bothering you like this."

"No, it's okay. Either you must really care, or you're just as crazy as she is." I shook my head. "To be honest, you're all she ever talks about lately; therapy, therapy, and more therapy."

"Really?"

"Yes, therapy and that gym she wants so much to own."

"Thanks. That's all I needed to hear. I'm about to go out on a limb, and I needed to know where I stand."

"Smart move." I stood up. "Why don't you join my father

and Aunt Dorothy at our church on Sunday? You can all try to get Taylor to come."

"Sounds like a plan."

"Unfortunately, I'll be gone for a while."

"When will you be back?"

"I was supposed to only be gone for a week, but now I don't know." I shook my head. "I guess I'll have to see."

"Again, I'm sorry, but I just had to know. I think I'm in love with your sister." Keith admitted.I smiled. "You think?"

"Okay, I know I'm in love with your sister."

On the outside, I smiled because I was happy that Taylor had found someone to love her, but on the inside, I was sad I had lost the one who loved me. "God bless you, then."

"Thanks." Keith turned and started to walk away.

"Bye." I was ready to leave all of this behind and to embark on a new journey.

I put on my shades, looked through the plane window, and let the tears run down my face. I couldn't believe I had lost Joshua forever. My secret was out, and my life was over. The only reason I was still going to Africa was because I needed to escape. Very simply escape. There was no place else I wanted to go. The wedding was off, the love of my life was gone. My reputation at the church and at the affiliated college was smeared forever, which meant I couldn't go back to either of them. I put my head into my hands and let the emotions of the past few days cleanse my soul.

I had never been on a missions trip, and even though this was clearly supposed to be about public relations, I knew I would be staying closely with missionaries. I also knew where my heart truly was and that was in helping people. Public relations? Could I truly do the job and be concerned only with the image and not necessarily with the people? That really wasn't me, and I knew it, but I was still willing to give this new position a try. Not only did I need the money, but after what happened between Joshua and me, I really needed the time away. Time away seemed like an understatement. I had the rest of my life to be away because Joshua wanted no parts of me after my lies and deception. I remembered the way he looked at me with disgust when he found out. Why didn't I just come forward and say it a long time ago before it got too serious, before the stakes became too high? I looked at my empty ring finger again and ached for what would have been.

My flight stopped in London where I had to switch to a British Airways flight, but what would happen once I reached Kenya?

Chapter Forty-three

I arrived in Kenya at the Jomo Kenyatta International Airport, the largest airport in the country. Greeted by Sister Martha and Sister Ethel from Missionary Chapel Church, it felt good to see familiar faces. They had been there for a week already with a group of ten. Sister Martha was wrapped from head to toe in traditional African garb, so much so that I almost didn't recognize her. Sister Ethel, however, wore a long sleeved dress and a wide brimmed straw hat. "Sister Alex. We're so glad you decided to join us." Sister Martha hugged me with her wide arms.

"Yes, we are." Sister Ethel did the same with her smaller ones.

"Thank you." I smiled. "I'm glad to be here, and I'm anxious to get started."

"Well, you're going to have to wait a little bit for that. First our driver is going to take you on a little tour. Dr. Harding insists that anyone who comes here must get an idea of what they're dealing with before you're thrown into the fire." Sister Martha laughed, but I wasn't really sure what was funny.

I was already nervous about being here to do this public relations thing. I certainly didn't have time for jokes.

"Then we'll show you where you can get settled in." Sister Ethel's words were more of a comfort.

"Okay, that's fine." I wasn't sure if it was fine or not, but since I was in unfamiliar surroundings, I didn't complain. In fact, I had never been farther than South Carolina my entire life. Neither had Taylor. A pang of guilt went through me as I thought of her back home in Brooklyn, crumpled over in her wheelchair. I shook the image from my head.

They led me to the 4x4 Landcruiser parked out front and introduced me to the driver. "Jambo," he said. He was a tall, well built man with incredibly smooth, dark skin."Jambo," I answered, which meant hello in Swahili.

As we boarded the vehicle, I saw that it had a game viewing roof since, as they explained to me, it was usually used for safaris. Immediately, I noticed the rolling hills, grassy plains, and humid feel to the air. All of the roads were tarred yet some were rougher than others. The driver cruised down rugged hills and flat lowlands at high speeds. Pedestrians chatted casually while crossing the roads. The driver explained issues of poverty, HIV, cultural, and political importance. While listening to him, I noticed many nice parks and reserves. I also noticed safari vans full of people on their way to study the beautiful wildlife. The mystery of mountain forests, stony Northern deserts, and high moors was inescapable.Then we saw the Great Rift Valley that stretched from Jordan toMozambique. The driver told us that we would have an opportunity for mountain climbing atop Mt. Kenya, which kind of interested me because I always liked heights. I saw beautiful beaches along the coast and the tropical climate soothed me.

"Now this would be a nice place for a honeymoon. Maybe you and Deacon Joshua can check it out." Sister Martha pointed to the beach.

Sister Ethel just giggled.

"Yeah, maybe." Sadly I looked away and hid my naked ring finger underneath my bag. Of course they didn't know yet. It was too soon, and they were thousands of miles away from Missionary Baptist Church, so they hadn't heard.

While we were still riding, it started to rain, and the driver explained that it was the rainy season. Finally, we ended our tour in the colonial-built capital, Nairobi. The Methodist Guest House, where were staying, was located in the Lavington Green section of Nairobi. The rooms were a fair size and were equipped with thirteen-inch television sets. There were only about six or eight channels, nothing like the cable I was accustomed to, but it was better than nothing. There was a business center where we could use the Internet and public telephones, so for that I was grateful. There was a small gift shop and a western-style mall named Yaya Center that we could walk to if we wanted. There was also a place for group seating to encourage fellowship amongst the missionaries. I went into my room, closing the door behind me. I kicked off my sandals, peeled off my denim outfit, and took a shower in the small bathroom. When I came out, I threw myself across the bed. I looked at my empty ring finger and began to cry. I had gambled and lost Joshua. I had been living a lie, trying to be self-righteous, and yet I had done the most unrighteous thing.

It was a wonder that I could even lift my head daily and go on with my sham of a life for as long as I did, avoiding innocent children, ducking and hiding like some kind of bandit. For so long I had randomly selected children from a crowd, seeking solace in their eyes, seeking redemption and wondering what if. Not only was I ashamed, but I was missing my calling. What a waste my life was.

Before I could truly sink into the abyss of depression, there was a knock at the door.

"Sister Alex, are you ready?" Sister Ethel's soft voice summoned me.

"Five minutes, please." I jumped off of the bed and into my clean underwear.

"We'll meet you out front," Sister Martha said.

I grabbed a long sleeved, pink cotton shirt to go along with my khaki skirt. Dr. Harding had spent a considerable amount of time telling us about the modest dress codes. He made it very clear, no tank tops, sleeveless outfits or low rider jeans. Believe me, I got the picture. I pulled my hair back into a ponytail, put a pink Nike cap on my head, and sunglasses on my face. I wore no jewelry or makeup. I grabbed my Bible and a small umbrella, then stuffed them into my canvas bag. I looked around, careful not to leave anything of value in the room. Now I was ready for ministry.

When we entered the Land Cruiser this time, it was filled with other American missionaries. The driver took us to the largest slum in Kenya, Kibera. We climbed up a hillside where I saw a mess of rusted metal roofs joined together. There were windows without glass panes. There was sewage from outside the city running into the city to join with the sewage from inside the city that already had no way out. Consequently, the stench was horrible. We met families of eight who lived in one room shacks without a toilet. The conditions were horrendous, and I immediately felt the pain of these people. I could see that just as I had heard about, sanitation was one of their biggest issues. Yet because of their ability to survive on a dollar in Kibera, and the close proximity to the rich who would hire them, they continued to live in this slum. I shook my head because these made the slums back home look like paradise.

As we talked with some of the natives, who spoke a mixture of broken English and Swahili, I discovered that some of them were quite happy where they were, helping each other and enjoying a great sense of community. One lady explained how a neighbor had given her sugar cane for her and her son. Another told us how her neighbors helped with chores when she was sick. We prayed with them, sang songs out in the fields, and passed Bible tracs out to the occasional passerby. The next day the entire missionary group was up at dawn. We had devotion together, and then Sister Martha dispersed the assignments for the day, which I wouldn't be able to participate in. Instead, I had a press conference scheduled at the Minister for Education's office. Unfortunately, it was time to start fulfilling my public relations obligations, which I was not at all excited about. I could probably do the job with my hands behind my back, but missions seemed much more interesting.

The only bright spot, however, was Missionary Seger Abasi, who was also on assignment from the United States. He was actually a native Kenyan who had been working in The United States for the past ten years. He had quite a sense of humor, and after all I had been through, surprisingly, he was able to make me laugh.

Upon entering the office of the minister for education, Dr. Wanjii greeted me with, "Jambo."

"Jambo," I replied. Then he proceeded to speak in his native language. So I pulled out my notes and said, "Sisemi kiswahili, lakini" which meant that I didn't speak Swahili. We spoke briefly in English. Then when the press arrived, I took my place in front of the camera and simply shared all the information I had about Missionary Bible College. That was the easy part because after working there for three years, I knew it inside and out. I not only discussed all of the academic programs, but I highlighted all of the outreach programs as well. Needless to say, the crowd seemed to be impressed. Dr. Wanjii spoke of modeling one of the newer Bible schools like ours. He introduced me to a few of his colleagues, and we spoke intensely about the vision of Missionary Bible College. I knew it well. Then we all sat down to eat nyama choma-grilled goat and Sukumu wiki-collard greens. At the end of our meeting we said, "kwaheri" to each other, which means good-bye.

After the van dropped me off at the guest house, upon seeing that everyone was still out on their afternoon duties, Seger and I left to take a short walk. Down through the brush and up a slippery hillside, I found a tiny one room schoolhouse. I peeked inside the window and saw young children between the ages of five and ten sitting on the floor. The children fascinated me in every way. I stood gazing at them through the window until their teacher soon invited me in.

"I'm sorry. I don't mean to disturb you." I turned to go, filled with embarrassment.

The teacher put her hand on my shoulder to stop me. "No problem. You here to help us, to teach us."

"Oh no, just the Bible, not—" I shook my head frantically.

She put the chalk in my hand. "This is Vacation Bible School. You teach us."

I looked at the teacher, then the chalk, then into the eyes of the students who sat silently waiting for what I had to say.

So Seger and I walked in and started talking about Jesus, His life, His love, and how He died on the cross for our sins. The next thing I knew, I was talking about how precious life is, and going on and on about the goodness of God. I always did love talking about the Lord, and if the right folk were asked, they'd say I always loved to talk period. We sang "Jesus Loves Me" and I was filled. Following the children's lead and the beat of my own heart, I didn't return to the guesthouse until dinnertime.

The missionaries and I worked very closely every day, especially Seger and me. He seemed to love teaching also. Daily we walked barefoot through the tall thick trees, eating papayas, and talking about the vision God had placed in his heart, and about the vision I was discovering in mine. I could tell that he was beginning to like me. Once when we were walking by a waterfall, he reached out for my hand, but I resisted.

"I can tell you've been hurt," he said with his Kenyan accent.

"Yes, I have. Twice, actually."

"I'm sorry."

"Don't be. It's just life. Besides, the second time was my fault."

Seger smiled. "I don't believe that."

"It's true. I wasn't honest about my past so—"

"But why should something from the past make such a difference to the present?"

"Well, it's hard to explain, but it did."

"I don't care about anything from your past. I just want you in my future."

He had smooth, dark, Belgium chocolate colored skin and eyes that sparkled like fine onyx. When he put his hand under my chin and lifted it, I thought I was ready, but as much as I wanted to forget about Joshua, I couldn't.

"I'm sorry. I need more time," I said.

"He must be someone really special."

"He is."

"I understand. Your wounds are fresh. But I promise to make you forget all about him."

I smiled as I watched him walk away.

Chapter Forty-four

Joshua walked out of class at Missionary, past Alex's desk. I could picture her sitting there with her warm smile and big, bright eyes. She was the only woman who could make my heart skip a beat. I also missed those curvy hips, and that sassy walk wrapped up in the classiest exterior a man could imagine. No, really that woman could melt an iceberg with her walk. I sighed as I walked down the lonely hallway and out of the front door. I couldn't believe it was all over. I guessed she would be impressing some other guy now, but I sure did miss her. Since I had been going to counseling, I was better able to accept this, and better able to forgive.

Before I could get to my car, my phone rang, and I saw on my caller ID that it was Yvonne. What did that woman want now? I was tired of her always calling me. "I need this. I want that." Didn't she know any of the other brothers in the church? I had better things to do. I wasn't even going to answer the call until I thought of Sister Winifred's nagging lips.

"Yeah? What?" I answered, obviously irritated.

"Now what kind of way is that for a future minister to answer his phone?"

"I don't have time for this, Yvonne."

"Well, I'm sorry to disturb you, but I need you to come over quickly. I've got . . . it's an emergency," Yvonne whined.

"Okay, okay. I'm leaving school now. Give me ten minutes," I sighed. "What's this all about anyway?"

But she had already hung up. I was in no mood for her female antics. This was getting out of hand.

When I arrived at Sister Winifred's door, I noticed that the house was quiet. I rang the doorbell, and Yvonne came to the door. She peeked out, and then let me in quickly. It was dark, so I couldn't see a thing.

"Can you please turn on a light, or is that the problem?" I asked.

"No, the problem is the heat." Yvonne said.

"The heat? Did your air conditioning or power go out?"

"I'm hot." Yvonne clicked on a lamp, and I saw that she was wearing a very thin robe. Suddenly, I could see curves everywhere, imprints of every body part. When I stopped staring, I closed my mouth.

"My Lord. I thought you were genuinely in trouble."

"I am." Yvonne moved closer to me.

I backed away. "I'm a man of God. Did you genuinely think that I'd be so weak?"

"Maybe." Yvonne giggled.

"Yes, men are weak in the flesh, but thank God for the Spirit. Get dressed."

She caught up to me and threw her body against mine. It was all I could do to pry her off of me. "Good-bye, Yvonne."

"But I thought—"

"I'm in love with Alex. I always have been." I stood in the doorway with the door open. I was so disgusted. "I was trying to help you out."

"Oh, so that's all it was?"

"Yeah, that's all it ever was. I'll be a minister soon, and I ain't going out like this."

"Where are you going?"

"I'm going to do what I shoulda done from the beginning. Leave you the heck alone."

***

It was a breezy day at the Long Island Cemetery. I knelt to place fresh lilies on Delilah's grave. They were her favorite. I used my finger to outline her name on the tombstone. Then I buried my face in my hands as I remembered the way she died, like a piece of meat on a slab. Being here was rough, but I knew I could handle it now. The scriptures Pastor Martin had given me to meditate on had helped. I hadn't visited her grave since she was buried two years ago, but through God's grace, I wasn't angry anymore. My eyes filled up with tears, and for the first time, I didn't wipe them away. After continuous counseling with Pastor Martin, I learned to forgive Delilah, no matter how wrong she had been. When I finally stood up, I caught a glimpse of a familiar face. I saw Alex's sister, Taylor, humped over a grave a few feet away. She seemed to be placing fresh lilies on a grave, and I just knew it was her mom's. Then I saw her father farther away in the distance, going down the trail while Taylor lingered behind.

Before she rolled away from the gravesite in her wheelchair, I called out to her softly. "Taylor."

"Joshua?" Taylor rolled over to me.

"How are you?" I smiled, but couldn't look her in the eyes. I was ashamed of how I had treated her sister.

"I'm cool, but what's up with you?"

"I'm miserable without your sister." I was sure I probably looked miserable also.

"That's funny. I'm usually miserable with my sister. Just kidding." Taylor threw her head back and laughed hard.

"Why don't you call her?"

"Oh, is she back from Kenya?"

"No."

"I don't think she'll want to talk to me after the way I put her off. Besides she's in love with someone else."

"Are you kidding me? My sister is in love with you, only you."

"Are you sure?"

"I'm her twin, okay? I know what I'm talking about."

"But would she forgive me?"

"Look. You're pathetic. She ain't no saint, but if anyone would forgive you, it would be Alex. We don't always get along, but she's cool people."

"You're right about that. She's a giving person, and I let her go."

Taylor smacked her gum and blew a small bubble. "Yeah, whatever."

"That's why I feel so bad."

"Look, life is too short for feeling bad. It's time to get on with the business of living, don't you think?"

"What did you say?"

"I said it's time to get on with the business of living."

"That's funny. My pastor told me the exact same thing."

"Cool. Look, I've got to go and catch up with my father. See ya around."

I watched her start down the winding trail with her electric wheelchair and wondered how any disabled person could survive without one. Taylor had come a long way.

When I left the cemetery, I immediately went to see my parents. I met them in the informal living room. The sunlight flowed in from the huge cathedral windows. They were both seated on the velvet sofa. I sat down in a high backed armchair.

I took a deep breath. "Mom and Dad, I know what you're going to say, but I want to reconcile with Alex." Mom stood up immediately.

"What do you mean you want to reconcile with her?"

"I love her. I made a mistake." I was excited.

"Are you sure, son?" Dad looked into my eyes as if he were peering into my soul.

"I've never been surer in my life," I answered.

Dad nodded his head in agreement. "All right then, I support your decision. I just want you to be sure and to be happy."

"What? Have you two lost your minds?" Mom stood up and started pacing.

"Mom, what happened with her was a long time ago, and she's not that person anymore." I stood up too.

"That's what they all say." Mom squinted up her narrow eyes and threw her hands into the air.

"Mom, don't." I didn't want to hear anything negative about Alex.

"What about your ministry?" Mom continued to pace the marble floors.

"What about it? Alex has been the most supportive of my ministry."

Mom stood still for a moment. "Yes, I know she's been dabbling in ministry at our little sister church, but will she stand by you when it's time for you to take over Kingdom House of Prayer?"

"First of all, that's if God calls me to take over the church. What if God calls me to start my own? I don't know which direction the ministry will take at this point. But I do know that Alex will be by my side." I stood next to my mother.

"What do you mean if you take over the church? Of course you will. You're your father's only son," Mom said as she reached up, grabbed me by the shoulders and shook me.

"Ever since I told you two that I was going into the ministry, you've been trying to control me." Now I was angry. "I have to live my own life."

Mom narrowed her glare. "Like you lived your own life when you went against us and married Delilah?"

I slammed my fist against the wall. "Alex is not Delilah."

"How do you know that?" Mom started walking again, breathing hard this time. "Mirriam." My father started.

"No, don't Mirriam me. This is my only son, and I want

the best for him. That's why I found that gentleman," Mom said.

"What gentleman?" Dad looked at my mom. "What do you mean found?"

"Do you think that low life just showed up and showed interest in Alex after all these years? No, he didn't just show up. I dug him up." Mom's eyes looked small and beady.

"What?" I asked.

"Tell me you're kidding." Dad covered his face in shame.

"No, I'm not kidding. I paid a private investigator to dig up Alex's old college boyfriend. It wasn't hard at all. I knew there would be something scandalous there. I just didn't know what it was," Mom said.

"There is no scandal, Mom." I couldn't believe she did that. "Why would you, on purpose, try to destroy my life?"

Mom fell back onto the couch. "Because I didn't want anyone to hurt you again like Delilah did. I wanted to be sure Alex was all she claimed to be, so I paid that hoodlum to come to New York City, to become involved in her life again."

"I don't believe this." I was shocked.

"It wasn't hard. He said he had real feelings for the girl once and that he wouldn't mind seeing her again anyway." Mom threw her hands in the air. "So what was the harm in that? If she loved Joshua, she wouldn't have been moved by an old fling, right?"

"Mom, you almost messed up my whole life. Now I have to see if she'll take me back. I don't know if she will, but she's all I want." I didn't know how to do it, but I knew I had to act fast.

"Go handle your business, son." Dad patted me on the back, and then turned to my mother. "I'll handle your meddling mother."

"Joshua," Mom said.

I was determined. "Leave me alone, Mom. I'm going to really pray hard for you. Pastor Martin was right about everything. I've got to put all this mess behind me if I want to go forward."

Mom yelled out. "Son, I'm just concerned about your future. You're making a huge mistake."

"Then let me make it." I opened the front door. "But Alex is all I want right now, and I'm going to get her back."

Chapter Forty-five

After the initial week in Kenya, I realized that I was in no way ready to go home. Besides, I had nothing to go home for. I couldn't explain it, but I felt a strong urging to stay and commune with God under the stars. Then there were the dreams I kept having, not my usual nightmares, but ones of me speaking to a crowd of women. So I said good-bye to Sister Martha, Sister Ethel and the other eight missionaries from the church. Their two week assignment was over. I, however, knew that after only a week, my real assignment was just beginning. I called Dr. Harding and asked if I could extend my visit to do some additional missionary work. I explained to him that it was something I felt the Lord was calling me to do and that I needed an indefinite leave of absence. Hesitantly, he agreed, reiterating the importance of me making up my mind about the public relations position once and for all. He agreed to put a temp in my current position for a little while so I could have time to sort out my affairs if I would do one more public relations assignment while I was here in Nairobe. I was glad we had a deal since I was sure that at any given moment some religious know it all would come marching into Dr. Harding's office demanding my resignation.

I continued to stay at the guesthouse, but this time the group staying with me was from a church in London. Seger stayed on in Kenya as well because his was a six month assignment. One evening during the church service, a group of natives from Kibera that we had evangelized to earlier, came in and sat down. We were so happy about their hunger for God. Pastor Njoki preached, and everyone in the service fell under the power of the Holy Ghost.

The next day I called home to speak to Taylor. I reminded her to check up on Michelle for me, and she promised she would. We chatted briefly about Dad, Aunt Dorothy, and Keith. It felt good to hear her voice, yet the entire time we were talking, the subject of young women kept rising in my spirit. I tried to block it out. Taylor also told me that she had seen Joshua at the cemetery and that he asked about me. I wasn't sure why, but I was too hurt to ask.

After the call, I went to use the computers located in a small area of the guesthouse. I looked up information on young women in Kenya, and through the Internet I found out that two hundred and fifty two thousand fifteen through nineteen-year-old Kenyan girls seek abortions every year. I also saw that twenty-seven percent of nineteen-year-old women in the Nyanza Province of Kenya were either pregnant or already mothers. When I discovered that one in ten women in Kenya would die from abortions, that was the end of the line for me. I decided to find these women.

As I went through the villages interviewing young women, I was drawn by their stories of miseducation, confusion, and desperation, which in turn, set the tone for the illegal butchering they'd subjected themselves to. So I began to work with the young women as well as the children, and surprisingly, it was very good. As we trudged through the village, we brought food, toys, medicine, and books, all the comforts we so easily took for granted in America. The missionaries, Seger, and I went walking from house to house praying without ceasing. It was refreshing to see people who had so little, love God so much. I sat down on the shore sinking my toes into the sand, letting the tide wash against my feet. I threw my head back and looked up into the distant sky. It was a lavender grayish color, more beautiful than I could've imagined. Seger came and sat next to me.

"I love it here," I said.

"Me too."

"I just want to give of myself, to make a difference in the lives of children and their mothers."

"It's good to know what you want."

"Children's ministry. That's my heart."

"Mine too, really." I looked up into Seger's dark eyes. "It's just been so long since I've been away from it."

"So? What's stopping you from coming back?"

"Nothing, I guess."

"You can pick up where you left off. That's the wonderful thing about the God we serve. You can lose your way, and when you realize it, He'll take you back and fix you up like nothing ever happened."

"You're right about that. But have you ever gone so far you didn't know how to get back?"

"Yes, I have, but the scripture says if we acknowledge Him in all our ways, that He'll direct our path. You're a child of the Most High, and you're loved, remember? You can't lose." Seger was so full of faith.

I wanted some of his spirit to rub off on me. "I never forget He loves me, but sometimes I forget the details."

"I understand." Seger covered his head with a plastic bag as the rain began to fall. "But it's there, in our minds, that Satan attacks us."

I started running toward the jeep. "Tell me about it." The rain came down heavier as we sped away.

Most of my days were spent down at the little schoolhouse, with Seger and me working diligently with the children, feeding them naturally and spiritually. It was exhilarating. One day Seger took me down to the Masaii Mara, a beautiful landscape in the African Rift Valley. There I saw hippos in the river, giraffes grazing in the trees, and herds of zebras on the plains. We saw the villagers building a school there.

"This organization is committed to building schools here, and so far the project has been very successful," Seger said.

"Sounds good."

"The Masaii have the highest primary school dropout rate here in Kenya."

"Oh, no." I found a spot in the grass to sit down. "Why?"

Seger sat down next to me. "Most of these children start school late because schools are usually too far away from their communities."

"Wow, how sad."

"Oh, for the Masaii, it gets sadder."

"Really?"

"Most times the kids can't go to school because they've got to tend to the fields, the goats, and cattle."

"That's terrible."

"Then most of the schools are in really bad condition. That's why I wanted to bring you here. That's why this school and the others are so important."

I looked down at the bag of coloring books I carried. "I see. I'm glad I can be a part of this."

After spending the entire month of August in Kenya, for the first time in my entire adult life, I was totally satisfied. I wasn't worried about my reputation. In fact, I didn't know what they were saying about me back in Brooklyn, and I didn't care. I wasn't worried about money because I had just taken a leave from my job, and yet God was providing. I wasn't worried about Michelle because she had her parents. I wasn't worried about my sister because apparently she had been doing just fine without me. Besides, she had Keith to help her. And despite my feelings for Joshua, I wasn't worried about not being his wife. I just figured it wasn't God's will, and that was finally enough for me.At the end of the day Seger and I walked down the hillside toward the guesthouse. I took a banana out of my bag and began to peel it. Seger smiled as he always did. The sunset was beautiful. Before we reached our destination, Seger stopped and pulled the banana from my hand. He took my hands in his.

"Seger, I—"

"No, don't say a word." Seger put his finger to my lips. Then I watched him move in for a kiss.

Chapter Forty-six

Before I could even react, I heard a rustling sound in the bushes. I turned away from Seger to follow the noise. The air was humid and smelled of wet grass. Then I heard that strong familiar voice.

"Alex," Joshua said.

I jumped to face the unexpected. "Joshua?"

"Yes, it's me. I'm here. Will you come with me to talk, please?" Joshua looked directly into my eyes.

I was so surprised to see him standing there in his caramel tallness with his low-cut hair and smooth shaven face. He smelled of cologne, and although I couldn't name the brand, it was raw and masculine. His brown eyes were piercing, and they drew me into his web.

"Yes, we can talk." Then I turned to Seger to make the obligatory introduction. Seger, this is Mr. Joshua Bennings from the United States. He's a deacon at Brooklyn Missionary Chapel. Joshua, this is Seger Abasi. He's a missionary here."

"It's good to meet you, sir," Seger said.

"Right," Joshua looked Seger up and down.

"Seger, thanks for everything, but I'll see you tomorrow." I signaled that it was all right for him to leave.

"Are you sure?" Seger looked concerned.

I nodded my head. "Yes, I'm sure." Seger said goodnight and walked on ahead of us. My mind raced with thoughts of why Joshua was here. Then Joshua and I continued the lonely walk down the hillside and stopped near the guesthouse.

"How did you find me?" I asked.

"Dr. Harding gave me all the information I needed."

"Of course." I didn't dare look into his eyes. "So what brings you to Kenya, Joshua?"

"I missed you." Joshua reached up and touched my face.

"You missed me?" I tried to be cold as ice, but with the warmth of hishands, my resolve was melting.

"Yes, badly. I made a big mistake."

"A mistake?"

"Yes. I shouldn't have given you up." Joshua took my hand. "I'm sorry."

I looked at my hand in his. "I'm sorry too."

"What has been going on with you? It has been really bad not knowing—"

"Well, a lot has happened in the weeks since we've been apart." I wanted to be totally honest, no matter what.

"First of all, what about that guy I saw you with at the church?"

"Ahmad."

"Do you love him?"

"No, of course not. He's just a guy from my awful past. He just showed up somehow."

"Yes, unfortunately my mother had something to do with that."

I wasn't surprised. "What?"

"I'm sorry, but she was involved with that dude showing up."

"Really? How did—" That woman never liked me.

"Look, we'll talk about her later. I want to talk about you now."

"Well, I know you heard everything I said. I mean there I was unprepared and spilling all of my business to the masses."

"Yeah, I heard."

"So you know my issue." I began to fumble with my shoes.

"Yeah."

"And you also know that I haven't been happy with my whole life. I've been as paralyzed as my sister is."

"Okay."

"Stagnant. I've wanted to teach for a long time, but it took me going halfway across the world, here to the Motherland, to accept that." Overcome with emotion, I buried my face in my hands. "I wasn't willing to go forward and do what it takes . . . until now."

"So?"

"I'm a different person now. I'm going back to school. I want to make a difference in the lives of children. And I'm also going to work with young ladies, teaching them to love themselves as God loves them. In fact, I'm going to adopt a child from Africa one day. I decided that just yesterday."

"I see. It seems like you've done a lot of growing since you've been here."

"I have. There is so much I know God wants me to do."

"I'm happy for you," Joshua said.

"I've always wanted this. It's just that I had been carrying the burden of . . ." My words trailed off.

"The abortion?"

"Yes, and it had been giving me nightmares."

"Nightmares?"

"Yes, they'd calmed down for a few years, but when we got together and you started bringing up motherhood and Lilah, they came back. I thought I was over it, had buried it, but it came back to haunt me."

"Why didn't you tell me? I mean, this thing you did was so long ago."

"Ten and a half years ago, to be exact. I was scared and blind." I wiped the tears that had emerged. "I didn't want to lose you."

"I've got to admit I was shocked when I heard you confess everything at church, but it all makes sense now; your commitment to Michelle, your reluctance with Lilah, everything." Joshua's eyes pleaded for forgiveness. "I'm sorry I didn't understand."

"I didn't expect you to understand. I didn't even understand it myself. And to be honest, I don't think you were ready, until now, to hear it. But now that you know about it, I've got to tell you everything." I sat down on a rock.

"You don't have to—"

"Yes, I do. It's important, and it could affect our future, now that I think you might want one with me."

Joshua sat on the ground. "All right then, go on."

"I never told you much about my college sweetheart, Ahmad, because it hurt too much. We broke up right before my junior year."

"Right."

"I was so sure he was the one. We had dated for the entire sophomore year, and I thought I was going to marry him. In fact we even planned to work together and everything. I thought he was going to be my husband, not that he was even marriage material. But in the romanticism of my young mind, I made just one compromise and that mistake cost me everything. I became pregnant, he ran off to California to become an actor, and the rest is history." I looked up into Joshua's brown eyes.

"You don't have to—"

"Yes, I do." I paused, and then continued. "I snuck down to one of those inner city clinics, and before I knew it they had me up on a table and in stirrups. I waited for him. He was supposed to meet me, but I never heard from him again. Without even knowing, I had let them kill two babies."

"Two babies?"

"Twins. I didn't know I was carrying twins until it was too

late. Anyway what's done is done." I sighed and looked down at the ground.

"What did your family say?"

"No one ever knew, only Taylor. She was the only one who was there for me. But she was taking her personal trainer exam that day so I never even told her I was going. She never knew until it was over."

"That was a lot to go through by yourself."

I looked into Joshua's eyes and knew he was a good man. Mom had always told us to find a good man. "And when you find him," she'd say, "marry him." She believed in keeping it simple and keeping it holy.

"I thought I was saving my life, my reputation, my career. I didn't know at the time that I was destroying a life. Theirs and mine."

"So that is what the nightmares have been about?"

"Every last one of them. I've had to live with myself ever since. That's why I couldn't teach. I couldn't work around kids, not after what I had done. Every time I'd look into one's eyes, I'd see my babies. My twins. I'd hear them crying, and I could never turn it off."

Joshua put his arms around me. "You should've told me sooner. We could've had this resolved."

"I couldn't. I felt like I had done the worst thing in the world until I had to speak for Michelle. It was like I was also speaking for myself or at least like the Holy Spirit was speaking through me."

"That's the past. You've already repented, so God has already forgiven you and cleansed you from all unrighteousness. He did that the day you got born again, remember?"

"I know, but I've only recently come to accept His forgiveness for that particular thing. I'm sorry I couldn't tell you before."

"I understand. We've all done things before we knew Christ

that we're ashamed of. We regret it, but we can't take it back.
God wipes it out, and we keep on going in Jesus' name."

"Amen."

"I have a confession to make," Joshua said.

"What is it?"

"I felt paralyzed too. Pastor Martin helped me to see that."

"Oh?"

"Yes, I've been in counseling since you've been gone."

"How were you paralyzed?"

"I wanted to marry you ever since the first week I met you. I
knew you were special when I joined your church and saw you
on the praise team, but I . . ." Joshua stood up. "I just couldn't
find the courage, even when we were engaged, to open up to
you."

"What could you possibly be afraid of?"

"Of losing you like I lost Delilah."

"I know that feeling of loss. It's hard."

"Yes, it is."

I picked up a stick and started writing in the dirt. "What
about Yvonne?"

"Are you kidding? She never was anything at all. Just an
innocent distraction."

"Innocent? I don't know about that."

"I'm sorry it didn't seem that way, but I never had any interest in Yvonne.

Unfortunately, I found out the hard way what she had in
mind for me. I should've listened to you." Joshua took the
stick out of my hand and threw it. Then he took my hands
in his.

"Oh, really?"

"Yep. Don't worry; I put her in her place."

I gently pulled my hands out of his. "But she was always
there, always around. You let her be around. At first it didn't
bother me too much, but after awhile, it was threatening."

"It was my fault. I should've cut it from the jump."

Little hot tamale Yvonne, always following Joshua around like a little puppy dog on the pretense of church business. It was ministry all right, the ministry of how Miss becomes a Mrs. No, I didn't think so. And then she was so bold that she tried to steal Joshua right up under my nose. Yeah right; like I was going to sit back and let that happen. That girl had so many tricks up her sleeve, but not one I didn't recognize. The only reason she was able to get as far as she did was because I was so busy covering up my own mess, I didn't even realize I was out of the game. "When you broke up with me I thought my whole life was over, but through the blood of Jesus, I'm more than a conqueror," I said.

"You're a strong woman. I want to be as strong as you," Joshua said.

"When God heals your heart, you'll know you're strong," I said. "When the time is right, you'll know you're strong."

Joshua took my hands. "But that time is now."

"What?"

"I've been praying for courage for a long time. Like you, I've been trying to help people when I couldn't help myself." Joshua squeezed my hands as he gazed into my eyes.

Apprehensive, I pulled my hands away. "But what's different now?"

"Now I've been delivered from fear. I had to do a lot of praying, souls searching, and counseling, but I know exactly what I want in my future."

"Are you sure?"

"Very sure, and I bind up any hindrances in the mighty name of Jesus." Joshua held one hand up toward the sky.

"Well, amen to that." I remembered our better days, back at Missionary and at the college, praying and serving together, discussing his vision for the future; our future. "So?"

"So what?" Now I was lost.

"Will you?" Joshua asked, getting down on one knee in the grass.

"Will I what?"

"Will you marry me? I'll accept everything you've got, if we have kids together or if we can't, even the child you want to adopt from Africa. We'll adopt together." Joshua offered me back my beautiful ring. "I don't care anymore. I just want to be with you."

I took the ring from him and held onto it. "Yes, Joshua, I'll marry you, but only after I get situated in school and in this young women's ministry. Can you give me six months this time?"

Joshua breathed out a sigh of relief. "I'll give you anything you need."

"You see, I've been delivered too. And I must fulfill God's will for my life. I've waited long enough," I said.

"That's fine with me. I won't pressure you. I'll wait." Joshua hugged me as if he didn't want to let go. Then he placed the engagement ring back on my finger.

And we laughed and talked until both of us were filled with love. Then we prayed together before it was time for Joshua to go back to his hotel room. It hadn't been the most romantic evening, but it certainly was spiritual, so I felt at peace.

When I finally went to bed, I had no nightmares. I only had dreams about my bright future.

Chapter Forty-seven

When Joshua left after a week, it was back to business as usual. I spent the remainder of my time with the children I knew that God had assigned to me. I stayed for another four weeks delivering supplies, working in the fields, teaching at Vacation Bible Schools and attending occasional public relations events. I was even able to help a few of the villagers to build a bridge. One day Pastor Njoki invited the missionaries and me to his parents' home at The Mount Kenya Game Ranch, which was just outside the city of Nairobe. An older, distinguished couple, they gave us a warm greeting as we arrived. There I saw another side of Kenya, a land of lavish living nestled in the foothills of the mountains, exclusive residences, and panoramic views of the forests of Kenya National Park. For the first time during my trip, I was able to kick back and just have fun. Since the climate was very moderate in the mountains, it was virtually pest free, so there were no screens on the windows and doors. We not only soaked up the sun, but we also went on a helicopter safari, and went fly fishing. A few people from the group went to play tennis or golf, but since I'd never played, I stayed away from that. At nightfall we admired the majestic snow covered peaks of Kerinyaga, called God's Mountain.

Although the temperature that night was cool, the private estate was cozy with a log fireplace. We had dinner there. Pastor Njoki prayed for us, and then we were on our way back to the guesthouse in Nairobe.

It was raining when we returned. We stepped out of the van and ran through the wet grasslands up to the front door. Seger stopped me on the porch before I went in.

"So you'll be going back to the States soon?"

"Yes."

Seger narrowed his gaze. "I don't want you to go."

"I've enjoyed my time here, but my fiancé is waiting for me."

"I know, but are you happy with him?" Seger lifted my chin so that he could stare directly into my eyes.

"I'm very happy."

"But I thought he didn't understand you, didn't want to accept all of you, your past included."

"That was before, but he's okay now."

"Really. How do you know this?"

I sighed before answering him because I didn't want to hurt his feelings. He was a good man. "We've reconciled everything. Things are good between us."

"What if things get not so good again?"

"Then I will look toward the hills from whence cometh my help." Nothing would stand between Joshua and me ever again.

Seger let out a hearty laugh. "Good answer, Sister Alex."

"Thank you, Brother Seger." I took in the sparkle of his eyes. "I'd better go now. Goodnight."

"Goodnight," Seger said.

As soon as I went inside the guesthouse, I used the Internet to e-mail Joshua.

Dear Joshua,

I miss you so much, and I am so glad you returned your heart to me. During the weeks when I was away from you, I tried to bury your memory. I never knew you'd still want me after finding out about my flaws. So now you have it.

I'm not flawless. Neither of 'us is. Let's make this thing work
with Jesus being the flawless one.
    Alex

The next day I checked my e-mail, and Joshua had written
me back.

Dear Alex,
    I'm so sorry I made you feel like you couldn't come to me. I
guess I was just caught up in my own problems. I didn't have
time for yours, really. I was selfish, judgmental, and I didn't make
things easy for you to come clean, I know. Again I'm sorry. Forgive
me for being so darned self-righteous. Please forgive me. I don't know
what I was doing, trying to go on without leaving the bitterness I
had for Delilah behind. Never even grieving for my lost child or
my lost wife. Just going on as a shell of a man. I'm sorry I wasn't
a complete man for you then. I've finally buried the past. Through
God, I know I'm a whole man now, ready to be a good hus-
band. Ready to love you like you deserve to be loved. Please come
home to me and be my wife. I promise to spend the rest of my life
trying to make you happy.
    Joshua

After reading his e-mail, the words became real to me, and
I knew in my heart, it was time for me to leave. I had spent
three months here, and it was time to go home. It was time
to prepare to be Joshua's wife. Although I called Dr. Harding to tell him that I was coming home and that I would not
be accepting the promotion, he seemed to understand. My
destiny was finally clear to me, and public relations was not
a part of it. I headed out toward the school to say good-bye,
and at that very moment the clouds darkened and hung low.
When I looked up into the sky it was as if the heavens had

opened up for me once again. The rain began to fall all over me, and within seconds, I was drenched. Knowing it was the rainy season, I should've taken my umbrella. There wasn't a dry spot on my body, and yet I felt magnificent. I knew this purifying rain was a sign from God and that He had filled me with everything that had been missing. I had a second chance to start over and right the wrongs of yesterday. I ran through the puddles, deep inside the marshes and ended up at the little schoolhouse with the mud roof.

The people in the villages, especially the children, were sad to see me go, but I promised them all that I would return. One particular boy at an orphanage, named Kiano, who Seger and I had bonded with, cried because I was leaving. "I'll be back," I promised him as I headed out the front door. Both Pastor Njoke and Seger escorted me to the airport, although Seger was obviously disappointed that I was engaged again. I was excited to be going home, whole, for the first time in a long time.

Back in Brooklyn, the weather had changed. It was the second week of October now, and the red and orange leaves were scattered onto the pavement. I buttoned up my leather jacket as I sat in the leather guest chair, waiting patiently for Pastor Martin to end his phone call. I observed his various degrees from college and graduate school, his ordination certificates from various churches, and other honors of all kinds. I was impressed that his sense of direction seemed to have always been so clear.

Finally, Pastor Martin hung up the phone and rubbed his balding head. "I'm glad you finally came to see me."

"So am I."

"That was some speech you made a month ago."

"I'm a little ashamed." I looked down at my feet.

He smiled. "You shouldn't be."

"Believe me, it wasn't planned." I looked up into Pastor Martin's face. "It was only the Holy Spirit."

"I know that. I wouldn't have let you take over my pulpit if it weren't." Pastor Martin smiled.

"Yes, sir." I let out a deep breath and began to sit up straight in my chair.

"I knew that you'd been hurting for a long time. My wife and I both sensed it, and we had been praying for you, like we do for all our members. The Holy Spirit never shared with us why you were hurting, just that you needed special prayer."

This statement took me by surprise. "I had no idea."

"I know you didn't."

"I'm so ashamed though."

"You shouldn't be. Old things are passed away. Behold all things are become new."

I felt a hint of excitement run through me. "Pastor, since my trip to Kenya, I do feel new. I know that was what I needed; to be away from everything and everyone that I knew, just to hear God's voice."

"I'm glad you finally received the blessing, Sister Alex. It has been there all along."

My tears began to fall from my eyes. "I know that now."

"God forgave you a long time ago. I'm glad you finally decided to forgive yourself."

"You're right, Pastor."

"It's all behind you now. God is a forgiving God. You know that. He's a God of the second chance, third chance, and so on. God loves you."

"I know."

"They were twins, weren't they?"

"Yes. How did you know that?"

"The Holy Spirit just told me." Pastor Martin looked down at his desk. "You'll meet them someday."

"I know."

"It doesn't make the pain any less real, but . . . my wife and I lost our first child, and we still remember. We still feel the loss even twenty-five years and six kids later. But we go on, and that's what you have to do. Go on. Get on with the business of living."

"My mom used to say that all the time."

"Your mother was a faithful woman. We really miss her here at the church."

"I miss her too. But you're right. I must go on. I feel like I have to do something, like there is a ministry in me, something that was missing or undeveloped before. I learned so much while I was in Kenya. Now the ministry is big in me."

"I know that feeling when it's ripe. It's your season, Sister Alex."

"Yes, it's my season." I sighed. "I want to help others like me and like Michelle, like I want to mentor young women, particularly in the area of abstinence."

"Maybe you can start here at the church." Pastor Martin appeared to be searching for something.

"Sounds great." I jumped to my feet. "When can I start?"

"As soon as you're really ready. Pray about it, get your information organized, and we'll have a meeting with the board on next week."

"Thank you, Pastor. I've been praying for answers a long time, and now I finally understand what I have to do."

"I'm glad."

I picked up my leather purse from the chair. "I'm going to graduate school, and I'm going to major in education. I'm also going to take a few classes in Christian counseling at the Bible college."

"Good for you. I'm happy that you've found God's will."

"This time I have." I was finally certain about what I wanted to do with my life.

Pastor Martin stood up and smiled. "Well my dear, then you're on your way."

Chapter Forty-eight

The next few weeks I spent meditating in the Word of God; letting it transform me. I knew I needed this preparation if I were ever going to become Joshua's wife. Surprisingly, Taylor decided to join me in my divine quest. She and Keith had become quite close while I was gone, and part of their weekly routine was none other than doing Bible study. Leave it to Keith to get Taylor on track. Finally, I got the call from my Aunt Dorothy that Michelle was in the hospital.

I drove to Brooklyn Hospital, remembering the uneasy feeling I had the first timeI met with Michelle's parents about her pregnancy. I checked her room number at the front desk, then took the elevator upstairs to the labor and maternity suites. I noticed that Mr. Harris stood in the doorway of her room as if he were protecting it. He smiled and invited me in.

The room was decorated with pastel lilac colored walls, modern cherry wood furniture, and carefully tucked away warmers. Admiring the decor, I looked up at the ceiling and noticed concealed ceiling lights. Now this was the kind of room I would want to deliver my children in.

As I entered I saw Sister Harris holding the sleeping newborn.

I walked quietly over to Michelle. "Hello, everyone."

"Hi, Sister Alex." Michelle reached around my neck with her free arm to hug me.

"Oh, Michelle, he's beautiful." I smiled at her mother.

"It's good to see you, Alex." Sister Harris politely smiled back.

"Thanks," Michelle said to my compliment toward her beautiful son.

"What's his name?" I asked.

Michelle smiled, obviously proud of her child. "His name is Elijah, and he's going to be a prophet."

"Amen to that." I held up my hand in typical church style. "May I hold him?" I reached out for the plump cheeked baby. "Are you kidding me? You're the reason he's here," Michelle said.

Sister Harris stood up and placed the baby in my arms. I felt all the emotion run through my body, but this time it was a warm feeling, and my eyes began to fill up with tears. "I'm glad he's healthy, and I'm glad he's here."

"Me too." Michelle leaned over to see her baby's face. "His father joined the army, so hopefully I'll be getting child support to help too."

"That's good." I smiled. "You made the right choice, the only choice."

"I know. One time I thought about putting him up for adoption, but after talking it over with my parents and my baby's father, I decided to keep him. Thank you again for not letting me . . ."

I was so glad the whole ordeal was over. "Don't worry about it. Your experience actually helped me."

"Helped you?"

"Yes, saving your baby forced me to face my own fears about not saving my own babies. I've grown a lot since that day. In fact, when I'm done with my training, I'm going to start a not for profit organization to help young mothers to keep their babies."

Michelle sat up in bed. "That's a great idea."

"No, that's a God idea," Sister Harris said. "You see, every-

Ashea S. Goldson

one doesn't have the spiritual guidance or family support that you have. Some girls are really all alone and desperate. I don't think they should be. Every girl deserves to know that Jesus loves her regardless of what she's done. Every girl deserves to know that she can have a second chance at life without condemnation." It was my vision, and I couldn't let it go now.

"When Elijah gets a little older, I'd like to help out at your center," Michelle said.

"You just do whatever it takes to finish school and get to college, young lady. There will always be a place for you and Elijah at the center." I handed Michelle her baby.

"I'm going to college right here in New York City, hopefully to City College. I'm going to become an obstetrician." Michelle kissed her baby's cheek, and I could feel the love.

"You'll make it if you keep yourself focused." I stood up and started walking toward the door. "May God's will be done in your life."

"And in yours, Sister Alex," Michelle said.

"I guess I'll see you on Sunday." I walked toward the door.

"I'll see ya then, and thanks for coming by." Michelle held the baby close to her chest with one arm and waved with the other.

"Good-bye, Minister Harris and Sister Harris," I said.

"See you Sunday, dear," Sister Martin hugged me before I went out the door.

"Thanks for stopping by, Sister Alex." Minister Martin held the door open for me.

I looked back at Michelle, and she looked so happy. "Take good care of Elijah."

"I will," Michelle said.

I rode away with the wind in my hair and a song in my heart. Michelle's new life had begun. Unfortunately, the moment I walked through the door of my apartment, I heard that Taylor's life was over.

Chapter Forty-nine

Taylor sobbed uncontrollably. I stepped over a pile of dirty clothes in the middle of the floor and almost tripped over a pair of shoes as I walked toward her "What happened?"

"My life is officially over." Taylor sat, slumped over in her wheelchair.

I bent down in front of her wheelchair. "What's wrong? Tell me what happened."

A cool breeze blew in from the half cracked window. I noticed that her laptop was on the floor and papers were also scattered as well. "I received an e-mail today from Ms. Arlene about The Push It Fitness Center, so I called." Taylor smelled like mints, and I wondered what she had been eating.

"Okay?"

"I called her, and she told me that she was ready to accept Shayla McConnell's offer since it was the only on the table. I begged her, and she told me she'd give me three weeks more and that's it." Taylor shook her head.

"Well, it's nice of her to give you three more weeks. She likes you."

"Likes me? That ain't helping. I don't have a dime to my name and haven't been able to borrow anything. I stalled by asking her for more time, but I don't have a clue what to do. It's just hopeless. My life is over."

"Look, don't say that. We've come too far for you to say that."

"Too far?"

"God spared your life for a reason." I grabbed onto Taylor's shoulders and shook her lightly. "You could've died in that car."

"Maybe I should've died." Taylor reversed her wheelchair and wheeled herself away from me.

"Oh, come on. I'm not gonna stay here and let you wallow around in self pity." It was hard for me to hear her talking like this, giving up on all she had worked her whole life for. I wanted to instantly fill her with faith, but I knew she was a work in progress.

Taylor sniffled. "Then don't stay here. Go, then; just go."

"I'm not going anywhere. Neither are you."

"What am I supposed to do now?"

"You're supposed to stand and fight." I caught up to Taylor and rubbed her back. "I don't know what we're going to do, but we're not going to give up. Now let's pray."

"Okay." Taylor nodded as the tears continued to roll down her face.

"Father God, we come before you, not in desperation, but in complete expectation and gratitude. We already know who you are and what you've said in your Word. We believe and we continue to stand on your Word. Please give us the wisdom and the courage to go forth in your name and to possess the land. In the precious name of Jesus. Amen."

"Amen." Taylor turned her back to me. "Look, you can pray, but it won't work for me like it does for you, Alex."

I saw the disbelief in her eyes. I felt her disappointment, but I couldn't succumb to the circumstances. "Don't say that."

"I've never wanted anything more than The Push It Fitness Center, and I know it was a pretty big dream since I don't have any money. Now it's over."

I let her lean her head on my shoulder. "Sweetie, it ain't over till God says it's over." A week later as I was reading the morning paper, I ran across an article on Mark McConnell,

Shayla McConnell's husband, and the financial challenges that he had been having as a result of the changing economic times. I took the article to Taylor who slapped me five, but Taylor still worried about where she would get money for the down payment she needed. Ms. Arlene was going to give up the center and retire on schedule, no matter what. Ms. Arlene had waited long enough and couldn't afford to wait for Taylor's dreams to manifest.

Chapter Fifty

I was in the kitchen preparing banana pancakes and cheese omelets for breakfast when the doorbell rang. I was surprised to see my dad and Keith at the door together.

"Hi, Daddy. What are you doing here so early?"

"I just wanted to see my baby girls and spend some time with you two today. I missed you when you were gone. Plus I haven't seen Taylor in a couple of weeks, so you know . . . it's time."

"I understand, Daddy," I said.

"Hi, Alex." Keith waved his hand as I let him in.

"Hi, Keith." I faced Taylor's room. "Get up, Taylor. You've got company."

"I'm here, and it's time for our session." Keith's voice swept through our small apartment.

I peeped in at Taylor, looked over at the clock, and realized that she had overslept. A huge art deco mirror hung over her bed. She moved around under the covers to position herself upright. Suddenly, Taylor let out a scream. "Come on in. I've got a terrible cramp in my leg."

I opened the door wide.

"What do you mean a cramp in your leg?" I wasn't sure I heard her correctly.

"Can you feel your leg?" Keith yelled out before he burst into the room with Daddy right on his heels.

Still half asleep, I don't think Taylor even realized what she said right away. "Wait, I can feel something in my legs, like a cramp."

"Are you sure?" I jerked the covers off of her, revealing her bare thighs and legs. "Yes, I'm sure. I can feel a cramp in my left leg." Taylor covered her mouth with her hands.

Taylor looked up at Keith, but I'm sure she didn't have time to be embarrassed. It all happened so fast. Daddy cracked the bedroom door just a little.

"Good morning, Taylor." Daddy sat down on the edge of her bed.

Taylor yelled out. "Morning, Daddy."

Keith moved in for closer observation, and he began poking and prodding Taylor.

"Ow, be careful," Taylor said.

"Oh my goodness. That's the breakthrough." I danced and shouted around the room. "Hallelujah. That's the breakthrough."

"That's great. This is a miracle." Keith lifted her up out of the bed and spun her around before placing her gently back in bed. Then he calmly took out his pad and pen to document everything.

I could hardly believe it myself, that what she was feeling was actually real, that she could feel her legs in any capacity, something she hadn't done for many months. "Good, then let's work on these legs." Keith began pushing and pulling gently, bending her knees, massaging her legs and feet, and asking questions of all kinds.

For the first time since the accident, she said she felt his hands when they were on her body, every finger, every knuckle.

Then Taylor began to cry. "Thank you, Jesus. Thank you, Lord. Father, forgive me for running from you, for isolating myself from my family, and for being so hard hearted. I'm sorry, and I ask that you make me right, clean. I believe you died on the cross for my sins. Please accept me into your kingdom, the one that Mom and Alex, Aunt Dorothy, Dad, and

Keith have been nagging me about this whole time. In Jesus' name. Amen."

Dad and I put our arms around Taylor, and we were a family like we hadn't been in years. Our worship lifted us out of the room and into the Spirit where we could all move about freely, walk and run and dance.

For two weeks, after careful examination by her doctors, Keith and Taylor worked harder than ever. She was determined to break medical barriers, and she said she knew the Lord would help her, even though she had a long road ahead, and even though she still could not walk on her own.

I was happy that she acknowledged that it was God who had brought her this far, and that He wouldn't let her down.

Then one day Keith showed up at our door. "Hi, Keith," I said.

"Hello, Alex." Keith whispered. "I came over because I have a surprise forTaylor."

"Okay. Come on in." I watched Taylor's face light up when she saw Keith. "We were just sitting here talking."

"Really? I don't want to interrupt." Keith gave Taylor a hug and sat down on the couch next to her.

I sat on the loveseat.

"Hi, Keith." Taylor couldn't stop smiling.

"So what were you guys talking about if you don't mind me asking?"

Taylor poked out her lips. "We were talking about my business deadline and how there's no chance of me meeting it. No money, no hope."

I picked up a throw pillow and squeezed it. "I told her not talk like that, that nothing is impossible for God, but she won't listen."

"Oh, come on. I'm sure Shayla McConell's offer has already been accepted by now," Taylor said.

"Why would you say that? Didn't Ms. Arlene say she'd give you three more weeks?" Keith shifted his position so he could look directly at Taylor.

"Yeah, she did, but I've only got a week left of that extension and nothing has changed for me. Plus I'm sure Shayla is hounding her everyday about the center. She wants it almost as bad as I do, just for the wrong reasons." Taylor looked down at the floor.

"I don't think Shayla has been hounding Ms. Arlene about the center," Keith said.

"Why not?" Taylor asked.

Keith pulled out a newspaper. "Because she's got bigger problems with her husband filing for bankruptcy."

Bankruptcy?" Taylor snatched the paper out of Keith's hands. "You're kidding, right?"

"Nope," Keith said.

I threw my hands in the air. "God is good."

"Okay so Shayla has some money problems, and she probably can't buy the center right now, but neither can I." Taylor rolled her eyes. "Ms. Arlene is going to get rid of it regardless."

"That brings me to my surprise," Keith stood up and started fumbling around in his pockets.

"What is it?" Taylor asked.

Keith bent down and kissed Taylor on the forehead. "I'm proud of how hard you've been working in therapy and on your research for the business. I know your boss is selling the center now, and you didn't even have a chance to get it like you wanted."

"It's just funny, though. A few months ago the Push It Fitness Center was all I cared about. I was so bitter, but now I've got you, my big headed sister over there, and my dad. The accident was sad, but with God's help, I was able to get through it all."

"And come out a better person," I added.

"Yeah, that's right. A whole person. Now I just want to be able to start my own center one day. I'm grateful for my disability check in the meantime, though." Taylor held Keith's hand.

"I'm glad you said one day because that day is now." Keith reached into his jacket pocket and pulled out an envelope. "This is for you."

Taylor looked up at him. "What is it?"

"It's the down payment for Ms. Arlene's place and a loan application where I've co-signed for you." Keith looked like he could hardly contain his excitement.

"What are you saying?" Taylor leaned forward in her chair.

"Well, I've been thinking about how determined you've been and about how you really deserve to own The Push It Fitness Center. I figured you'd need a partner, maybe a physical therapist."

"Oh, Keith, are you sure?" Tears started to stream down Taylor's eyes.

"I've never been surer of anything," Keith said.

Taylor reached up to hug him. "You're the best."

"That's wonderful. I'm so happy for you." I leaned down to hug Taylor.

"Oh, and there is just one more thing . . ." Keith reached back into his pocket and pulled out a small ring box. When he opened it, the brightest diamond sparkled in her face. "Well, what do you think? Will you become my partner for life?"

"For life? I don't know. That sounds like a long commitment."

"I know you're committed to the center, but will you make the commitment to me?" Keith pushed the ring on her finger.

"As soon as I can walk down the aisle." Taylor smiled at her ring.

"That's good enough for me," Keith said.

I grabbed Keith and gave him a big hug. "Welcome to the family."

"Hey, hey, hands off. You've already got your man." Taylor laughed through her tears and planted a big kiss on Keith.

Chapter Fifty-one

It was a week before Thanksgiving, and the day was special. Dark clouds hovered overhead, threatening a heavy downpour, reminding me of my trip to Kenya during the rainy season. It also reminded me of that day so many years ago, when one decision changed the course of my life forever. Yet, here I was standing boldly on the newly renovated stage of The Harvey Theater at The Brooklyn Academy of Music, waiting to share one of the most pivotal events of my thirty-year existence.

The Harvey was a self contained venue located on Fulton Street, restored and uniquely decorated. The academy, which had its history dating back to its first performance in 1861, had grown into a successful urban center over the years, bringing performing arts and film from all around the world to Brooklyn. I remembered the first time my mother brought my sister and me to attend a play there. What a magical experience it was, sitting in the balcony watching world class actors put on the performance of a lifetime. Now I stood here, all grown up, not to entertain, but to enlighten. Pastor Martin held the microphone. "And now I introduce to you Sister Alex Carter, a fine young lady, a member of Missionary Chapel Church since she was a little girl, a member of the praise team, a diligent worker on nearly every church committee there has ever been, an employee at Missionary Bible College, and I could go on, but I'll stop now. Suffice it to say that Sister Alex has taken a trip to Kenya and has come back with a powerful message from the Lord." Pastor Martin started off the applause, and I came forward.

I waited for the applause to stop. Then I looked out into the eight hundred and seventy full seats and felt nothing but gratitude. "Welcome to Giving Life Women's Ministry. This ministry is not just about being pregnant or giving birth, at least not to babies, but it's also about giving birth to vision. God's vision through activism, planting Word seed, speaking life, carrying life, and protecting it. It is our mission to carry and protect life. That is our ultimate vision. As Christian women, we're nurturers of life so we cannot give in to societal pressures and join others in destroying life. We are not the ultimate creator of life. Therefore, we have no right to be the ultimate destroyer of life.

"Believe it or not, I was a destroyer of life. You see about ten and a half years ago, when I was about the same age of some of you here, I thought I was in love. I became pregnant. The truth is that he didn't love me, just used me. That's why God tells us to wait on our husbands, but like so many of us, I didn't listen. But that's all right because Jesus loved me the whole time. But sadly, before I knew that Jesus loved me, I was pregnant. I was pregnant and alone." I sighed at the memory.

So I went to have an abortion at a cheap clinic in the town I went to college in. My twins, yes they were twins, were sucked out of me at only three months into the pregnancy. They never had a chance. And I never told a living soul how that procedure affected me physically or emotionally.

"Physically, I suffered an infection in the womb and fallopian tubes, which is a very fragile organ. In fact, I was blessed that my tubes were not sealed shut. That can happen when you develop pelvic inflammatory disease. I'm still not sure if other permanent damage was done. I'll have to trust God to heal me if it was.

"No one knew how I hemorrhaged and lay in a pool of my own blood, enduring side splitting pain for days. This was all because I was too scared to return for my post operative exam and because I had retained some fetal and placental tissue inside my womb. I almost died, trying to kill my babies. But no one knew. I was in college far away from home, so no one knew. No one except God, that is," I said.

The crowd was silent.

"Emotionally, I cried every day for months. I couldn't concentrate in my classes, so my grades dropped. I had nightmares for years afterward. I gave up my chosen career because I couldn't face children. I didn't think I deserved the right to work with children. Now some of you might think how silly is that, but that's how I felt. So I gave up my career aspirations of being a teacher, and then I avoided anyone with a baby because I couldn't stand to look in their eyes.

So the biggest thing is not only did I end two lives, but to make matters worse, I couldn't even do the will of God for my own life. In fact, I almost sabotaged my relationship with my fiancé and his daughter because of my fear. She was the sweetest little girl, but I didn't want anything to do with her because of my own issues. I almost lost the opportunity to be her mother.

"I kept praying and waiting for answers, but the answer was in me all the time. I had to tell my story and get free. God had already set me free, but I had to forgive myself. I had to tell this story to free others too."

"Why did you do it?" one girl yelled out.

"To preserve myself, because I listened to Satan's suggestions on saving myself, my reputation, and my life. As a result, I ended two lives that never had a chance." My eyes overflowed with tears. "I made a deal with the devil and lost. I lost my children, and I lost myself. For a long time I had lost my own life." I wiped my eyes with a tissue.

I walked away from the podium and stood in front of it. "Like Pastor Martin said I did take a trip to Kenya and God did give me a message there, but not because the problems with abortion are limited to Kenya. According to the Center For Disease Control, in 1990, abortions in the United States rose to a high of one point six million.According to information obtained primarily from The Center For Disease Control, since the Roe vs. Wade court decision, the annual number of legal induced abortions since 1973 has increased gradually up to 1990, which was a peak point, and then declined. In 2003, a total of eight hundred and forty-eight thousand, one hundred and sixty-three legal induced abortions were reported to CDC by forty-nine reporting areas. Have been forty eight million, five hundred eighty nine thousand, nine hundred and ninety three. In 2003, one point thirty-one million pregnancies were terminated by abortion in the United States. That means two point one percent of all women from the ages of fifteen to forty-four had an abortion in 2000. Unfortunately, over the years abortion has become one of the most common surgical procedures.

"The saddest news, I'm ashamed to say, is that a great percentage of these women are Christians."

The audience gasped, and then began to whisper.

"Why did these women do what they did? Some of the reasons I found were interference with school or work responsibilities, not being able to afford it, not wanting to be a single parent, or having problems with one's partner. But I say, don't we trust God enough to stay in the Spirit so we don't fulfill the lust of the flesh? Apparently not. "We should be separate, holy, and set apart until marriage. No matter what the world teaches us. We get our teaching not from the media, not from our peers, but from the Word of God. So join with us, ladies, at this teen summit in a declaration of abstinence. Let's be holy together until we can give that precious gift to our husbands. Now, I have a special guest who would like to say a few words."

Michelle came up, holding Elijah in her arms. "Hi, I'm Michelle, and this is my baby. His name is Elijah, and one day he'll be a prophet. Now can you imagine if I had destroyed his life? I would have done exactly that if it weren't for Sister Alex."

The crowd roared.

"She intervened in my life 'cause, Satan had me under a spell. Now I regret ever thinking about abortion, but it's out there, and it's real. The judgment I experienced, especially at my church, cut through to the core of my heart. My fellow members insulted me, and I felt cut down in my spirit. I felt like Jesus didn't love me, but I know now that's not true. Satan tried to oppress, depress, control, and confine me all in my mind. But Jesus saved me. He never did stop loving me. It ain't easy, but this is Elijah, and like I said before, one day he'll be a prophet. Thank you." Michelle handed the microphone back to me.

The crowd applauded. Then I came forward, holding the microphone with one hand and holding the other hand in the air. Then with everything that was in me, I began to sing Tramaine Hawkins's "Holy One." Tears rolled down my cheeks as I entered into praise and worship. *No, Lord, I'll never let you down any more.* The crowds applauded and cried out with adulation. The atmosphere was filled with joy as Sister Martin thanked us both.

Afterward, I made my way behind the curtain to meet my friends and family backstage. Joshua immediately handed me a bouquet of long stemmed red roses. Lilah actually jumped into my arms and gave me a big kiss. Daddy, Aunt Dorothy, and Marisol hugged me and gave me their best wishes. Yet the one I searched through the crowds for, the one I was the most excited to see was Taylor. Taylor appeared slowly, wearing her metal leg braces and holding onto a walker struggling to get to me. I met her halfway.

"I'm proud of you." Taylor's eyes were filled with tears.

I threw my arms around her, careful not to make her lose her balance. "Girl, please."

"For everything you're doing for those young girls, for everything you do for the Lord, for not letting stuff get you down." Taylor held onto her walker.

"Well, stuff has had me down for a long time." I smiled at her.

"But you don't stay down. I didn't say you was perfect." Taylor laughed hard. "What about you? Not so long ago you were too afraid to get out of bed and even get into a wheelchair, but look at you now, walking again, about to run your own center," I said.

"That ain't nothing special." Taylor laughed. "God did all the work."

"I know, but you're a living testimony," I said.

Just then Keith broke through the crowd and put his arm around Taylor. "Great job, Sister Alex."

I smiled. "Thanks."

"I'm waiting for another miracle, you know." Taylor turned around and looked at Keith.

"Oh?" I wasn't sure which miracle she was referring to. So much had already happened for both of us.

"The miracle of me being able to walk again," Taylor said.

"But you're walking now."

"No, I mean without all of this." Taylor directed her eyes toward all the metal equipment she needed to hold her steady. "I'm taking one step at a time, but one day I'm gonna put that tiara on my head, gonna throw away these braces and this walker, and I'm gonna walk right down the aisle at my wedding. I'm a diva, remember?" Taylor wiped away her budding tears.

"I know you will," I said. "If your faith is nearly as big as your mouth, you will."

Taylor and Keith both laughed.

Since I had lost a few pounds and toned up a lot, Taylor and I looked more alike than we had in a long time. I smiled at the fact that we not only had the same looks, but because we also had the same heart. Twins. We walked arm in arm, side by side, enjoying the goodness that is God, with a million tears left behind them and nothing but grace ahead. Today confirmed the fact that although that rainy day eleven years ago may have altered my course, it didn't alter my destiny. That was something God designed, and I still had a right to it. No matter what trials we faced, no matter how dark it got, no matter what weeping we may endure for a night, joy always comes in the morning.

Epilogue

Here we were back in Kenya on our long awaited honeymoon. Sister Ethel and Sister Martha were right about this being the perfect romantic spot. Besides, we wanted to start our international adoption proceedings right away. As the reddened sun faded onto the purplish horizon, we walked along the beach and everything was perfect. After a whirlwind courtship and a tumultuous engagement, we were finally Mr. and Mrs. Joshua Bennings and that was all that mattered.

It had been a beautiful spring wedding, compliments of Daddy and The Benningses. Everything had gone smoothly. Pastor Martin presided over the ceremony. Lilah had been the sweetest flower girl ever. Daddy had walked me gracefully down the aisle. Taylor had been my maid of honor, of course. Marisol and Michelle had been my bridesmaids. Deacon Jacob had been Joshua's best man. The entire Bennings family had been seated on one side with their skeptical, elitist expressions. Aunt Dorothy had been seated on the other side, where my mother would have been, six foot one, two hundred and seventy-five pounds, and proud as ever. The entire Missionary Chapel congregation had been invited to the ceremony, even Sister Winifred and Yvonne. They never came though. Haters.

Anyway, here we were, wrapped in our blanket on the sand, basking in the joy that was our love, when I noticed a group of what seemed to be missionaries walking toward us. One of them handed us a tract. "Jesus loves you," one woman said.

Epilogue

Joshua smiled at them and took the tract. "Thank you."

"We know God is good." I looked over at Joshua and grabbed his hand. "We're on our honeymoon."

"Oh, how nice." The woman spoke with an accent and appeared to be a native.

Joshua and I looked at each other and grabbed hands. The sun reflected itself on the rippling waters, and I was at peace.

Reading Group Discussion Questions

1) Why do you think Alex was apprehensive when Joshua proposes to her?

2) Why was helping Michelle so important to Alex? Should she have just distanced herself from the entire situation?

3) Why wasn't Alex willing to consider Dr. Harding's offer at first? What changed her mind?

4) Why was Joshua so uptight and moody? Why do you think he didn't communicate his issues to Alex?

5) Why do you think Taylor was so rebellious and stubborn toward the things of God? What changed her toward the end?

6) Why do you think Alex kept bumping into Ahmad, despite her needing to stay away from him? Did she do the right thing by talking to him?

7) How could Alex have handled the Yvonne situation differently? Should she have confronted Joshua about her concerns earlier?

8) Should Joshua have been spending so much time with Yvonne, even as an obligation to Sister Winifred? What, if anything, should Alex have done to help Taylor get back into the church, without offending her?

Reading Group Discussion Questions

Do you think that Alex made the right decision in planning to go away to Kenya a few weeks before her wedding? And if so, why?

Should Joshua have reacted differently when he found out that his mother was involved in his and Alex's breakup?

As a man of God, should Joshua have talked to Alex first and not called off the engagement, or should he have just forgiven her sooner?

Do you think Alex did the right thing in marrying Joshua or should she have started over and considered Serge?

What made Taylor and Keith end up together? Do you think it was a good idea for Taylor to say she would marry him when she could walk down the aisle? Why or why not?

Urban Christian His Glory Book Club!

Established in January 2007, *UC His Glory Book Club* is another way to introduce **Urban Christian** and its authors. We are an online book club supporting Urban Christian authors by purchasing, reading, and providing written reviews of the authors' books. *UC His Glory Book Club* welcomes both men and women of the literary world who have a passion for reading Christian-based fiction.

UC His Glory Book Club is the brainchild of Joylynn Jossel, author and Executive Editor of Urban Christian and Kendra Norman-Bellamy, author and copy editor for Urban Christian. The book club will provide support, positive feedback, encouragement, and a forum whereby members can openly discuss and review the literary works of Urban Christian authors. In the future, we anticipate broadening our spectrum of services to include online author chats, author spotlights, interviews with your favorite Urban Christian author(s), special online groups for *UC His Glory Book Club* members, ability to post reviews on the website and amazon.com, membership ID cards, *UC His Glory* Yahoo! Group and much more.

Even though there will be no membership fees attached to becoming a member of *UC His Glory Book Club*, we do expect our members to be active, committed, and to follow the guidelines of the book club.

Urban Christian His Glory Book Club

UC His Glory Book Club **members pledge to:**
- Follow the guidelines of *UC His Glory Book Club*.
- Provide input, opinions, and reviews that build up, rather than tear down.
- Commit to purchasing, reading, and discussing featured book(s) of the month.
- Respect the Christian beliefs of *UC His Glory Book Club*.
- Believe that Jesus is the Christ, Son of the Living God.

We look forward to the online fellowship.

Many Blessings to You!

Shelia E. Lipsey
President
UC His Glory Book Club

**Visit the official Urban Christian His Glory Book Club website at www.uchisglorybookclub.net

ORDER FORM
URBAN BOOKS, LLC
78 E. Industry Ct
Deer Park, NY 11729

Name: (please print): _____

Address: _____

City/State: _____

Zip: _____

QTY	TITLES	PRICE
	A Man's Worth	$14.95
	Abundant Rain	$14.95
	Battle Of Jericho	$14.95
	By The Grace Of God	$14.95
	Dance Into Destiny	$14.95
	Divorcing The Devil	$14.95
	Forsaken	$14.95
	Grace And Mercy	$14.95
	Guilty & Not Guilty Of Love	$14.95
	His Woman, His Wife His Widow	$14.95
	Illusion	$14.95
	The LoveChild	$14.95

Shipping and Handling - add $3.50 for 1st book then $1.75 for each additional book.
Please send a check payable to:
    Urban Books, LLC
Please allow 4 - 6 weeks for delivery

ORDER FORM
URBAN BOOKS, LLC
78 E. Industry Ct
Deer Park, NY 11729

Name: (please print): _____

Address: _____

City/State: _____

Zip: _____

QTY	TITLES	PRICE
	16 ½ On The Block	$14.95
	16 On The Block	$14.95
	Betrayal	$14.95
	Both Sides Of The Fence	$14.95
	Cheesecake And Teardrops	$14.95
	Denim Diaries	$14.95
	Happily Ever Now	$14.95
	Hell Has No Fury	$14.95
	If It Isn't love	$14.95
	Last Breath	$14.95
	Loving Dasia	$14.95
	Say It Ain't So	$14.95

Shipping and Handling - add $3.50 for 1st book then $1.75 for each additional book.
Please send a check payable to:
Urban Books, LLC
Please allow 4 - 6 weeks for delivery